# *Junky*

## *The Definitive Text of "Junk"*

## WILLIAM S. BURROUGHS

Edited and with an Introduction by
Oliver Harris

Grove Press
*New York*

First published in the United States of America by Ace Books in 1953.

This edition with material by Allen Ginsberg and edited with an introduction
by Oliver Harris published by arrangement with Penguin Classics, an imprint of
Penguin Books

*Printed in the United States of America*
*Published simultaneously in Canada*

ISBN: 978-0-8021-2042-7
e-Book ISBN: 978-0-8021-9405-3

Grove Press
an imprint of Grove/Atlantic, Inc.
841 Broadway
New York, NY 10003

Distributed by Publishers Group West

www.groveatlantic.com

12 13 14 15   10 9 8 7 6 5 4 3 2 1

# CONTENTS

# ACKNOWLEDGMENTS

I would like to thank James Grauerholz for all his scholarly support and generous practical help, not only on this project but over the years. Thanks also to John Bennett of Ohio State University; to the staff in Green Library at Stanford University; and to those in the Butler Library at Columbia University.

For permission to quote previously unpublished materials, thanks are due to: Bob Rosenthal of the Allen Ginsberg Trust; and to Peter Matson.

For permission to print previously published materials, thanks are due to HarperCollins.

Finally, I'd like to dedicate this edition to Ian MacFadyen, for being quite simply a great reader of Burroughs.

# INTRODUCTION

## "WHAT YOU SEE IS WHAT YOU GET"

If you're looking for books about narcotic addiction, the supply has never been better. There are social histories, public health polemics, and political critiques of the war on drugs; cultural studies and ethical analyses; surveys of narcotic legislation, addict psychology, pharmacology and treatment methods; personal memoirs, trash novels, and classic works of literature. The junkie is a modern icon, and heroin has a history and a mythology as well as a chemistry. And if you're looking for books by William Burroughs, there are over two dozen to choose from, most if not all of which make reference to narcotics and addiction. Junk and Burroughs go together, he's *the* addict-artist of the twentieth century, but he never wrote another book remotely like this, his very first.

Descriptions such as "down-to-earth and honest prose"; "what you see is what you get"; "an honest account of the 'vicious circle' of addiction"—readers' comments from an online bookstore Web site, these are not terms anyone would ever use for *Nova Express*, *The Wild Boys*, or *The Western Lands*. One thing you can say about any book by William Burroughs, however, is that whenever you think you've got it pinned down, that's when it has just slipped between your fingers. This is true of the book you are holding now, even though, of all Burroughs' works, it is the only one that is more often read outside the rest of the oeuvre than as part of it, devoured by readers who admit they choked on *Naked Lunch*, whereas this one, it seems, is a straight read from cover to cover.

Both more and less than a record of Burroughs' early years on heroin, this book is, to borrow a phrase from Luc Sante (author of *Low Life*, a classic study of crime and drugs), crowned with many hats. Having things to say about marijuana, cocaine, Benzedrine, Nembutal, peyote, yagé, and antihistamines, as well as opium and its derivatives, it's halfway to being a pharmacopoeia. Reflecting Burroughs' studies in anthropology (first at Harvard and then Mexico City College), it mimics the ethnographic field report, detailing the territories and habits of various urban American subcultures and documenting their emergence or decline in the immediate postwar era. Its attention to hipster idiom and criminal argot makes it a study of underworld linguistics. Not only does it recount the practices of narcotics police, lawyers, doctors, and psychiatrists in federal hospitals, but it also contains a surprising amount of information on the economics of crop farming, tips on the dynamics of luck, and meditations on loyalty and betrayal, existential loneliness, and the abject horrors of our own flesh. It is a work of journalistic reportage, a species of confessional autobiography, and a novel informed by Ernest Hemingway, Dashiell Hammett, John O'Hara, and F. Scott Fitzgerald, as well as the dialogue of Hollywood B movies. This is reckoned to be Burroughs' one straightforward story, a simple, informative account written in a plain, dry style. But read it again and you come across little pearls of prose and strange, spectral images, weird moments of pure menace or utter ambiguity that give the lie to the notion of terse, gritty realism and whose effects are all the more unsettling because they didn't seem to be there before. Read it a third time and, far from being dull and flat-footed, the writing now appears spry and subtle, capable of sharp comic touches and guilty of devious tricks. Look at it from different angles and the thing changes before your eyes, like a trompe l'oeil picture.

This strange, double-take logic comes in many guises. Here's just one variety. William Lee says: "You need a good bedside manner with doctors or you will get nowhere." At first, the joke is on the doctors, and this looks like the deadpan irony of such phrases as "a hard-working thief," and a host of others where normally positive cultural terms are given a deft, subversive twist. But look again and the key words are no longer "bedside manner" and "doctors" but the twice-repeated "you": suddenly, Lee isn't talking about doctors, he's telling *you* how to score from them. This recurrent tactical trap, insinuating the reader's complicity in the criminal world and making visible our voyeurism, is a unique feature of Burroughs' style here. The closest equivalent to it is a line in Hammett's *Red Harvest*: "He wasn't the sort of man whose pocket you would try to pick unless you had a lot of confidence in your fingers"—which tempts us to wonder just how much confidence *do* we have in our fingers, whether to pick or not to pick the pocket? In other words: What side of the criminal fence are you really on, just where do you draw the line?

It's tempting to conclude that Burroughs' chillingly cool and seductive book is complex and ironic, to say that its apparent simplicity is a sophisticated ruse designed to fool you, but this is too simple and won't do either. In fact, Burroughs' first novel is both absolutely distinct from everything he would write after it, and yet impossible to read without encountering at every turn phantom traces of the writing to follow. It's like reading two books simultaneously, one atypically straight, the other characteristically twisted. This is its paradoxical situation, its destiny, as the original work of one of America's great original writers.

## ". . . FOR REASONS UNKNOWN TO ME"

The story of how this debut novel came to be written in the first place, of how and why Burroughs began his career with it, this is a mystery that is bound to interest us. But our appetite for the hard facts is always balanced by an intuitive sense that the mystery of such beginnings should remain intact. Perhaps this is because writers must, at some level, remain mysteries to themselves in order to write at all, and we respect that truth as much as we want to violate it. In any event, there's a contradiction here that goes to the heart of Burroughs' novel, one captured in two of its most characteristic lines. "Here are the facts," is the first of them, which promises to give us everything we want to know, and this the other, that takes it all back again: "There is no key, no secret someone else has that he can give you."

To get a measure of this book, and to understand what this new edition seeks to add to our appreciation of it, the simplest place to start is with the significant but unexpected mystery of what I have so far avoided—its title. Titles are not supposed to be mysterious. They're meant to fix a work, to give it a clear identity, to define in miniature the author's intention. Not so this one, whose history of slight but crucial changes is a version of the novel's curious editing fate writ small.

Burroughs began his "book about junk" at the dead center of the twentieth century, only a couple of months after relocating his family to Mexico City in late fall 1949. Escaping the punitive regime of Cold War America after a string of drug busts, Burroughs was beginning what would turn into a quarter of a century as a writer-in-exile. He broke the news to Jack Kerouac in a letter dated March 10, 1950, and interesting news it must have been. Five years earlier they had actually collaborated on a novel together, but whereas Kerouac was now more passionate than ever about his literary vocation—his own first novel, *The Town and the City*, had just been published—Burroughs had since given up on writing. In later years, he would say Kerouac was the one who kept telling him he was a writer, but there was no mention of this in March 1950. He called his novel simply "Junk," and at the end of the year this was what he typed on the title page of his first-draft manuscript, followed by his *nom de plume* (borrowed from his character's appearance in Kerouac's novel): "William Dennison." When the novel appeared in 1953, both title and pseudonym had changed. *Junk* by William Dennison had become *Junkie: Confessions of an Unredeemed Drug Addict* by William Lee.

Burroughs himself chose the new name—a *very* equivocal choice, in fact: he said he needed a pseudonym to conceal his identity from his family, but perversely he chose "Lee," his mother's maiden name, and so revealed the very thing he claimed to want to hide. Both the title and subtitle, however, were chosen behind Burroughs' back by the publishers, Ace Books, in one of a series of cuts and changes they forced on his novel. Allen Ginsberg, who at that time was acting as Burroughs' agent, had already fought and lost the case before the deal with Ace was signed, in July 1952. "I really feel that JUNK is an inspired title," he wrote to A. A. Wyn, the publisher, that April. "It's funny, it's straightforward, original, and yet very typical of junkie's talk, and characteristic of author. I think it would be a real sad mistake to change, and advise against it."[1] Why was his advice and Burroughs' choice ignored? According to Carl Solomon, who had acquired the book for Ace, it was because they thought it would give the impression the book *was* junk.

These anecdotes tell us a good deal about Burroughs' situation as a first-time novelist, and they hint at the larger story of writing and publishing in that particular era, but their interest doesn't stop there. Almost twenty-five years later the title would change once again, this time to *Junky*, for the unexpurgated and expanded Penguin edition that has been in print since 1977. Burroughs authorized the changes made for that edition, but there was still one decision taken out of his hands. In August 1976, he wrote

---

1. Ginsberg to A. A. Wyn, April 12, 1952 (Ginsberg Collection, Columbia University).

his agent Peter Matson: "I would suggest that the title of this new edition be JUNK, rather than JUNKIE. JUNK was the original title which I gave the book, and this was changed by A. A. Wyn for reasons unknown to me." The next month, Matson reported the verdict of Penguin's editor: "Dick Seaver likes JUNKY, thinking that, without the 'Y' it sounds too much like garbage, if you'll excuse the expression."[2]

Taken together, what do these identical behind-the-scenes anecdotes about a title add up to? From an editor's point of view, they make visible the sheer *contingency* of Burroughs' novel, the part played in it by chance events or the decisions of others, only some of which can ever be known. From a critical point of view, they offer a different kind of warning about "the facts," since interpretations of literature are typically based on silent assumptions that may well turn out to be false. In their different ways, Ginsberg, A. A. Wyn, and Richard Seaver all knew that a book called *Junk* means something quite different to one called *Junkie* or *Junky*. And more generally, these anecdotes give an absolutely material dimension to the truism that we never read the same novel twice. Every book changes to some extent over time and in new contexts, but Burroughs' first novel has changed literally again and again in name and in content. You might think that the author's own wishes should finally be respected now, albeit posthumously, and this new edition be given the title *Junk*. However, publishing remains as bound by pragmatic concerns today as it was twenty-five or fifty years ago, and the fact is that, in the end, the sales department is right: in bookstores, people will still go on asking for *Junky*. But in scholarly circles, too, another change would only mean one more confusion because, over time, the familiar title has accrued a body of meanings, a certain weight, a particular status:

2. Burroughs to Peter Matson, August 25, 1976, and Matson to Burroughs, September 10, 1976 (Matson Collection, Columbia University).

for better or worse, *Junky* is canonical now. And so it has been left to the subtitle—*The Definitive Text of "Junk"*—to indicate that this text represents the last stage in a fifty-year history. The aim of this edition, then, is to clarify and settle that history, and to do so by going back to Burroughs' original manuscripts, to fully restore the original text, if not his original choice of its title.

### ". . . AN AMERICAN BOY"

How autobiographical is *Junky*? Or to put it another way, what relation does William Burroughs have to William Lee? These questions need answering because Burroughs' first novel was the most mined source of information about his life for some thirty-five years, until publication of Ted Morgan's biography in 1988. In particular the Prologue, where Burroughs filled in the narrative's missing background, used to be taken as a wholly reliable biographical resource: most of the details do turn out to be correct, even the most unlikely ones (case records from the Payne Whitney Psychiatric Clinic prove that Burroughs' doctors really had "never heard of Van Gogh," for example), but recent Burroughs criticism has nevertheless shown the artful, rather than artless nature of its presentation of facts. And what of the rest of the narrative? Ginsberg was first to point out the obvious in the "Appreciation" he wrote in 1952 (see Appendix 4): "It is the autobiography of one aspect of the author's career, and obviously cannot be taken as an account of the whole man." Now that we have two biographies (the other by Barry Miles), a volume of letters covering the period, and a mass of interviews, journalism, and critical material, it's possible to see just how partial the account given really is.

Rather than go into the fine details of the narrative's accuracy or selectivity, it is, I think, more instructive to focus on the holes in it that are so large they are easy to overlook. For example, there are portraits of Herbert Huncke, the Times Square hustler who passed the word "beat" to Kerouac and who appears in *Junky* as Herman, and of the thief Phil White, a.k.a. "the Sailor," to whom Burroughs initially planned to dedicate his novel and who appears in it as Roy. But there's not one word referring to the two key figures he befriended at this time—Ginsberg and Kerouac. These significant absences make for a revealing contrast to Kerouac's work: although Burroughs read *The Town and the City* just weeks into the writing of his own first novel, *Junky* did not follow that path of group myth-making, autobiographical fiction that characterized Beat Generation writing.

There is also very little about his wife, Joan Vollmer Adams. Given his focus, there was never going to be much, but after the shooting accident in September 1951 that killed her, Burroughs was put on the spot when Ace pressured him for more: "About death of Joan. I do not see how that could be worked in," he wrote Ginsberg in April 1952. "I did not go into domestic life in *Junk* because it was, in the words of Sam Johnson, 'Nothing to the purpose.' "[3] Later that month he complained that Ace's demands left him feeling like a man "being sawed in half by indecisive fiends," but it's clear from following letters that the indecision was his own, as were the fiends: "If they want it I will write it. Alternatively they could simply cross out all references to her." In the end, the disappearance of Lee's wife, like her presence, remains anomalous: occasional references have the unsettling effect of making the reader want either more, or none at all.

Burroughs' indecision suggests the difficulty he had in maintaining, over time, a consistent relation to his persona and therefore a single style of writing. At first, the chronology of his experience

3. Apart from those referenced in footnotes, all quotations from Burroughs' letters are from *The Letters of William S. Burroughs: 1945–1959* (Penguin, 1993), edited by Oliver Harris.

provided a minimal structure—you couldn't call it a "plot"—but this would come to pose increasing problems. In part, this was because Burroughs had a technical and temperamental difficulty with sustaining realist narrative, a conventional weakness he would later turn into an experimental advantage. Indeed, in the effort to keep it "straight," he decided to cut some of the most interesting sections, which he recognized as digressions from the main narrative line. But the problem can only have become worse as he ceased writing about events set safely in the past, and began having to deal with experiences from the more immediate present. Living with the trauma of a self-inflicted tragedy, and unable either to write about it or to ignore its effects, Burroughs completed *Junky* during increasingly difficult times, and in the last quarter of the novel it shows.

If there was a logic to excluding his fellow writers Ginsberg and Kerouac, this doesn't explain another key decision, namely why Burroughs made his alter ego so *un-literary:* the passing references Lee makes to popular culture (George Raft, Jimmy Durante, Louis Armstrong—an interesting trio) contrast sharply to those he makes in *Queer,* the novel he wrote while still finishing *Junky* (Frank Harris and Jean Cocteau). In letters, Burroughs would sometimes call opium "Cocteau's kick," referring to *Opium: Diary of a Cure,* but such an allusion to the French writer would be completely out of place for the Lee of *Junky.* In fact, there are European literary references in the Prologue—to "Oscar Wilde, Anatole France, Baudelaire, even Gide"—although they're used to distinguish the young Burroughs/Lee from "an American boy of that time and place." The Prologue is also the place where Burroughs speaks of being "greatly impressed by an autobiography of a burglar, called *You Can't Win,* " and in many ways this is the key reference, the one that tells us most about *Junky* and the particular relation it fashions between literature and life.

Sixty years after reading it for the first time, Burroughs took the chance to pay back the pseudonymous Jack Black by writing a foreword to the republication of *You Can't Win* (New York: Amok Press, 1988). Here Burroughs recalls how he was "fascinated by this glimpse of an underworld of seedy rooming-houses, pool parlors, cat houses and opium dens, of bull pens and cat burglars and hobo jungles." There are two things to say about this, one self-evident, the other easily missed. The first is the sheer pleasure Burroughs takes in the lingo of Jack Black's wild frontier locales, the way he savors the phrases, so clearly redolent for him of a lost world, of a nighttime netherworld glazed with a sheen of nostalgia. Burroughs, who also enjoyed the colorful urban world of Damon Runyon, had a double fascination with the criminal milieu and its vivid argot that is reflected throughout *Junky*. He would have found this in *You Can't Win* ("The underworld is quick to seize upon strange words," Black observes), and probably a little later in David Maurer's *The Big Con* (1940), a classic work on the routines and slang of the confidence man in his Golden Age, up to the early 1920s.[4] Maurer's rich gallery of grifters belonged to the vivid but vanishing life that lay outside the sheltered suburbs of Burroughs' midwestern childhood, and in *Junky* he brought something like it alive: Subway Mike, George the Greek, Pantopon Rose, Louie the Bellhop, Eric the Fag, and the Black Bastard—these are blood relatives of the Hashhouse Kid and Slobbering Bob in Maurer's book or the Sanctimonious Kid, Smiler, and Salt Chunk Mary in Jack Black's.

Prompted by such sources, in *Junky*, Burroughs shows his grasp of the different functions served by a specialized argot. We see how it can map the thief's or addict's clandestine life and make it seem a whole alternative world: "Life telescopes down to junk, one fix and looking forward to the next, 'stashes' and 'scripts,' 'spikes' and

4. See David W. Maurer, *The Big Con: The Classic Story of the Confidence Man and the Confidence Trick* (1940: London: Century, 1999).

'droppers.'" For the addict, the slang also doubles the social role of the substance itself. "Heroin was our badge," said Rodney King, onetime partner of Charlie Parker, the great bebop junkie. "It was the thing that said, 'we know. You don't know.' It was the thing that gave us membership in a unique club, and for this membership we gave up everything else in the world."[5] Alert to the decline of old subcultures and the emergence of new ones, late on in *Junky*, Burroughs reports news of changes in the New York scene since he was last there, to suggest how a shift in key terms can define an existence, and, like passwords, admit entry into it: "I learned the new hipster vocabulary: 'pot' for weed, 'twisted' for busted, 'cool,' an all-purpose word."

Cab Calloway in *A Hepster's Dictionary* said the term *hip* meant "wise, sophisticated, anyone with boots on"—where the last phrase signifies living on the street, being streetwise—and Burroughs must have been drawn by this sense that an outsider from official culture gets to possess insider knowledge, gets to know the score. His own glossary definition of *hip* spells out this logic as a sly challenge to the reader: "The expression is not subject to definition because, if you don't 'dig' what it means, no one can ever tell you." As Burroughs would show at the start of *Naked Lunch*, a square who "wants to come on hip" makes a perfect mark; to the reader hungry for the vicarious thrill of knowledge without the risk of experience, *Junky* gives a warning all the better to set the trap, like one of Maurer's con games.

Early on in *You Can't Win*, Black describes his youthful fascination with Jesse James—this would be the early 1880s—and concludes: "Looking back now I can plainly see the influence the James boys and similar characters had in turning my thoughts to adventure and

5. Quoted in Jill Jonnes, *Hep-Cats, Narcs, and Pipe Dreams: A History of America's Romance with Illegal Drugs* (New York: Scribner, 1996).

later to crime." Adventure and crime: the point Burroughs makes in his Prologue to *Junky* is that, trapped in an haute bourgeois suburb of St. Louis and insulated from city life by his family's money, the terms appeared synonymous. *You Can't Win* surely turned Burroughs' thoughts to adventure and crime, and later to writing. But there remains one thing that goes unsaid in the Prologue, and is only hinted at in passing in Burroughs' Foreword to *You Can't Win*, via the phrase "opium dens." Although this is absolutely typical of *Junky*—in giving autobiographical details that are entirely accurate, while omitting to provide the key—the question arises: why did Burroughs neglect to mention the fact that Jack Black was an addict, when this was surely a part of his book's allure for the young Burroughs and so directly relevant to *Junky*?

The most likely explanation is that he wanted to avoid any suggestion of the *literariness* of both his experiences and his own writing, the idea that either were inspired by reading books. This move helped keep *Junky* at a clear remove from the great Romantic tradition, of Coleridge and De Quincey, that he knew so well. If Burroughs stripped Lee of his own literary knowledge and ambition, and gave priority to the anonymous confessions of an American thief rather than to Romantic poets or European modernists, it was surely because he wanted his writing to appear with boots on.

## "SUBJECT IS HOT NOW"

Looking back from the vantage point of half a century, the tribute that Burroughs himself would pay to *You Can't Win* can just as well be said of *Junky*: "He has recorded a chapter of specifically American life that is now gone forever." In summer 1952, however, as he worried over negotiations with A. A. Wyn, Burroughs had very contemporary works in mind. In June he wrote Ginsberg: "Is he or is he not going to publish JUNK? Two books already out on the

subject—DOWN ALL YOUR STREETS and H IS FOR HER-
OIN. I think this beginning of deluge. *NOW* is time to publish
or we bring up rear and lose advantage of timeliness. . . . Subject
is hot now but it won't be hot long."[6] Although he was wrong on
the last score—the subject would never cool down—his reference
points here are revealing.

*Down All Your Streets*, a long first novel about crime and drugs
in New York City, won modest critical acclaim as well as good
sales for Leonard Bishop when Dial Press published it in 1952.
David Hulburd's *H Is for Heroin* ("A Teen-Age Narcotic Tells Her
Story") was a twenty-five-cent paperback from the Popular Library.
By this point, Burroughs had accepted that Ace, a relatively new,
middle-range player in the pulp paperback industry, was his best
bet for *Junky*. But to begin with he had his sights set on New
Directions, the one-man press run by James Laughlin, famous for
his extraordinary list of modernist literature and for publishing
interesting new talent.

For over a year both Ginsberg and Kerouac had lobbied Laughlin on Burroughs' behalf by recommending *Junky*, Kerouac closing a letter in February 1952 with the telling lines (given him by
Ginsberg): "It would be a shame if it was eventually swallowed up
by cheap paper covered 25 cent Gold Medal or Signet books like
'I, Mobster.'"[7] The Ace Double Book publication of *Junkie* (bound
back-to-back with a reprint of Maurice Helbrant's memoir, *Narcotic
Agent*, and priced at thirty-five cents) put Burroughs firmly in the
drugstore and newsstand pulp market rather than on the serious
hardback shelves. It's not an entirely idle thought to wonder what
would have happened to Burroughs' first novel as an imprint not

6. Burroughs to Ginsberg, June 15, 1952 (Ginsberg Collection, Columbia
University).
7. *Jack Kerouac: Selected Letters, 1940–1956* (New York: Viking, 1995),
edited by Ann Charters, 333.

of Ace Books but of New Directions—both in terms of reception (the Ace edition sold over a hundred thousand copies in its first year, but none to literary reviewers) and also in terms of actual content. As we'll see in more detail below, in important ways the final form and content of *Junkie* were shaped directly and indirectly by its publishers.

The market that Burroughs was destined to enter also made for a telling contrast to a much more famous novel on the subject that he must have known: Nelson Algren's *The Man with the Golden Arm*. Nominated for a Pulitzer Prize, the book had made Algren an instant celebrity in 1950, and his depiction of Frankie Machine, the low-life, poker-dealing junkie of the title, had an equal impact: as David Courtwright notes in his history of opiate addiction in America, Algren's hero marked a crucial generational shift in the cultural stereotype of the addict, now defined for the postwar public in the image of the hustling street criminal.[8] The irony, however, is that Algren's literary ambition and experience of narcotics were aloof from street level. In fact, it was his agent who encouraged him to use junk as a peg for his plot at a time when Algren, corresponding with Simone de Beauvoir and financed by literary fellowships, barely knew any actual junkies.

In March 1950, while Burroughs was beginning work on *Junky*, Algren was receiving invitations to Hollywood (the movie of his novel, directed by Otto Preminger and starring Frank Sinatra, came out in 1955), and was being presented with the National Book Award for Fiction by Eleanor Roosevelt at the Waldorf-Astoria. While the prospect of the latter fate would not have tempted Burroughs, it's necessary to see how materially the publishing context defined by Ace Books ensured that in 1953 Burroughs' novel, not

8. See David T. Courtwright, *Dark Paradise: A History of Opiate Addiction in America* (Cambridge: Harvard University Press, 2001).

printed under his own name or even using his title, bypassed any chance of a literary reputation or critical reception.

In 1952 Burroughs was well aware that the subject of *Junky* was hot, in several senses of the word. From a publishing point of view, it was the type of story that would sell paperbacks, a new and booming industry. But the paranoid and reactionary national mood—this was the era of McCarthyism—meant that the subject was also dangerous to handle. Amid wider fears about popular culture and its capacity to incite imitation, the paperback industry was itself subject to congressional investigation in 1952, and found guilty. A pulp novel about drug addiction therefore combined two moral panics for the price of one.

*Junkie* was a product of these times, as Ace Books sought both to exploit the interest—packaging the novel inside an especially lurid and voyeuristic cover—and to defend their backs, by inserting a series of nervous disclaimers. This attempt to censor Burroughs' novel had unforeseen ironic effects, however. Perversely, the notes inserted into the text imply one of two things: either that whenever there *isn't* a disclaimer or a rebuttal ("This statement is hearsay," or "This is contradicted by recognized medical authority"), the text can *only* be telling the truth; or that this censorious voice is inadvertently pinpointing the really important facts. Ace also added a Publisher's Note (see Appendix 5), which proposed the novel's function as a deterrent; it would, they claimed, "discourage imitation by thrill-hungry teen-agers." The irony of these measures would not have been lost on Burroughs, and his original introduction to "Junk" (see Appendix 2) spelt out his own position in blunt terms: "Official propaganda opposes any factual statement about junk, so that almost nothing accurate has been written on the subject." Cutting through the myths mattered because, as he knew from firsthand experience as an addict, America in 1950 was at the peak of a postwar epidemic. Whatever else it is, *Junky* remains a precise eyewitness report to essential changes on the ground.

Early on and near the end of *Junky*, Burroughs makes reference to the Harrison Narcotics Act of 1914. The key statute in the history of addiction legislation, the act was actually drafted as a tax measure to regulate the market, but it was soon interpreted as a law prohibiting the supply of opiates. Born in February 1914, Burroughs' life coincided with the world of narcotic prohibition, although the coincidence had not only a symbolic meaning, but a close family connection. After becoming addicted to morphine in the course of medical treatment, his uncle, Horace Burroughs, committed suicide just days after the Harrison Act came into effect in March 1915; finding his condition suddenly criminalized was too much for Burroughs' already troubled uncle, but he was only among the first of many such victims. Interestingly, however, in *Junky*, Burroughs doesn't single out the Harrison Act as the event that forced addicts into a world of crime because it cut off their legal supplies. He therefore avoided making a case that recent historians of addiction have shown to be something of a popular myth, a simplification that overlooks the emergence of addict subcultures well before the national legislation. Rather, Burroughs observes a range of behavior that details the transformation of narcotic use over a forty-year period with remarkable accuracy and eye for significant detail.

Take the very first reference in the book. In the Prologue, Burroughs describes as a child hearing his maid talk about opium smoking, and records its impact on him: "I will smoke opium when I grow up." The truth of this anecdote does not depend on whether it actually happened, but on its historical accuracy. According to David Courtwright, the white, as distinct from Chinese, opium smoker emerged in America in the late nineteenth century, and was always associated with the lower-class underworld: prostitutes, gamblers, petty criminals—even unsavory maids caring for the impressionable sons of haute bourgeois families. Indeed, there were widespread fears that opium smoking was spreading to the upper classes, especially the idle rich. The decadent aristocrat enchanted by the opium pipe became a stock character, an image Burroughs would later parody in a self-portrait that continued where the Prologue to *Junky* left off: "As a young child I wanted to be a writer because writers were rich and famous. They lounged around Singapore and Rangoon smoking opium in a yellow pongee silk suit."[9] But besides the aristocratic and artistic associations, the opium smoker is a significant first reference because when imports of smoking material were banned, under the Smoking Opium Exclusion Act of 1909, the use of heroin accelerated to take its place.

Heroin's rise coincided with a major shift in the profile and milieu of the typical addict, and the substance of these changes is documented in Burroughs' novel through details that might otherwise appear insignificant. To give only a few isolated examples: *Junky* begins in New York in 1945, the urban center of heroin use at the point when supply lines resumed after wartime shortages; Burroughs gives the moniker "Short Count Tony" to his Italian connection on the Lower East Side, and it was when Italian gangsters replaced Jewish dealers that the purity of street heroin declined sharply, which in turn led to a rise in intravenous use to maximize the hit; the key transformation in addiction, the reason it moved into the underworld, was the shift from its medical origins, so that a character like Matty, encountered by Lee in Lexington, defines the older generation ("A doctor had got Matty on stuff. 'The Jew bastard,' Matty said . . . 'But I made him wish he'd never seen me'"); early on, Burroughs focuses on a particular Broadway block to define the territory as well as type of addict ("The hipster-bebop junkies never showed at 103rd Street. The 103rd Street boys were all oldtimers"), so making an important spatial and temporal distinction that anticipates the one he gives later on in Mexico

9. *The Adding Machine* (London: Calder, 1985), 2.

("No zoot-suiters. The hipster has gone underground"), which in turn conveys an ethnic dimension (zoot suits, with broad, padded shoulders, were worn by Mexican-Americans, and associated with racial tension and riots in southern California during 1943) and marks the rise of a true heroin counterculture; the end of *Junky* describes the "nationwide hysteria" that spread from the "police-state legislation" passed in Louisiana, referencing the Boggs Act of 1951, which imposed harsh mandatory sentences at a time when the postwar epidemic was actually in decline—a sign, as Burroughs claimed in a letter at this time, that the "real significance of these scandalous laws is political."

Finally, the long section of *Junky* set in the Public Health Service Narcotic Hospital at Lexington is especially significant, because it gives a firsthand description of the key federal institution, important not only for the treatment of addiction, but for medical research (from the 1950s, this included secret CIA experiments) and the development of policy over four decades. Lexington opened in 1935 when addiction was seen in public health terms as a contagious sickness, and the narcotic farm was designed, as Caroline Acker has shown, to segregate addicts out of the prison system and, maybe, to rehabilitate them using techniques of moral and social adjustment.[10] In 1946, Lexington's intake was 600; in 1949, there were nearly 3,000 admissions; in 1950, over 5,500. This massive increase featured two key demographic changes: as Jill Jonnes notes, there were 214 black admissions in 1949; in 1950, the figure was 1,460. The other feature was an equally spectacular rise in the number of young addicts, and in 1951 a special new juvenile ward was opened to cope with the problem; as Bill Gains

10. See Caroline Jean Acker, *Creating the American Junkie: Addiction Research in the Classic Era of Narcotic Control* (Baltimore: Johns Hopkins University Press, 2002).

says, with a gloating smile for emphasis, "Yes, Lexington is full of young kids now."

Bill Gains, in fact, deserves a special mention. With his cruel, vampiric smile, he is a significant exception that proves a particular rule in *Junky*. "If you have a commodity you naturally want customers," Lee notes; but "Gains was one of the few junkies who really took a special pleasure in seeing non-users get a habit." Burroughs' observations of peddling drugs emphatically contradict one of the tenets of what, in his original introduction to "Junk," he called "the officially sponsored myth": *"Addicts want to get others on the stuff."* Ironically, Burroughs implies that, with the odd exception, the economics of the junk trade are *more* rather than less ethical than those of the above-ground business world. To the prevailing cold war rhetoric of imitation and deterrence and the insistence on striking a moral position, Burroughs just said *no*.

Commissioner of Narcotics Harry J. Anslinger—who also published a book in 1953, *The Traffic in Narcotics*—maintained the official myths as long as possible. But, as David Courtwright notes, hard epidemiological data, like the Lexington intake figures, actually supports Burroughs' insistence throughout *Junky* that addiction is not a moral failing or a psychopathology demanding punitive treatment but a disease of exposure. Burroughs, who spent two weeks in Lexington during January 1948, was a statistic in the manifest failure of politically motivated and increasingly draconian prohibition laws. Fifty years later, at a time when America has incarcerated half a million drug offenders—an astonishing development beyond even Burroughs' powers of prophecy—his point-blank refusal in *Junky* to dodge the moral, medical, legal, and political hypocrisy that surround the subject of addiction is, regrettably, more relevant now than it ever was.

Nevertheless, it would be a mistake to conclude on this note, just as it would be a mistake to read Burroughs' descriptions of junk peddling as only a critique of capitalism or a riposte to tales of the "heroin menace." In the end, and not just for literary reasons, Burroughs' novel is more than—*other than*—a bold piece of clear-eyed reportage. His clinical observations give rise to speculative insights, to flights of scientific fantasy about addiction, and from his original introduction it is clear that these pointed toward a *thesis*. Here he made explicit, for example, the logic behind the many images in the novel that imply *junk itself* is a kind of spectral vampire preying on its users: "You cannot avoid the feeling that junk is in some way alive," "junk is a parasite," and so on. Before being able to take the idea further, Burroughs would have to write *Queer*—a slighter text in many obvious ways, and yet, in other respects, more crucial to his development—but this is Burroughs taking the first steps toward his theory of the *virus*, a central concern in his writing from *Naked Lunch* onwards. In other words, *Junky* is in embryonic form an exploratory novel, an *experimental* text, like all those Burroughs would write after it, and the final lines of the introduction he cut could stand as the maxim for his entire oeuvre. "I am using the known facts as a starting point in an attempt to reach facts that are not known."

•

Burroughs began "Junk" in early 1950, and Ace Books published it as *Junkie* on April 15, 1953, but what happened to his manuscript—both in between and since then—reveals a good deal about his early career that significantly changes the established understanding of how Burroughs began as a writer. Since this is a fascinating and complex episode in a much larger history that I have related elsewhere,[11] I will focus here on the most immediate

11. See *William Burroughs and the Secret of Fascination* (Carbondale: Southern Illinois University Press, 2003).

issue; namely, how piecing together this story makes visible for the first time the true editing and publishing history of Burroughs' first novel, up to and including this present edition. The history of Burroughs' manuscript can be divided in three parts. By the end of 1950, he had completed a one-hundred-and-fifty-page draft, typed up for him by Alice Jeffries, the wife of a friend in the expatriate community of Mexico City. The manuscript he mailed Lucien Carr that December—Ginsberg's role as amateur literary agent came later—was organized into twenty-nine chapters (numbered up to thirty, but, mysteriously, there was no Chapter 8), and ended at the point when Lee first meets Old Ike in his lawyer's office (pages 107–8). Burroughs scholars have long assumed this "original" manuscript was lost; in fact, with a few pages missing, it is the one preserved at Columbia University. Burroughs revised quite a few details during 1951 and 1952, but he never replaced this manuscript as such. Then, starting in March 1951, he wrote and inserted a few short expansions, began what he called the "Mexican section," and in April decided to make one significant cut: removal of Chapter 28, a long digression that applied the theories of Wilhelm Reich to addiction. The next phase began in early 1952, when Burroughs wrote more short inserts and in March made a second significant cut: removal of Chapter 27, a long detour into the economics of the Rio Grande Valley. "The idea," he told Ginsberg, "is cut down to straight narrative."

Part three of the manuscript history is the most significant and revealing, but because so many of the pieces were scattered or thought lost, until now no accurate account was possible. It dates from the point in April 1952 when Ginsberg informed A. A. Wyn that Burroughs had begun *Queer*, which, even though it was written in the third person, started as a sequel to "Junk." Much to Burroughs' annoyance, Wyn stalled negotiations until he had seen the new manuscript, with the idea of adding it onto the end of "Junk"; but when in June he saw what Burroughs had written so far, he rejected it (less due to its homosexual content than to its quite different quality of writing). Wyn now demanded forty more pages for "Junk" before he would agree to the contract. Burroughs was furious—Wyn had already required him to write the autobiographical Prologue—and he in turn refused to start work on the new material until the contract was signed, which it was on July 5. By a deadline of August 15, he duly completed both the Prologue and a thirty-eight-page manuscript ("I am not completely satisfied," he told Ginsberg, "especially not with that fucking preface").[12]

Apart from a two-page insert made in 1977, this additional manuscript corresponds to the final quarter of the published novel (pages 108–44). Now, because of the events they describe, the last eight pages of this new manuscript could only have been written from scratch in July 1952, while the first ten might have drawn on the "Mexican section" Burroughs began in spring of 1951. The large middle portion, however, over half of this manuscript, can now be identified as a light reworking of material taken from the first half of *Queer*. Precise comparison of newly discovered manuscripts in turn reveals exactly how, where, and why Burroughs edited one to fit the other; in fact, it shows the way he literally *cut up* his carbon copies and pasted the fragile pieces together. This cannibalization of material—which would become an essential trademark of Burroughs' practice as a writer—lets us see for the first time and very exactly the relationship between these two novels, enabling a new understanding for readers—and critics— baffled by the sudden and striking difference between them.

Once Ace Books had Burroughs' manuscript, the editors set to work. In December 1952, they made the decision to bind it

12. Burroughs to Ginsberg, August 20, 1952 (Ginsberg Collection, Columbia University).

back-to-back with *Narcotic Agent* ("an appalling idea," Burroughs groaned, although he later admitted the memoirs were "not so bad as I expected"). Then, having reorganized the novel into fifteen chapters, they cut numerous passages, made two dozen separate bowdlerizations (some small: "Fucking punks" became "Nowhere punks"; others more substantial), and inserted seven editor's notes. Finally, in February 1953 Ace held up the publication schedule once they knew that Burroughs, now traveling through Central and South America, was planning to write about his expedition to find the drug *yagé*. Burroughs declined to be screwed twice—"They are up to their old tricks: 2 books, 1 advance"—and two months later the book was on sale in rail stations across America.

The first Ace edition sold 113,170 copies between April and the end of 1953 (96,382 in the United States, 16,578 in Canada, the rest unaccounted for) and earned $1,129.60, but Burroughs never received proper royalty payments and would complain repeatedly that Ace failed to honor its contract. Ginsberg, meanwhile, had another complaint. After a meeting with Wyn in October, he covered all the stalls and bookstores around Times Square, 42nd Street, and Greenwich Village in search of *Junkie*, and found no copies for sale. Since these were, as he later protested to Wyn, the hottest areas for junk and therefore for a book called *Junkie*, it raises the interesting question as to where those one hundred thousand readers of Burroughs' novel came from, who they were, and what they made of it.

Apart from a British reprint by Digit Books in 1957, *Junkie* wasn't published separately—let alone under Burroughs' own name—until the Ace edition of 1964, which they reprinted in 1970 and 1973, while other editions appeared from Olympia Press (1966, reprinted in 1969 and 1972) and Bruce and Watson (1973). It was translated into languages from Dutch to Japanese, including an Italian edition (titled *La scimmia sulla schiena—Monkey on the Back*) that featured an article on the apomorphine cure which Burroughs asked to be reprinted in the 1964 Ace edition ("the article would lend dignity and purpose to the publication"),[13] but to no avail. In the mid-1970s Burroughs, through his agent Peter Matson and lawyer Eugene Winick, finally took action against Ace Books for breach of contract, presented an overwhelming case, and secured reversion of the rights. This paved the way for the new Penguin edition of 1977, and for the many changes, corrections, and restorations of material carried out by James Grauerholz and authorized by Burroughs.

The differences between *Junky* and the first edition of *Junkie* are extensive but can be given briefly: The title was changed (and the subtitle dropped); the dedication was cut ("To A.L.M."—a cryptic reference to Adelbert Lewis Marker, the real-life original of Allerton, Lee's object of desire in *Queer*); Carl Solomon's Publisher's Note was replaced with a new introduction by Allen Ginsberg; Ace's chapters were replaced by a continuous text, divided only by spacing; paragraphing was reorganized; the bowdlerizations were undone and a dozen or so original names restored; the editor's notes were deleted; the glossary was relocated to after the narrative; a number of errors were corrected; a number of new errors were introduced (some due to mistakes in the 1973 Ace reprint, the one used as the basis for the Penguin edition); and, finally, various unused parts of Burroughs' original manuscripts were inserted, including the long Rio Grande Valley section. All in all, some 250 deletions, corrections, and additions were made, and in the narrative itself the net result was that when *Junkie* became *Junky* it gained 3,850 words, lost just under a hundred, and in other, more subtle ways, it both looked and read like a different novel.

*Junky* (1977) was completely unexpurgated but not "complete"—in the sense of restoring a single, authoritative manuscript—since, properly speaking, no such object ever existed. The use of manuscripts is always a matter of delicate decisions (you can draw up

13. Burroughs to Carl Solomon, October 11, 1964 (New York University).

principles, but have to apply them flexibly) and of chance factors (unlike a jigsaw puzzle, you can never say there aren't more small pieces still to discover), as well as of interpretation (finding more evidence doesn't always resolve ambiguities). Apart from making just over a hundred small corrections or changes, this present edition adds to *Junky* approximately the same amount of new material (around four thousand words) as *Junky* added to *Junkie*, but the way it does so is, and had to be, quite different.

This edition of *Junky* takes advantage of important new manuscript discoveries, and a better understanding of old ones: the middle half of the July 1952 manuscript, the whole chapter on Wilhelm Reich, Burroughs' original introduction and draft glossary, the *Queer* manuscripts—these and other fragments were all unavailable or presumed lost in 1977. On the other hand, the imprimatur of Burroughs himself is no longer available. This is one reason I have gone into the details, to make the process of change between editions as visible as possible, and why, where the authority is uncertain or the impact questionable, I have intervened cautiously. Despite the great interest of almost all of it, around three-quarters of the new material has not been inserted into the text. Over five hundred words from the manuscripts of *Junky* and *Queer* have been given in notes, and the bulk of it, starting with the most important material, has been put into a short section of appendices.

Appendix 1, the long-lost Chapter 28 (found in the Ginsberg Collection at Stanford University), is so significant that it is tempting to think it should have been restored to *Junky*. It is certainly more revealing than the Valley section that immediately preceded it in the manuscript, and that Burroughs also decided to cut. But it is not just a question of disregarding the author's past unambiguous decision. ("Reich will be deleted bag and baggage," he told Ginsberg in May 1951; "I do not feel that the part about Reich and the philosophical sections belong there cluttering up the narrative," he repeated in April 1952.) It is also a question of the effect that restoring this material would have on everything else around it.

Although it suspends the narrative, and the prose here is oddly wooden, lacking the deceptive fluency and rhythm elsewhere, the real reason Burroughs wanted it cut is surely because it cast the rest of the novel in an entirely different light. Suddenly Burroughs breaks into his *own* voice, as if relieved to escape the constraint of his narrator's, and the person that emerges is a speculative philosopher, a *theorist* of addiction. It is impossible to imagine William Lee reading Reich's *The Cancer Biopathy* (as Burroughs did in June 1949) or building an orgone accumulator (as he did that November), but the effect of this section is to draw attention to the presence of similar material scattered throughout the novel that is otherwise quite easily overlooked. It also reveals something else about Burroughs. Reich was once one of Europe's leading psychoanalytical thinkers, but in postwar America he came to be regarded as a science crank and a medical charlatan. Some of Burroughs' speculations about addiction have turned out to be extraordinarily prescient, literally prophetic, but others show him up as an amateur on his soapbox, a crackpot eccentric; talking about "orgones," Burroughs admits here that he might be taken "for a lunatic." So there were several reasons why Reich was cut, "bag and baggage."

Burroughs' original introduction (also from the Ginsberg Collection at Stanford) has much in common with Chapter 28, and it's no coincidence that he decided to revise it in April 1952, the same time he reconfirmed Reich was to be cut. Burroughs recognized that with constant revisions his novel had changed and, while a few pieces of Chapter 28 survived in the new autobiographical Prologue he was asked to write, none of this original introduction did. Again, it is a highly revealing text, speculating about the endocrine balance of addicts, promoting the value of antihistamine treatments (as a wonder drug, the clear forerunner of apomorphine for Burroughs), and making absolutely explicit his determination to go beyond the misinformation of prevailing myths.

Burroughs' letter to A. A. Wyn (Ginsberg Collection, Columbia University), which was written some time in 1959, but possibly never mailed, is included here for two reasons. Firstly, it provides a warrant for correcting several unauthorized changes made to Burroughs' novel by Ace Books, changes that are themselves given as representative instances, only "the more flagrant mutilations" of his manuscript. Secondly, it shows Burroughs' attention to detail, concerning not just accurate idiomatic usage, but the novel as a whole: "I spent a year working on this manuscript. I checked over every word many times." This could be read as a corrective to those who assume Burroughs tossed off his writing carelessly. But to be more exact, it suggests that, whereas for *Naked Lunch*—first published in 1959—and his early cut-up texts, he *did* embrace accidents and overlook what other authors would call mistakes, this did not apply to his first novel.

Appendix 4, Ginsberg's "Appreciation" from April 1952 (previously published in *Deliberate Prose: Selected Essays, 1952–1995*), is no less interesting for being full of factual errors about Burroughs' life. In fact, the contrast it makes with the Prologue by Burroughs that Ace did publish is intriguing, especially if, as the internal evidence suggests, Burroughs modeled his own autobiographical sketch on Ginsberg's draft. This is true for many local details: like Ginsberg, Burroughs would mention Gide and Baudelaire among his reading, but not Cocteau's *Opium* (for reasons I suggested above) or W. B. Yeats' *A Vision* (a work of philosophy too recondite and eccentric); Burroughs would keep the finger-cutting incident, but not the shooting of Joan; and the writing of his first mature attempt at fiction, "Twilight's Last Gleaming" (described by Ginsberg as a "20-page playlet"), would also be left out, along with any suggestion of a literary background to *Junky*. Equally, this piece is interesting for showing Ginsberg's immediate grasp that

Burroughs had written "an important document"; "an archive of the underground." On the other hand, it also shows how bound Ginsberg was, or felt he had to be, by the language of moral judgment (speaking of "subterranean vices" when he meant homosexuality) that characterized the early 1950s.

One final point is worth noting. This only hints at the efforts Ginsberg made to promote Burroughs' novel, at a time when few were willing. Planning to have it appear under the names of Kerouac and John Clellon Holmes (both already recognized as Beat Generation figures), Ginsberg even wrote a gossip column piece to coincide with publication, intended for David Dempsey in *The New York Times*—only to have Kerouac angrily refuse to lend his name to it (either out of fear of guilt-by-association with narcotics, or because of his on-off literary rivalry with Holmes). Ginsberg's tireless support for *Junky* cannot be overstated.

The last three appendices are reprinted here to complete the publishing record, since each appeared as an introductory text to the three main previous editions. The first of Carl Solomon's two pieces, an anonymous Publisher's Note that preceded the first edition of *Junkie*, is the more revealing of the two and of clear historical interest. Ginsberg's introduction to the 1977 Penguin edition accurately describes Solomon's involvement in the Ace edition, just one part of its very instructive and still valuable narrative of events. The account is not entirely reliable, however. Ginsberg implies, for example, that the Rio Grande Valley section was blue-penciled by Ace, when the evidence shows it was cut by Burroughs. More importantly, his claim that Burroughs wrote *Junky*, in effect, *for* Ginsberg, sending him chapters as part of their long-distance correspondence, is contradicted by all the evidence (a correction that has far-reaching implications within the larger history I have related). The alternative account of how Burroughs began the novel, given by both his biographers, is that when his oldest friend, Kells Elvins, moved to Mexico City in January 1950 he simply encouraged Burroughs to write up like a diary his past experiences as an addict, which, although it's partial and inadequate, is what he probably did.

But it would be wrong to end this introduction to *Junky* with a quibble about Ginsberg's accuracy as an historian of its writing. He was the one who was there, and there when it mattered, making sure Burroughs' novel got published in the first place—and besides, who can ever truly say, "Here are the facts"? This is the peculiar interest of *Junky;* that it began at a point when Burroughs seemed to believe he could say this, and was finished at a time when he knew that he couldn't. If Burroughs never demystified the origins of his writing, this may be because incomplete or inaccurate accounts suited someone with things to hide (which he certainly had), but also because he doubted the value and suspected the power of claims to true knowledge. Even so, the novel itself points to the unaccountable, to that which, like the junkie identity, "escapes exact tabulation" and so remains irresistibly elusive, leading us on but always slipping away. "There is no key, no secret someone else has that he can give you"—Burroughs leaves us with a paradoxical key, a perverse secret, a confession perhaps, and most definitely a warning.

Oliver Harris

September 2002

# *Junky*

# Prologue

I was born in 1914 in a solid, three-story, brick house in a large Midwest city. My parents were comfortable. My father owned and ran a lumber business. The house had a lawn in front, a back yard with a garden, a fish pond and a high wooden fence all around it. I remember the lamplighter lighting the gas streetlights and the huge, black, shiny Lincoln and drives in the park on Sunday. All the props of a safe, comfortable way of life that is now gone forever. I could put down one of those nostalgic routines about the old German doctor who lived next door and the rats running around in the back yard and my aunt's electric car and my pet toad that lived by the fish pond.

Actually my earliest memories are colored by a fear of nightmares. I was afraid to be alone, and afraid of the dark, and afraid to go to sleep because of dreams where a supernatural horror seemed always on the point of taking shape. I was afraid some day the dream would still be there when I woke up. I recall hearing a maid talk about opium and how smoking opium brings sweet dreams, and I said: "I will smoke opium when I grow up."

I was subject to hallucinations as a child. Once I woke up in the early morning light and saw little men playing in a block house I had made. I felt no fear, only a feeling of stillness and wonder.

Another recurrent hallucination or nightmare concerned "animals in the wall," and started with the delirium of a strange, undiagnosed fever that I had at the age of four or five.

I went to a progressive school with the future solid citizens, the lawyers, doctors and businessmen of a large Midwest town. I was timid with the other children and afraid of physical violence. One aggressive little Lesbian would pull my hair whenever she saw me. I would like to shove her face in right now, but she fell off a horse and broke her neck years ago.

When I was about seven my parents decided to move to the suburbs "to get away from people." They bought a large house with grounds and woods and a fish pond where there were squirrels instead of rats. They lived there in a comfortable capsule, with a beautiful garden and cut off from contact with the life of the city.

I went to a private suburban high school. I was not conspicuously good or bad at sports, neither brilliant nor backward in studies. I had a definite blind spot for mathematics or anything mechanical. I never liked competitive team games and avoided these whenever possible. I became, in fact, a chronic malingerer. I did like fishing, hunting and hiking. I read more than was usual for an American boy of that time and place: Oscar Wilde, Anatole France, Baudelaire, even Gide. I formed a romantic attachment for another boy and we spent our Saturdays exploring old quarries, riding around on bicycles and fishing in ponds and rivers.

At this time, I was greatly impressed by an autobiography of a burglar, called *You Can't Win*. The author claimed to have spent a good part of his life in jail. It sounded good to me compared with the dullness of a Midwest suburb where all contact with life was shut out. I saw my friend as an ally, a partner in crime. We found an abandoned factory and broke all the windows and stole a chisel. We were caught, and our fathers had to pay the damages. After this my friend "packed me in" because the relationship was endangering his standing with the group. I saw there was no compromise possible with the group, the others, and I found myself a good deal alone.

The environment was empty, the antagonist hidden, and I drifted into solo adventures. My criminal acts were gestures, unprofitable and for the most part unpunished. I would break into houses and walk around without taking anything. As a matter of fact, I had no need for money. Sometimes I would drive around in the country with a .22 rifle, shooting chickens. I made the roads unsafe with reckless driving until an accident, from which I emerged miraculously and portentously unscratched, scared me into normal caution.

I went to one of the Big Three universities, where I majored in English literature for lack of interest in any other subject. I hated the University and I hated the town it was in. Everything about the place was dead. The University was a fake English set-up taken over by the graduates of fake English public schools. I was lonely. I knew no one, and strangers were regarded with distaste by the closed corporation of the desirables.

By accident I met some rich homosexuals of the international queer set who cruise around the world, bumping into each other in queer joints from New York to Cairo. I saw a way of life, a vocabulary, references, a whole symbol system, as the sociologists say. But these people were jerks for the most part and, after an initial period of fascination, I cooled off on the set-up.

When I graduated without honors, I had one hundred fifty dollars per month in trust. That was in the depression and there were no jobs and I couldn't think of any job I wanted, in any case. I drifted around Europe for a year or so. Remnants of the postwar decay lingered in Europe. U.S. dollars could buy a good percentage of the inhabitants of Austria, male or female. That was in 1936, and the Nazis were closing in fast.

I went back to the States. With my trust fund I could live without working or hustling. I was still cut off from life as I had been in the Midwest suburb. I fooled around taking graduate courses in psychology and Jiu-jitsu lessons. I decided to undergo psycho-analysis, and continued with it for three years. Analysis removed inhibitions and anxiety so that I could live the way I wanted to live. Much of my progress in analysis was accomplished in spite of my analyst who did not like my "orientation," as he called it. He finally abandoned analytic objectivity and put down an out-and-out con. I was more pleased with the results than he was.

After being rejected on physical grounds from five officer-training programs, I was drafted into the Army and certified fit for unlimited service. I decided I was not going to like the Army and copped out on my nut-house record—I'd once got on a Van Gogh kick and cut off a finger joint to impress someone who in-terested me at the time. The nut-house doctors had never heard of Van Gogh. They put me down for schizophrenia, adding paranoid type to explain the upsetting fact that I knew where I was and who was President of the U.S. When the Army saw that diagnosis they discharged me with the notation, "This man is never to be recalled or reclassified."

After parting company with the Army, I took a variety of jobs. You could have about any job you wanted at that time. I worked as a private detective, an exterminator, a bartender. I worked in factories and offices. I played around the edges of crime. But my hundred and fifty dollars per month was always there. I did not have to have money. It seemed a romantic extravagance to jeopardize my freedom by some token act of crime. It was at this time and under these circumstances that I came in contact with junk, became an addict, and thereby gained the motivation, the real need for money I had never had before.

The question is frequently asked: Why does a man become a drug addict?

The answer is that he usually does not intend to become an addict. You don't wake up one morning and decide to be a drug addict. It takes at least three months' shooting twice a day to get any habit at all. And you don't really know what junk sickness is until you have had several habits. It took me almost six months to get my first habit, and then the withdrawal symptoms were mild. I think it no exaggeration to say it takes about a year and several hundred injections to make an addict.

The questions, of course, could be asked: Why did you ever try narcotics? Why did you continue using it long enough to become an addict? You become a narcotics addict because you do not have strong motivations in any other direction. Junk wins by default. I tried it as a matter of curiosity. I drifted along taking shots when I could score. I ended up hooked. Most addicts I have talked to report a similar experience. They did not start using drugs for any reason they can remember. They just drifted along until they got hooked. If you have never been addicted, you can have no clear idea what it means to need junk with the addict's special need. You don't decide to be an addict. One morning you wake up sick and you're an addict.

I have never regretted my experience with drugs. I think I am in better health now as a result of using junk at intervals than I would be if I had never been an addict. When you stop growing you start dying. An addict never stops growing. Most users periodically kick the habit, which involves shrinking of the organism and replacement of the junk-dependent cells. A user is in continual state of shrinking and growing in his daily cycle of shot-need for shot completed.

Most addicts look younger than they are. Scientists recently experimented with a worm that they were able to shrink by withholding food. By periodically shrinking the worm so that it was in continual growth, the worm's life was prolonged indefinitely. Perhaps if a junkie could keep himself in a constant state of kicking, he would live to a phenomenal age.

Junk is a cellular equation that teaches the user facts of general validity. I have learned a great deal from using junk: I have seen life

measured out in eyedroppers of morphine solution. I experienced
the agonizing deprivation of junk sickness, and the pleasure of relief
when junk-thirsty cells drank from the needle. Perhaps all pleasure
is relief. I have learned the cellular stoicism that junk teaches the
user. I have seen a cell full of sick junkies silent and immobile in
separate misery. They knew the pointlessness of complaining or
moving. They knew that basically no one can help anyone else.
There is no key, no secret someone else has that he can give you.

I have learned the junk equation. Junk is not, like alcohol or
weed, a means to increased enjoyment of life. Junk is not a kick.
It is a way of life.

My first experience with junk was during the War, about 1944 or 1945. I had made the acquaintance of a man named Norton who was working in a shipyard at the time. Norton, whose real name was Morelli or something like that, had been discharged from the peacetime Army for forging a pay check, and was classified 4-F for reasons of bad character. He looked like George Raft, but was taller. Norton was trying to improve his English and achieve a smooth, affable manner. Affability, however, did not come natural to him. In repose, his expression was sullen and mean, and you knew he always had that mean look when you turned your back.

Norton was a hard-working thief and he did not feel right unless he stole something every day from the shipyard where he worked. A tool, some canned goods, a pair of overalls, anything at all. One day he called me up and said he had stolen a Tommy gun. Could I find someone to buy it? I said, "Maybe. Bring it over."

The housing shortage was getting under way. I paid fifteen dollars per week for a dirty apartment that opened onto a companionway and never got any sunlight. The wallpaper was flaking off because the radiator leaked steam when there was any steam in it to leak. I had the windows sealed shut against the cold with a caulking of newspapers. The place was full of roaches and occasionally I killed a bedbug.

I was sitting by the radiator, a little damp from the steam, when I heard Norton's knock. I opened the door, and there he was standing in the dark hall with a big parcel wrapped in brown paper under his arm. He smiled and said, "Hello."

I said, "Come in, Norton, and take off your coat."

He unwrapped the Tommy gun and we assembled it and snapped the firing pin.

I said I would find someone to buy it.

Norton said, "Oh, here's something else I picked up."

It was a flat yellow box with five one-half grain syrettes of morphine tartrate.

"This is just a sample," he said, indicating the morphine. "I've got fifteen of these boxes at home and I can get more if you get rid of these."

I said, "I'll see what I can do."

●

At that time I had never used any junk and it did not occur to me to try it. I began looking for someone to buy the two items and that is how I ran into Roy and Herman.

I knew a young hoodlum from upstate New York who was working as a short-order cook in Riker's, "cooling off," as he explained. I called him and said I had something to get rid of, and made an appointment to meet him in the Angle Bar on Eighth Avenue near 42nd Street.

This bar was a meeting place for 42nd Street hustlers, a peculiar breed of four-flushing, would-be criminals. They are always looking for a "set-up man," someone to plan jobs and tell them exactly what to do. Since no "set-up man" would have anything to do with people so obviously inept, unlucky, and unsuccessful, they go on looking, fabricating preposterous lies about their big scores, cooling off as dishwashers, soda jerks, waiters, occasionally rolling a drunk or a timid queer, looking, always looking, for the "set-up man" with a big job who will say, "I've been watching you. You're the man I need for this set-up. Now listen . . ."

Jack—through whom I met Roy and Herman—was not one of these lost sheep looking for the shepherd with a diamond ring and a gun in the shoulder holster and the hard, confident voice with overtones of connections, fixes, set-ups that would make a stickup sound easy and sure of success. Jack was very successful from time to time and would turn up in new clothes and even new cars. He was also an inveterate liar who seemed to lie more for himself than for any visible audience. He had a clean-cut, healthy country face, but there was something curiously diseased about him. He was subject to sudden fluctuations in weight, like a diabetic or a sufferer from liver trouble. These changes in weight were often accompanied by an uncontrollable fit of restlessness, so that he would disappear for some days.

The effect was uncanny. You would see him one time a fresh-faced kid. A week or so later he would turn up so thin, sallow and old-looking, you would have to look twice to recognize him. His face was lined with suffering in which his eyes did not participate. It was a suffering of his cells alone. He himself—the conscious ego that looked out of the glazed, alert-calm hoodlum eyes—would have nothing to do with this suffering of his rejected other self, a suffering of the nervous system, of flesh and viscera and cells.

He slid into the booth where I was sitting and ordered a shot of whisky. He tossed it off, put the glass down and looked at me with his head tilted a little to one side and back.

"What's this guy got?" he said.

"A Tommy gun and about thirty-five grains of morphine."

"The morphine I can get rid of right away, but the Tommy gun may take a little time."

Two detectives walked in and leaned on the bar talking to the bartender. Jack jerked his head in their direction. "The law. Let's take a walk."

I followed him out of the bar. He walked through the door sliding sideways. "I'm taking you to someone who will want the morphine," he said. "You want to forget this address."

We went down to the bottom level of the Independent Subway. Jack's voice, talking to his invisible audience, went on and on. He had a knack of throwing his voice directly into your consciousness.

No external noise drowned him out. "Give me a thirty-eight every time. Just flick back the hammer and let her go. I'll drop anyone at five hundred feet. Don't care what you say. My brother has two 30-caliber machine guns stashed in Iowa."

We got off the subway and began to walk on snow-covered sidewalks between tenements.

"The guy owed me for a long time, see? I knew he had it but he wouldn't pay, so I waited for him when he finished work. I had a roll of nickels. No one can hang anything on you for carrying U.S. currency. Told me he was broke. I cracked his jaw and took my money off him. Two of his friends standing there, but they kept out of it. I'd've switched a blade on them."

We were walking up tenement stairs. The stairs were made of worn black metal. We stopped in front of a narrow, metal-covered door, and Jack gave an elaborate knock inclining his head to the floor like a safecracker. The door was opened by a large, flabby, middle-aged queer, with tattooing on his forearms and even on the backs of his hands.

"This is Joey," Jack said, and Joey said, "Hello there."

Jack pulled a five-dollar bill from his pocket and gave it to Joey. "Get us a quart of Schenley's, will you, Joey?"

Joey put on an overcoat and went out.

In many tenement apartments the front door opens directly into the kitchen. This was such an apartment and we were in the kitchen.

After Joey went out I noticed another man who was standing there looking at me. Waves of hostility and suspicion flowed out from his large brown eyes like some sort of television broadcast. The effect was almost like a physical impact. The man was small and very thin, his neck loose in the collar of his shirt. His complexion was fading from brown to a mottled yellow, and pancake make-up had been heavily applied in an attempt to conceal a skin eruption. His mouth was drawn down at the corners in a grimace of petulant annoyance.

"Who's this?" he said. His name, I learned later, was Herman.

"Friend of mine. He's got some morphine he wants to get rid of."

Herman shrugged and turned out his hands. "I don't think I want to bother, really."

"Okay," Jack said, "we'll sell it to someone else. Come on, Bill."

We went into the front room. There was a small radio, a china Buddha with a votive candle in front of it, pieces of bric-a-brac. A man was lying on a studio couch. He sat up as we entered the room and said hello and smiled pleasantly, showing discolored, brownish teeth. It was a Southern voice with the accent of East Texas.

Jack said, "Roy, this is a friend of mine. He has some morphine he wants to sell."

The man sat up straighter and swung his legs off the couch. His jaw fell slackly, giving his face a vacant look. The skin of his face was smooth and brown. The cheek-bones were high and he looked Oriental. His ears stuck out at right angles from his asymmetrical skull. The eyes were brown and they had a peculiar brilliance, as though points of light were shining behind them. The light in the room glinted on the points of light in his eyes like an opal.

"How much do you have?" he asked me.

"Seventy-five half grain syrettes."

"The regular price is two dollars a grain," he said, "but syrettes go for a little less. People want tablets. Those syrettes have too much water and you have to squeeze the stuff out and cook it down." He paused and his face went blank: "I could go about one-fifty a grain," he said finally.

"I guess that will be okay," I said.

He asked how we could make contact and I gave him my phone number.

Joey came back with the whisky and we all had a drink. Herman stuck his head in from the kitchen and said to Jack, "Could I talk to you for a minute?"

I could hear them arguing about something. Then Jack came back and Herman stayed in the kitchen. We all had a few drinks and Jack began telling a story.

"My partner was going through the joint. The guy was sleeping, and I was standing over him with a three-foot length of pipe I found in the bathroom. The pipe had a faucet on the end of it, see? All of a sudden he comes up and jumps straight out of bed, running. I let him have it with the faucet end, and he goes on running right out into the other room, the blood spurting out of his head ten feet every time his heart beat." He made a pumping motion with his hand. "You could see the brain there and the blood coming out of it." Jack began to laugh uncontrollably. "My girl was waiting out in the car. She called me—ha-ha-ha!—she called me—ha-ha-ha!—a cold-blooded killer."

He laughed until his face was purple.

●

A few nights after meeting Roy and Herman, I used one of the syrettes, which was my first experience with junk. A syrette is like a toothpaste tube with a needle on the end. You push a pin down through the needle; the pin punctures the seal; and the syrette is ready to shoot.

Morphine hits the backs of the legs first, then the back of the neck, a spreading wave of relaxation slackening the muscles away from the bones so that you seem to float without outlines, like lying in warm salt water. As this relaxing wave spread through my tissues, I experienced a strong feeling of fear. I had the feeling that some horrible image was just beyond the field of vision, moving, as I turned my head, so that I never quite saw it. I felt nauseous; I lay down and closed my eyes. A series of pictures passed, like watching a movie: A huge, neon-lighted cocktail bar that got larger and larger until streets, traffic, and street repairs were included in it; a waitress carrying a skull on a tray; stars in a clear sky. The physical impact of the fear of death; the shutting off of breath; the stopping of blood.

I dozed off and woke up with a start of fear. Next morning I vomited and felt sick until noon.

Roy called that night.

"About what we were discussing the other night," he said. "I could go about four dollars per box and take five boxes now. Are you busy? I'll come over to your place. We'll come to some kind of agreement."

A few minutes later he knocked at the door. He had on a Glen plaid suit and a dark, coffee-colored shirt. We said hello. He looked around blankly and said, "If you don't mind, I'll take one of those now."

I opened the box. He took out a syrette and injected it into his leg. He pulled up his pants briskly and took out twenty dollars. I put five boxes on the kitchen table.

"I think I'll take them out of the boxes," he said. "Too bulky."

He began putting the syrettes in his coat pockets. "I don't think they'll perforate this way," he said. "Listen, I'll call you again in a day or so after I get rid of these and have some more money." He was adjusting his hat over his asymmetrical skull. "I'll see you."

Next day he was back. He shot another syrette and pulled out forty dollars. I laid out ten boxes and kept two.

"These are for me," I said.

He looked at me, surprised. "You use it?"

"Now and then."

"It's bad stuff," he said, shaking his head. "The worst thing that can happen to a man. We all think we can control it at first.

Sometimes we don't want to control it." He laughed. "I'll take all you can get at this price."

Next day he was back. He asked if I didn't want to change my mind about selling the two boxes. I said no. He bought two syrettes for a dollar each, shot them both, and left. He said he had signed on for a two-month trip.

•

During the next month I used up the eight syrettes I had not sold. The fear I had experienced after using the first syrette was not noticeable after the third; but still, from time to time, after taking a shot I would wake up with a start of fear. After six weeks or so I gave Roy a ring, not expecting him to be back from his trip, but then I heard his voice on the phone.

I said, "Say, do you have any to sell? Of the material I sold you before?"

There was a pause.

"Ye-es," he said, "I can let you have six, but the price will have to be three dollars per. You understand I don't have many."

"Okay," I said. "You know the way. Bring it on over."

It was twelve one-half grain tablets in a thin glass tube. I paid him eighteen dollars and he apologized again for the retail rate.

Next day he bought two grains back.

"It's mighty hard to get now at any price," he said, looking for a vein in his leg. He finally hit a vein and shot the liquid in with an air bubble. "If air bubbles could kill you, there wouldn't be a junkie alive," he said, pulling up his pants.

Later that day Roy pointed out to me a drugstore where they sold needles without any questions—very few drugstores will sell them without a prescription. He showed me how to make a col-lar out of paper to fit the needle to an eyedropper. An eyedropper is easier to use than a regular hypo, especially for giving yourself vein shots.

Several days later Roy sent me to see a doctor with a story about kidney stones, to hit him for a morphine prescription. The doctor's wife slammed the door in my face, but Roy finally got past her and made the doctor for a ten-grain script.

The doctor's office was in junk territory on 102nd, off Broadway. He was a doddering old man and could not resist the junkies who filled his office and were, in fact, his only patients. It seemed to give him a feeling of importance to look out and see an office full of people. I guess he had reached a point where he could change the appearance of things to suit his needs and when he looked out there he saw a distinguished and diversified clientele, probably well-dressed in 1910 style, instead of a bunch of ratty-looking junkies come to hit him for a morphine script.

Roy shipped out at two- or three-week intervals. His trips were Army Transport and generally short. When he was in town we generally split a few scripts. The old croaker on 102nd finally lost his mind altogether and no drugstore would fill his scripts, but Roy located an Italian doctor out in the Bronx who would write.

I was taking a shot from time to time, but I was a long way from having a habit. At this time I moved into an apartment on the Lower East Side. It was a tenement apartment with the front door opening into the kitchen.

●

I began dropping into the Angle Bar every night and saw quite a bit of Herman. I managed to overcome his original bad impression of me, and soon I was buying his drinks and meals, and he was hitting me for "smash" (change) at regular intervals. Herman did not have a habit at this time. In fact, he seldom got a habit unless someone else paid for it. But he was always high on something—weed, benzedrine, or knocked out of his mind on "goof balls." He showed up at the Angle every night with a big slob of a Polack called Whitey. There were four Whities in the Angle set, which made for confusion. This Whitey combined the sensitivity of a neurotic with a psychopath's readiness for violence. He was convinced that nobody liked him, a fact that seemed to cause him a great deal of worry.

One Tuesday night Roy and I were standing at the end of the Angle bar. Subway Mike was there, and Frankie Dolan. Dolan was an Irish boy with a cast in one eye. He specialized in crummy scores, beating up defenseless drunks, and holding out on his confederates. "I got no honor," he would say. "I'm a rat." And he would giggle.

Subway Mike had a large, pale face and long teeth. He looked like some specialized kind of underground animal that preys on the animals of the surface. He was a skillful lush-worker, but he had no front. Any cop would do a double-take at sight of him, and he was well known to the subway squad. So Mike spent at least half of his time on the Island doing the five-twenty-nine for jostling.

This night Herman was knocked out on "nembies" and his head kept falling down onto the bar. Whitey was stomping up and down the length of the bar trying to promote some free drinks. The boys at the bar sat rigid and tense, clutching their drinks, quickly pocketing their change. I heard Whitey say to the bartender, "Keep this for me, will you?" and he passed his large clasp knife across the bar. The boys sat there silent and gloomy under the fluorescent lights. They were all afraid of Whitey, all except Roy. Roy sipped his beer grimly. His eyes shone with their peculiar phosphorescence. His long asymmetrical body was draped against the bar. He didn't look at Whitey, but at the opposite wall where the booths were located. Once he said to me, "He's no more drunk than I am. He's just thirsty."

Whitey was standing in the middle of the bar, his fists doubled up, tears streaming down his face. "I'm no good," he said. "I'm no good. Can't anyone understand I don't know what I'm doing?"

The boys tried to get as far away from him as possible without attracting his attention.

Subway Slim, Mike's occasional partner, came in and ordered a beer. He was tall and bony, and his ugly face had a curiously inanimate look, as if made out of wood. Whitey slapped him on the back and I heard Slim say, "For Christ's sake, Whitey." There was more interchange I didn't hear. Somewhere along the line Whitey must have got his knife back from the bartender. He got behind Slim and suddenly pushed his hand against Slim's back. Slim fell forward against the bar, groaning. I saw Whitey walk to the front of the bar and look around. He closed his knife and slipped it into his pocket.

Roy said, "Let's go."

Whitey had disappeared and the bar was empty except for Mike, who was holding Slim up on one side. Frankie Dolan was on the other.

I heard next day from Frankie that Slim was okay. "The croaker at the hospital said the knife just missed a kidney."

Roy said, "The big slob. I can see a real muscle man, but a guy like that going around picking up dimes and quarters off the bar. I was ready for him. I was going to kick him in the belly first, then get one of those quart beer bottles from the case on the floor and break it over his sconce. With a big villain like that you've got to use strategy."

We were all barred from the Angle, which shortly afterwards changed its name to the Roxy Grill.

●

One night I went to the Henry Street address to look up Jack. A tall, red-haired girl met me at the door.

"I'm Mary," she said. "Come in."

It seemed that Jack was in Washington on business.

"Come on into the front room," she said, pushing aside a red corduroy curtain. "I talk to landlords and bill collectors in the kitchen. We *live* in here."

I looked around. The bric-a-brac had gone. The place looked like a chop suey joint. There were black and red lacquered tables scattered around, black curtains covered the window. A colored wheel had been painted on the ceiling with little squares and triangles of different colors giving a mosaic effect.

"Jack did that," Mary said, pointing to the wheel. "You should have seen him. He stretched a board between two ladders and lay down on it. Paint kept dripping into his face. He gets a kick out of doing things like that. We get some frantic kicks out of that wheel when we're high. We lay on our backs and dig the wheel and pretty soon it begins to spin. The longer you watch it, the faster it spins."

This wheel had the nightmarish vulgarity of Aztec mosaics, the bloody, vulgar nightmare, the heart throbbing in the morning sun, the garish pinks and blues of souvenir ashtrays, postcards and calendars. The walls were painted black and there was a Chinese character in red lacquer on one wall.

"We don't know what it means," she said.

"Shirts thirty-one cents," I suggested.

She turned on me her blank, cold smile. She began talking about Jack. "I'm queer for Jack," she said. "He works at being a thief just like any job. Used to come home nights and hand me his gun. 'Stash that!' He likes to work around the house, painting and making furniture."

As she talked she moved around the room, throwing herself from one chair to another, crossing and uncrossing her legs, adjusting her slip, so as to give me a view of her anatomy in installments.

She went on to tell me how her days were numbered by a rare disease. "Only twenty-six cases on record. In a few years I won't be able to get around at all. You see, my system can't absorb calcium and the bones are slowly dissolving. My legs will have to be amputated eventually, then the arms."

There was something boneless about her, like a deep-sea creature. Her eyes were cold fish eyes that looked at you through a viscous medium she carried about with her. I could see those eyes in a shapeless, protoplasmic mass undulating over the dark sea floor.

"Benzedrine is a good kick," she said. "Three strips of the paper or about ten tablets. Or take two strips of benny and two goof balls. They get down there and have a fight. It's a good drive."

Three young hoodlums from Brooklyn drifted in, wooden-faced, hands-in-pockets, stylized as a ballet. They were looking for Jack. He had given them a short count in some deal. At least, that was the general idea. They conveyed their meaning less by words than by significant jerks of the head and by stalking around the apartment and leaning against the walls. At length, one of them walked to the door and jerked his head. They filed out.

"Would you like to get high?" Mary asked. "There may be a roach around here somewhere." She began rummaging around in drawers and ashtrays. "No, I guess not. Why don't we go uptown? I know several good connections we can probably catch about now."

A young man lurched in with some object wrapped in brown paper under one arm. "Ditch this on your way out," he said, putting it down on the table. He staggered into the bedroom on the other side of the kitchen. When we got outside I let the wrapping paper fall loose revealing the coin box of a pay toilet crudely jimmied open.

In Times Square we got in a taxi and began cruising up and down the side streets, Mary giving directions. Every now and then she would yell "Stop!" and jump out, her red hair streaming, and I would see her overhaul some character and start talking. "The connection was here about ten minutes ago. This character's holding, but he won't turn loose of any." Later: "The regular connection is gone for the night. He lives in the Bronx. But just stop here for a minute. I may find someone in Kellogg's." Finally: "No one seems to be anywhere. It's a bit late to score. Let's buy some benny tubes and go over to Ronnie's. They have some gone numbers on the box. We can order coffee and get high on benny."

Ronnie's was a spot near 52nd and Sixth where musicians came for fried chicken and coffee after one p.m. We sat down in a booth and ordered coffee. Mary cracked a benzedrine tube expertly, extracting the folded paper, and handed me three strips. "Roll it up into a pill and wash it down with coffee."

The paper gave off a sickening odor of menthol. Several people nearby sniffed and smiled. I nearly gagged on the wad of paper, but finally got it down. Mary selected some gone numbers and beat on the table with the expression of a masturbating idiot.

I began talking very fast. My mouth was dry and my spit came out in round white balls—spitting cotton, it's called. We were walking around Times Square. Mary wanted to locate someone with a "piccolo" (victrola). I was full of expansive, benevolent feelings, and suddenly wanted to call on people I hadn't seen in months or even years, people I did not like and who did not like me. We made a number of unsuccessful attempts to locate the ideal piccolo-owning host. Somewhere along the line we picked up Peter and finally decided to go back to the Henry Street apartment where there was at least a radio.

Peter and Mary and I spent the next thirty hours in the apartment. From time to time we would make coffee and swallow more benzedrine. Mary was describing the techniques she used to get money from the "Johns" who formed her principal source of revenue.

"Always build a John up. If he has any sort of body at all say, 'Oh, don't ever hurt me.' A John is different from a sucker. When you're with a sucker you're on the alert all the time. You give him nothing. A sucker is just to be taken. But a John is different. You give him what he pays for. When you're with him you enjoy yourself and you want him to enjoy himself, too.

"If you want to really bring a man down, light a cigarette in the middle of intercourse. Of course, I really don't like men at all sexually. What I really dig is chicks. I get a kick out of taking a proud chick and breaking her spirit, making her see she is just an animal. A chick is never as beautiful after she's been broken. Say, this is sort of a fireside kick," she said, pointing to the radio which was the only light in the room.

Her face contorted into an expression of monkey-like rage as she talked about men who accosted her on the street. "Sonofabitch!" she snarled. "They can tell when a woman isn't looking for a pickup. I used to cruise around with brass knuckles on under my gloves just waiting for one of those peasants to crack at me."

●

One day Herman told me about a kilo of first-class New Orleans weed I could pick up for seventy dollars. Pushing weed looks good on paper, like fur farming or raising frogs. At seventy-five cents a stick, seventy sticks to the ounce, it sounded like money. I was convinced, and bought the weed.

Herman and I formed a partnership to push the weed. He located a Lesbian named Marian who lived in the Village and said she was a poetess. We kept the weed in Marian's apartment, turned her on for all she could use, and gave her fifty percent on sales. She knew a lot of tea heads. Another Lesbian moved in with her, and every time I went to Marian's apartment, there was this huge red-haired Lizzie watching me with her cold fish eyes full of stupid hate.

One day, the red-haired Lizzie opened the door and stood there, her face dead white and puffy with nembutal sleep. She shoved the package of weed at me. "Take this and get out," she said. "You're both mother fuckers." She was half asleep. Her voice was matter-of-fact as if referring to actual incest.

I said, "Tell Marian thanks for everything."

She slammed the door. The noise evidently woke her up. She opened the door again and began screaming with hysterical rage. We could still hear her out on the street.

Herman contacted other tea heads. They all gave us static. In practice, pushing weed is a headache. To begin with, weed is bulky. You need a full suitcase to realize any money. If the cops start kicking your door in, there you are like with a bale of alfalfa.

Tea heads are not like junkies. A junkie hands you the money, takes his junk and cuts. But tea heads don't do things that way. They expect the peddler to light them up and sit around talking for half an hour to sell two dollars' worth of weed. If you come right to the point, they say you are a "bring down." In fact, a peddler should not come right out and say he is a peddler. No, he just scores for a few good "cats" and "chicks" because he is viperish. Everyone knows that he himself is the connection, but it is bad form to say so. God knows why. To me, tea heads are unfathomable.

There are a lot of trade secrets in the tea business, and tea heads guard these supposed secrets with imbecilic slyness. For example, tea must be cured, or it is green and rasps the throat. But ask a tea head how to cure weed and he will give you a sly, stupid look and come-on with some double-talk. Perhaps weed does affect the brain with constant use, or maybe tea heads are naturally silly.

The tea I had was green so I put it in a double boiler and set the boiler in the oven until the tea got the greenish-brown look it should have. This is the secret of curing tea, or at least one way to do it.

Tea heads are gregarious, they are sensitive, and they are paranoiac. If you get to be known as a "drag" or a "bring down," you can't do business with them. I soon found out I couldn't get along with these characters and I was glad to find someone to take the tea off my hands at cost. I decided right then I would never push any more tea.

In 1937, weed was placed under the Harrison Narcotics Act. Narcotics authorities claim it is a habit-forming drug, that its use is injurious to mind and body, and that it causes the people who use it to commit crimes. Here are the facts: Weed is positively not habit-forming. You can smoke weed for years and you will experience no discomfort if your supply is suddenly cut off. I have seen tea heads in jail and none of them showed withdrawal symptoms. I have smoked weed myself off and on for fifteen years, and never missed it when I ran out. There is less habit to weed than there is to tobacco. Weed does not harm the general health. In fact, most users claim it gives you an appetite and acts as a tonic to the system. I do not know of any other agent that gives as definite a boot to the appetite. I can smoke a stick of tea and enjoy a glass of California sherry and a hash house meal.

I once kicked a junk habit with weed. The second day off junk I sat down and ate a full meal. Ordinarily, I can't eat for eight days after kicking a habit.

Weed does not inspire anyone to commit crimes. I have never seen anyone get nasty under the influence of weed. Tea heads are a sociable lot. Too sociable for my liking. I cannot understand why the people who claim weed causes crime do not follow through and demand the outlawing of alcohol. Every day, crimes are committed by drunks who would not have committed the crime sober.

There has been a lot said about the aphrodisiac effect of weed. For some reason, scientists dislike to admit that there is such a thing as an aphrodisiac, so most pharmacologists say there is "no evidence to support the popular idea that weed possesses aphrodisiac properties." I can say definitely that weed is an aphrodisiac and that sex is more enjoyable under the influence of weed than without it. Anyone who has used good weed will verify this statement.

You hear that people go insane from using weed. There is, in fact, a form of insanity caused by excessive use of weed. The condition is characterized by ideas of reference. The weed available in the

U.S. is evidently not strong enough to blow your top on and weed psychosis is rare in the States. In the Near East, it is said to be common. Weed psychosis corresponds more or less to delirium tremens and quickly disappears when the drug is withdrawn. Someone who smokes a few cigarettes a day is no more likely to go insane than a man who takes a few cocktails before dinner is likely to come down with the D.T.'s.

One thing about weed. A man under the influence of weed is completely unfit to drive a car. Weed disturbs your sense of time and consequently your sense of spatial relations. Once, in New Orleans, I had to pull over to the side of a road and wait until the weed wore off. I could not tell how far away anything was or when to turn or put on the brakes for an intersection.

●

I was shooting every day now. Herman had moved into my apartment on Henry Street, since there was no one left to pay the rent for the apartment he had shared with Jack and Mary. Jack had taken a fall on a safe job and was in the Bronx County jail waiting for trial. Mary had gone to Florida with a "John." It would not have occurred to Herman to pay the rent himself. He had lived in other people's apartments all his life.

Roy was giving himself a long shore leave. He located a doctor in Brooklyn who was a writing fool. This croaker would go three scripts a day for as high as thirty tablets a script. Every now and then he would get dubious on the deal, but the sight of money always straightened him out.

There are several varieties of writing croakers. Some will write only if they are convinced you are an addict, others only if they are convinced you are not. Most addicts put down a story worn smooth by years of use. Some claim gallstones or kidney stones.

This is the story most generally used, and a croaker will often get up and open the door as soon as you mention gallstones. I got better results with facial neuralgia after I had looked up the symptoms and committed them to memory. Roy had an operation scar on his stomach that he used to support his gallstone routine.

There was one oldtime doctor who lived in a Victorian brownstone in the West Seventies. With him it was simply necessary to present a gentlemanly front. If you could get into his inner office you had it made, but he would write only three prescriptions. Another doctor was always drunk, and it was a matter of catching him at the right time. Often he wrote the prescription wrong and you had to take it back for correction. Then, like as not, he would say the prescription was a forgery and tear it up. Still another doctor was senile, and you had to help him write the script. He would forget what he was doing, put down the pen and go into a long reminiscence about the high class of patients he used to have. Especially, he liked to talk about a man named General Gore who once said to him, "Doctor, I've been to the Mayo Clinic and you know more than the whole clinic put together." There was no stopping him and the exasperated addict was forced to listen patiently. Often the doctor's wife would rush in at the last minute and tear up the prescription, or refuse to verify it when the drugstore called.

Generally speaking, old doctors are more apt to write than the young ones. Refugee doctors were a good field for a while, but the addicts burned them down. Often a doctor will blow his top at the mention of narcotics and threaten to call the law.

Doctors are so exclusively nurtured on exaggerated ideas of their position that, generally speaking, a factual approach is the worst possible. Even though they do not believe your story, nonetheless they want to hear one. It is like some Oriental face-saving ritual. One man plays the high-minded doctor who wouldn't write an unethical script for a thousand dollars, the other does his best to act like a legitimate patient. If you say, "Look, Doc, I want an M.S.

script and I'm willing to pay double price for it," the croaker blows his top and throws you out of the office. You need a good bedside manner with doctors or you will get nowhere.

Roy was such a junk hog that Herman and I had to shoot more than we needed to keep up with him and get our share. I began shooting in the main line to save stuff and because the immediate kick was better. We were having trouble filling the scripts. Most drugstores will only fill a morphine script once or twice, many not at all. There was one drugstore that would fill all our scripts anytime, and we took them all there, though Roy said we ought to spread them out so they would be harder for the inspector to find. It was too much trouble to walk around from drugstore to drugstore, so we usually ended up taking them to the same place. I was learning to hide my stuff carefully—"stash it," as they say in the trade—so Roy and Herman couldn't find it and take some.

Taking junk hidden by another junkie is known as "making him for his stash." It is difficult to guard against this form of theft because junkies know where to look for a stash. Some people carry their junk around with them, but a man who does that is subject to a charge of possession in the event of search by the law.

As I began using stuff every day, or often several times a day, I stopped drinking and going out at night. When you use junk you don't drink. Seemingly, the body that has a quantity of junk in its cells will not absorb alcohol. The liquor stays in the stomach, slowly building up nausea, discomfort, and dizziness, and there is no kick. Using junk would be a sure cure for alcoholics. I also stopped bathing. When you use junk the feel of water on the skin is unpleasant for some reason, and junkies are reluctant to take a bath.

A lot of nonsense has been written about the changes people undergo as they get a habit. All of a sudden the addict looks in the mirror and does not recognize himself. The actual changes are difficult to specify and they do not show up in the mirror. That is, the addict himself has a special blind spot so far as the progress of his habit is concerned. He generally does not realize that he is getting a habit at all. He says there is no need to get a habit if you are careful and observe a few rules, like shooting every other day. Actually, he does not observe these rules, but every extra shot is regarded as exceptional. I have talked to many addicts and they all say they were surprised when they discovered they actually had the first habit. Many of them attributed their symptoms to some other cause. As a habit takes hold, other interests lose importance to the user. Life telescopes down to junk, one fix and looking forward to the next, "stashes" and "scripts," "spikes" and "droppers." The addict himself often feels that he is leading a normal life and that junk is incidental. He does not realize that he is just going through the motions in his non-junk activities. It is not until his supply is cut off that he realizes what junk means to him.

"Why do you *need* narcotics, Mr. Lee?" is a question that stupid psychiatrists ask. The answer is, "I need junk to get out of bed in the morning, to shave and eat breakfast. I need it to stay alive."

Of course, junkies don't as a rule die from the withdrawal of junk. But in a very literal sense, kicking a habit involves the death of junk-dependent cells and their replacement with cells that do not need junk.

Roy and his old lady moved into the same tenement building. Every day we would meet in my apartment after breakfast to plan the day's junk program. One of us would have to hit the croaker. Roy always tried to put it on someone else. "I can't go myself this time, I had a beef with him. But listen, I'll tell you just what to say." Or he would try to get Herman or me to try a new croaker. "You can't miss. Just don't let him say no, because he will write. I can't go myself."

I had one of his sure-thing croakers reach for a telephone on me. I told Roy and he said, "Oh, I guess the guy's burned. Somebody made him for his bag a few days ago." After that, I kept away from strange croakers. But our Brooklyn boy was getting balky.

●

All croakers pack in sooner or later. One day when Roy came for his script, the doctor told him, "This is positively the last, and you guys had better keep out of sight. The inspector was around to see me yesterday. He has all the R-xes I wrote for you guys. He told me I'll lose my license if I write any more, so I'm going to date this one back. Tell the druggist you were too sick yesterday to cash it. You guys gave some wrong addresses on those scripts. That's a violation of Public Health Law 334, so don't say I didn't warn you. For God's sake, cover up for me if they question you. This could mean my whole professional career. You know I've always been right with you boys. I wanted to stop months ago. I just couldn't leave you guys stranded. So give me a break. Here's the script and don't come back."

Roy went back the next day. The doctor's brother-in-law was there to protect the family honor. He grabbed Roy by the coat collar and the back of the belt and threw him out onto the sidewalk.

"The next time I find you around here bothering the doctor," he said, "you won't be in a condition to walk away."

Ten minutes later, Herman arrived. The brother-in-law was giving him the same treatment when Herman pulled out a silk dress he had under his coat—as I recall somebody unloaded a batch of hot dresses on us for three grains of morphine—and turning to the doctor's wife who had come downstairs to see what all the commotion was about, he said, "I thought you might like this dress." So he got a chance to talk to the doctor who wrote him one last script. It took him three hours to fill it. Our regular drugstore had been warned by the inspector, and they would not fill any more scripts.

"You guys had better keep out of sight," the proprietor said. "I think the inspector has warrants out for all of you."

Our croaker had packed in. We split up to comb the city. We covered Brooklyn, the Bronx, Queens, Jersey City and Newark. We couldn't even score for pantopon. It seemed like the doctors were all expecting us, just waiting for one of us to walk into the office so they could say, "Absolutely no." It was as though every doctor in Greater New York had suddenly taken a pledge never to write another narcotics script. We were running out of junk. Patently, we would be immobilized in a matter of hours. Roy decided to throw in the towel and go to Riker's Island for the "thirty-day cure." This is not a reduction cure. They don't give any junk, not even a sleeping tablet. All they offer the addict is thirty days' detention. The place is always full.

Herman got picked up in the Bronx while he was looking for a croaker. No definite charge, just two detectives didn't like his looks. When they got him downtown they found out the narcotics squad had a warrant for him sworn out by the State Inspector. The charge was wrong address on a narcotics script. Some wagon-chasing lawyer called me up and asked if I would put up the money to buy Herman a bond. I sent two dollars for cigarettes instead. If a man is going to do time, he might as well start doing it.

I was all out of junk at this point and had double-boiled my last cottons. Junk is cooked up in a spoon and sucked into the dropper through a little piece of cotton to get it all out of the spoon. Some of the solution stays in the cotton, and addicts save these cottons for emergencies.

I got a codeine script from an old doctor by putting down a story about migraine headaches. Codeine is better than nothing and five grains in the skin will keep you from being sick. For some reason, it is dangerous to shoot codeine in the vein.

I recall one night Herman and I were caught short with nothing but some codeine sulphate. Herman cooked up first and shot one grain in the vein. Immediately he turned very red, then very pale. He sat down weakly on the bed. "My God," he said.

"What's the matter?" I asked. "It's perfectly all right."

He gave me a sour look. "All right, is it? Well, you shoot some then."

I cooked up a grain and got out my works ready to take the shot. Herman watched me eagerly. He was still sitting on the bed. As soon as I took the needle out of my arm I felt an intense and most unpleasant prickling sensation entirely different from the prickles you get from a good shot of morphine. I could feel my face swelling. I sat down on the bed next to Herman. My fingers were puffed up double size.

"Well," said Herman, "is it all right?"

"No," I said.

My lips were numb like I'd been hit across the mouth. I had a terrific headache. I began to pace up and down the room, since I had a vague theory that if I got the circulation going the blood would carry away the codeine.

After an hour I felt a little better and went to bed. Herman told me about a partner of his who passed out and turned blue after a shot of codeine. "I put him under a cold shower and he came around."

"Why didn't you tell me that before?" I demanded.

Herman was suddenly and unaccountably irritated. The sources of his anger were generally unfathomable.

"Well," he began, "you have to expect to take *some* chances when you're using junk. Besides, just because one person has a certain reaction doesn't necessarily mean that someone else will react in the same way. You seemed so sure it was all right, I didn't want to bug you by bringing anything up."

●

When I heard that Herman had been arrested I figured I would be next, but I was already sick and did not have the energy to leave town.

I was arrested at my apartment by two detectives and a Federal agent. The State Inspector had sworn out a warrant charging me with violation of Public Health Law 334 for giving a wrong name on a prescription. The two detectives were the con-man and tough-guy team. The con-man was asking me, "How long you been using junk, Bill? You know you ought to give a right name on those scripts." Then the tough-guy would break in, "Come on, come on, we're not boy scouts."

But they were not much interested in the case, and no statement from me was necessary. On the way downtown, the Federal man asked me some questions and filled out a form for their records. I was taken to the Tombs, mugged and fingerprinted. While I was waiting to go before the judge, the con-man gave me a cigarette and began telling me what a bad deal junk is.

"Even if you get by with it thirty years, you're only kidding yourself. Now you take these sex degenerates—" his eyes glistened—"the doctors say they can't help themselves."

The judge set bail at a thousand. I was taken back to the Tombs, ordered to take off my clothes and get under the shower. An apathetic guard poked through my clothes. I got dressed again, went up in the elevator, and was assigned to a cell. At four p.m. we were locked in our cells. The doors closed automatically from a master switch, with a tremendous clang that echoed through the cellblock.

The last of the codeine was running out. My nose and eyes began to run, sweat soaked through my clothes. Hot and cold flashes hit me as though a furnace door was swinging open and shut. I lay down on the bunk, too weak to move. My legs ached and twitched so that any position was intolerable, and I moved from one side to the other, sloshing about in my sweaty clothes.

A Negro voice was singing, "Get up, get up, woman, off your big fat rusty-dusty." Voices drifted back and forth. "Forty years! Man, I can't do no forty years."

At twelve that night, my old lady bailed me out and met me at the door with some goof balls. Goof balls help a little.

Next day I was worse and could not get out of bed. So I stayed in bed taking nembies at intervals.

At night, I would take two strips of benzedrine and go out to a bar where I sat right by the jukebox. When you're sick, music is a great help. Once, in Texas, I kicked a habit on weed, a pint of paregoric and a few Louis Armstrong records.

Almost worse than the sickness is the depression that goes with it. One afternoon, I closed my eyes and saw New York in ruins. Huge centipedes and scorpions crawled in and out of empty bars and cafeterias and drugstores on Forty-second Street. Weeds were growing up through cracks and holes in the pavement. There was no one in sight.

After five days I began to feel a little better. After eight days I got the "chucks" and developed a tremendous appetite for cream puffs and macaroons. In ten days the sickness had gone. My case had been postponed.

●

Roy came back from his thirty-day cure on Riker's Island and introduced me to a peddler who was pushing Mexican H on 103rd and Broadway. During the early part of the war, imports of H were virtually cut off and the only junk available was prescription M. However, lines of communication reformed and heroin began coming in from Mexico, where there were poppy fields tended by Chinese. This Mexican H was brown in color since it had quite a bit of raw opium in it.

103rd and Broadway looks like any Broadway block. A cafeteria, a movie, stores. In the middle of Broadway is an island with some grass and benches placed at intervals. 103rd is a subway stop, a crowded block. This is junk territory. Junk haunts the cafeteria, roams up and down the block, sometimes half-crossing Broadway to rest on one of the island benches. A ghost in daylight on a crowded street.

You could always find a few junkies sitting in the cafeteria or standing around outside with coat collars turned up, spitting on the sidewalk and looking up and down the street as they waited for the connection. In summer, they sit on the island benches, huddled like so many vultures in their dark suits.

The peddler had the face of a withered adolescent. He was fifty-five but he did not look more than thirty. He was a small, dark man with a thin Irish face. When he did show up—and like many oldtime junkies he was completely unpunctual—he would sit at a table in the cafeteria. You gave him money at the table, and met him around the corner three minutes later where he would deliver the junk. He never had it on him, but kept it stashed somewhere close by.

This man was known as Irish. At one time he had worked for Dutch Schultz, but big-time racketeers will not keep junkies on the payroll as they are supposed to be unreliable. So Irish was out. Now he peddled from time to time and "worked the hole" (rolling drunks on subways and in cars) when he couldn't make connections to peddle. One night, Irish got nailed in the subway for jostling. He hanged himself in the Tombs.

The job of peddler was a sort of public service that rotated from one member of the group to the other, the average term of office being about three months. All agreed that it was a thankless job. As George the Greek said, "You end up broke and in jail. Everybody calls you cheap if you don't give credit; if you do, they take advantage."

George couldn't turn down a man who came to him sick. People took advantage of his kindness, hitting him for credit and taking their cash to some other pusher. George did three years, and when he got out he refused to do any more pushing.

The hipster-bebop junkies never showed at 103rd Street. The 103rd Street boys were all oldtimers—thin, sallow faces; bitter, twisted mouths; stiff-fingered, stylized gestures. (There is a junk gesture that marks the junkie like the limp wrist marks the fag: the hand swings out from the elbow stiff-fingered, palm up.) They were of various nationalities and physical types, but they all looked alike somehow. They all looked like junk. There was Irish, George the Greek, Pantopon Rose, Louie the Bellhop, Eric the Fag, the Beagle, the Sailor, and Joe the Mex. Several of them are dead now, others are doing time.

There are no more junkies at 103rd and Broadway waiting for the connection. The connection has gone somewhere else. But the feel of junk is still there. It hits you at the corner, follows you along the block, then falls away like a discouraged panhandler as you walk on.

Joe the Mex had a thin face with a long, sharp, twitchy nose and a down-curving, toothless mouth. Joe's face was lined and ravaged, but not old. Things had happened to his face, but Joe was not touched. His eyes were bright and young. There was a gentleness about him common to many oldtime junkies. You could spot Joe blocks away. In the anonymous city crowd he stood out sharp and clear, as though you were seeing him through binoculars. He was a liar, and like most liars, he was constantly changing his stories, altering time and personnel from one telling to the next. One time he would tell a story about some friend, next time he would switch the story around to give himself the lead. He would sit in the cafeteria over coffee and pound cake, talking at random about his experiences.

"We know this Chinaman has some stuff stashed, and we try every way to make him tell us where it is. We have him tied to a chair. I light matches"—he made a gesture of lighting a match— "and put them under his feet. He won't say nothing. I feel so sorry for that man. Then my partner hit him in the face with his gun and the blood run all down his face." He put his hands over his face and drew them down to indicate the flow of blood. "When I see that I turn sick at my stomach and I say, 'Let's get out of here and leave the man alone. He ain't going to tell us nothing.'"

Louie was a shoplifter who had lost what nerve he ever had. He wore long, shabby, black overcoats that gave him all the look of a furtive buzzard. Thief and junkie stuck out all over him. Louie had a hard time making it. I heard that at one time he had been a stool pigeon, but at the time I knew him he was generally considered right. George the Greek did not like Louie and said he was just a bum. "Don't ever invite him to your home, he'll take advantage. He'll go on the nod in front of your family. He's got no class to him."

George the Greek was the admitted arbiter of this set. He decided who was right and who was wrong. George prided himself on his integrity. "I never beat nobody."

George was a three-time loser. The next time meant life as an habitual criminal. His life narrowed down to the necessity of avoiding any serious involvements. No pushing, no stealing; he worked from time to time on the docks. He was hemmed in on every side and there was no way for him to go but down. When he couldn't get junk—which was about half the time—he drank and took goof balls.

He had two adolescent sons who gave him a lot of trouble. George was half-sick most of the time in this period of scarcity, and no match for these young louts. His face bore the marks of a constant losing fight. The last time I was in New York I couldn't find George. The 103rd Street boys are scattered now and no one I talked to knew what happened to George the Greek.

Fritz the Janitor was a pale thin little man who gave the impression of being crippled. He was on parole after doing five years because he scored for a pigeon. The pigeon was hard up for someone to turn in, and the narcotics agent urgently needed to make an arrest. Between them they built Fritz up to a big-time dope peddler, and smashed a narcotics ring with his arrest. Fritz was glad to attract so much attention and he talked complacently about his "nickel" in Lexington.

The Fag was a brilliantly successful lush-worker. His scores were fabulous. He was the man who gets to a lush first, never the man who arrives on the scene when the lush is lying there with his pockets turned inside out. A sleeping lush—known as a "flop" in the trade—attracts a hierarchy of scavengers. First come the top lush-workers like the Fag, guided by a special radar. They only want cash, good rings, and watches. Then come the punks who will steal anything. They take the hat, shoes, and belt. Finally, brazen, clumsy thieves will try to pull the lush's overcoat or jacket off him.

The Fag was always first on a good lush. One time he scored for a thousand dollars at the 103rd Street Station. Often his scores ran into the hundreds. If the lush woke up, he would simper and feel the man's thigh as though his intentions were sexual. From this angle he got this moniker.

He always dressed well, usually in tweed sport coats and gray flannels. A European charm of manner and a slight Scandinavian accent completed his front. No one could have looked less like a lush-roller. He always worked alone. His luck was good and he was determined to avoid contamination. Sometimes, contact with the lucky can change a man's run of bad luck, but generally it works out the other way. Junkies are an envious lot. 103rd Street envied the Fag his scores. But everyone had to admit he was a right guy, and always good for a small touch.

●

The H caps cost three dollars each and you need at least three per day to get by. I was short, so I began "working the hole" with Roy. We would ride along, each looking out one side of the subway car until one of us spotted a "flop" sleeping on a bench. Then we would get off the train. I stood in front of the bench with a newspaper and covered Roy while he went through the lush's pockets. Roy would whisper instructions to me—"a little left, too far, a little back, there, hold it there"—and I would move to keep him covered. Often, we were late and the lush would be lying there with his pockets turned inside out.

We also worked on the cars. I would sit down next to the lush and open a newspaper. Roy would reach across my back and go through the lush's pockets. If the lush woke up, he could see that I had both hands on the paper. We averaged about ten dollars per night.

An average night went more or less like this. We started work about eleven o'clock, getting on the uptown IRT at Times Square. At 149th Street, I spotted a flop and we got off. 149th Street is a station with several levels and dangerous for lush-workers because there are so many spots where cops can hide, and it is not possible to cover from every angle. On the lower level the only way out is by the elevator.

We approached the flop casually, as though we did not see him. He was middle-aged, sprawled against the wall, breathing loudly. Roy sat down beside him and I stationed myself in front of them with an open newspaper. Roy said, "A little to the right, too far, back a little, there, that's good."

Suddenly the heavy breathing stopped. I thought of the scene in the movies where the breathing stops during the operation. I could feel Roy's tense immobility behind me. The drunk muttered something and shifted his position. Slowly the breathing started again. Roy got up. "Okay," he said, and walked rapidly to the other end of the platform. He took a crumpled mass of bills from his pocket and counted out eight dollars. He handed me four. "Had it in his pants pocket. I couldn't find a poke. I thought for a minute he was going to come up on us."

We started back downtown. At 116th we spotted one and got off, but the flop got up and walked away before we could get near him. A shabby man with a wide, loose mouth accosted Roy and started talking. He was another lush-worker.

"The Fag scored again," he said. "Two notes and a wristwatch down at 96th Street." Roy muttered something and looked at his paper. The man went on talking in a loud voice. "I had one come up on me, 'What are you doing with your hand in my pocket?' he says."

"For Chris' sake, don't talk like that!" Roy said and walked away from him. "Fucking wrong bastard," he muttered. "There aren't many lush-workers around now. Only the Fag, the Beagle, and that tramp. They all envy the Fag because he makes good scores. If a sucker comes up on him he pretends to feel his leg like he was a fag. Those tramps at 103rd Street go around saying 'Goddam Fag' because they can't score. He's no more a fag than I am." Roy paused reflectively. "Not as much, in fact."

We rode to the end of the line in Brooklyn without spotting a single flop. On the way back there was a drunk asleep in a car. I sat down beside him and opened my paper. I could feel Roy's arm across my back. Once, the drunk woke up and looked at me sharply. But both my hands were clearly visible on the paper. Roy pretended to be reading the paper with me. The drunk went back to sleep.

"Here's where we get off," Roy said. "We better go out on the street for a bit. Doesn't pay to ride too long."

We had a cup of coffee at the 34th Street automat and split the last take. It was three dollars.

"When you take a lush on the car," Roy was explaining, "you got to gauge yourself to the movement of the car. If you get the right rhythm you can work it out even if the mooch is awake. I went a little too fast on that one. That's why he woke up. He felt something was wrong, but he didn't know what it was."

At Times Square we ran into Subway Mike. He nodded but did not stop. Mike always worked alone.

"Let's take a run out to Queens Plaza," Roy said. "That's on the Independent. The Independent has special cops hired by the company, but they don't carry guns. Only saps. So if one grabs you, run if you can break loose."

Queens Plaza is another dangerous station where it is impossible to cover yourself from every angle. You just have to take a chance. There was a drunk sleeping full length on a bench, but we couldn't risk taking him because too many people were around.

"We'll wait a bit," Roy said. "Remember, though, never pass more than three trains. If you don't get a clear chance by then, forget it no matter how good it looks."

Two young punks got off a train carrying a lush between them. They dropped him on a bench, then looked at Roy and me.

"Let's take him over to the other side," said one of the punks.

"Why not take him right here?" Roy asked.

The punks pretended not to understand. "Take him? I don't get it. What does our queer friend mean?" They picked up their lush and carried him to the other side of the platform.

Roy walked over to our mark and pulled a wallet out of his pocket. "No time for finesse," he remarked. The wallet was empty. Roy dropped it on the bench.

One of the punks shouted across the tracks, "Take your hands out of his pockets." And they both laughed.

"Fucking punks," said Roy. "If I catch one of them on the West Side line I'll push the little bastard onto the tracks."

One of the punks came over and asked Roy for a cut.

"I tell you he didn't have nothing," said Roy.

"We saw you take out his wallet."

"There wasn't nothing in it."

A train stopped and we got on, leaving the punk there undecided whether or not to get tough.

"Fucking punks think it's a joke," Roy said. "They won't last long. They won't think it's so funny when they get out on the Island doing five-twenty-nine." We were in a run of bad luck. Roy said, "Well, that's the way it goes. Some nights you make a hundred dollars. Some nights you don't make anything."

●

One night, we got on the subway at Times Square. A flashily dressed man, weaving slightly, was walking ahead of us. Roy looked him over and said, "That's a good fucking mooch. Let's see where he goes."

The mooch got on the IRT headed for Brooklyn. We waited standing up in the space between cars until the mooch appeared to be sleeping. Then we walked into the car, and I sat down beside the mooch, opening *The New York Times*. The *Times* was Roy's idea. He said it made me look like a businessman. The car was almost empty, and there we were wedged up against the mooch with twenty feet of empty seats available. Roy began working over my back. The mooch kept stirring and once he woke up and looked at me with bleary annoyance. A Negro sitting opposite us smiled.

"The shine is wise," said Roy in my ear. "He's O.K."

Roy was having trouble finding the poke. The situation was getting dangerous. I could feel sweat running down my arms.

"Let's get off," I said.

"No. This is a good mooch. He's sitting on his overcoat and I can't get into his pocket. When I tell you, fall up against him, and I'll move the coat at the same time. . . . *Now!* . . . For Chris' sake! That wasn't near hard enough."

"Let's get off," I said again. I could feel the fear stirring in my stomach. "He's going to wake up."

"No. Let's go again . . . *Now!* . . . What in hell is wrong with you? Just let yourself flop against him hard."

"Roy," I said. "For Chris' sake let's get off! He's going to wake up."
I started to get up, but Roy held me down. Suddenly he gave
me a sharp push, and I fell heavily against the mooch.

"Got it that time," Roy said.

"The poke?"

"No, I got the coat out of the way."

We were out of the underground now and on the elevated. I was
nauseated with fear, every muscle rigid with the effort of control.
The mooch was only half asleep. I expected him to jump up and
yell at any minute.

Finally I heard Roy say, "I got it."

"Let's go then."

"No, what I got is a loose roll. He's got a poke somewhere and
I'm going to find it. He's got to have a poke."

"I'm getting off."

"No. Wait." I could feel him fumbling across my back so openly
it seemed incredible that the man could go on sleeping.

It was the end of the line. Roy stood up. "Cover me," he said.
I stood in front of him with the paper shielding him as much as
possible from the other passengers. There were only three left, but
they were in different ends of the car. Roy went through the man's
pockets openly and crudely. "Let's go outside," he said. We went
out onto the platform.

The mooch woke up and put his hand in his pocket. Then he
came out onto the platform and walked up to Roy.

"All right, Jack," he said. "Give me my money."

Roy shrugged and turned his hands out, palm up. "What
money? What are you talking about?"

"You know Goddamned well what I'm talking about! You had
your hand in my pocket."

Roy held his hands out again in a gesture of puzzlement and
deprecation. "Aw, what are you talking about? I don't know anything about your money."

"I've seen you on this line every night. This is your regular route." He turned and pointed to me. "And there's your partner right there. Now, are you going to give me my dough?"

"What dough?"

"Okay. Just stay put. We're taking a ride back to town and this had better be good." Suddenly, the man put both hands in Roy's coat pockets. "You sonofabitch!" he yelled. "Give me my dough!" Roy hit him in the face and knocked him down. "Why you—" said Roy, dropping abruptly his conciliatory and puzzled manner. "Keep your hands off me!"

The conductor, seeing a fight in progress, was holding up the train so that no one would fall on the tracks.

"Let's cut," I said. We started down the platform. The man got up and ran after us. He threw his arms around Roy, holding on stubbornly. Roy couldn't break loose. He was pretty well winded.

"Get this mooch off me!" Roy yelled.

I hit the man twice in the face. His grip loosened and he fell to his knees.

"Kick his head off," said Roy.

I kicked the man in the side and felt a rib snap. The man put his hand to his side. "Help!" he shouted. He did not try to get up.

"Let's cut," I said. At the far end of the platform, I heard a police whistle. The man was still lying there on the platform holding his side and yelling "Help!" at regular intervals.

There was a slight drizzle of rain falling. When I hit the street, I slipped and skidded on the wet sidewalk. We were standing by a closed filling station, looking back at the elevated.

"Let's go," I said.

"They'll see us."

"We can't stay here."

We started to walk. I noticed that my mouth was bone dry. Roy took two goof balls from his shirt pocket.

"Mouth's too dry," he said. "I can't swallow them."

We went on walking.

"There's sure to be an alarm out for us," Roy said. "Keep a look-out for cars. We'll duck in the bushes if any come along. They'll be figuring us to get back on the subway, so the best thing we can do is keep walking."

The drizzle continued. Dogs barked at us as we walked.

"Remember our story if we get nailed," Roy said. "We fell asleep and woke up at the end of the line. This guy accused us of taking his money. We were scared, so we knocked him down and ran. They'll beat the shit out of us. You have to expect that."

"Here comes a car," I said. "Yellow lights, too."

We crawled into the bushes at the side of the road and crouched down behind a signboard. The car drove slowly by. We started walking again. I was getting sick and wondered if I would get home to the M.S. I had stashed in my apartment.

"When we get closer in we better split up," Roy said. "Out here we might be able to do each other some good. If we run into a cop on the beat we'll tell him we've been with some girls and were looking for the subway. This rain is a break. The cops will all be in some all-night joint drinking coffee. For Chris' sake!" he rasped irritably. "Don't round like that!"

I had turned around and looked over my shoulder. "It's natural to turn around," I said.

"Natural for thieves!"

We finally ran into the BMT line and rode back to Manhattan.

Roy said, "I don't think I'm just speaking for myself when I say I was scared. Oh. Here's your cut."

He handed me three dollars.

Next day I told him I was through as a lush-worker.

"I don't blame you," he said. "But you got a wrong impression. You're bound to get some good breaks if you stick around long enough."

●

My case came to trial in Special Sessions. I drew a four-month suspended sentence. After I gave up lush-working I decided to push junk. There isn't much money in it. About all a using street-peddler can expect to do is keep up his habit. But at least when you are pushing, you have a good supply of junk on hand and that gives a feeling of security. Of course, some people do make money pushing. I knew an Irish pusher who started out capping a $^1/_{16}$-ounce envelope of H and two years later, when he took a fall and went away for three years, he had thirty thousand dollars and an apartment building in Brooklyn.

If you want to push, the first step is to find a wholesale connection. I did not have a connection, so I formed a partnership with Bill Gains, who had a pretty fair Italian connection on the Lower East Side. We bought the stuff for ninety dollars per quarter-ounce, cut it one-third with milk sugar and put it in one-grain caps. The caps sold for two dollars each, retail. They ran about ten to sixteen percent H, which is very high for retail capped stuff. There should be at least a hundred caps in one-quarter ounce of H before it is cut. But if the wholesaler is Italian he is almost sure to give a short count. We usually got about eighty caps out of these Italian quarter-ounces.

Bill Gains came from a "good family"—as I recall, his father had been a bank president somewhere in Maryland—and he had front. Gains' routine was stealing overcoats out of restaurants, and he was perfectly adapted to this work. The American upper-middle-class citizen is a composite of negatives. He is largely delineated by what he is not. Gains went further. He was not merely negative. He was positively invisible; a vague respectable presence. There is a certain kind of ghost that can only materialize with the aid of a sheet or other piece of cloth to give it outline. Gains was like that. He materialized in someone else's overcoat.

Gains had a malicious childlike smile that formed a shocking contrast to his eyes which were pale blue, lifeless and old. He smiled, listening down into himself as if attending to something there that pleased him. Sometimes, after a shot, he would smile and listen and say slyly, "This stuff is powerful." With the same smile he would report on the deterioration and misfortunes of others. "Herman was a beautiful kid when he first came to New York. The trouble is, he lost his looks."

Gains was one of the few junkies who really took a special pleasure in seeing non-users get a habit. Many junkie-pushers are glad to see a new addict for economic reasons. If you have a commodity you naturally want customers, provided they are the right kind. But Gains liked to invite young kids up to his room and give them a shot, usually compounded of old cottons, and then watch the effects, smiling his little smile.

Mostly, the kids said it was a good kick, and that was all. Just another kick like nembies, or bennies, or lush, or weed. But a few stayed around to get hooked, and Gains would look at these converts and smile, a prelate of junk. A little later, you would hear him say, "Really, So-and-so must realize that I can't carry him any longer." The pledge was no longer being rushed. It was time for him to pay off. And pay off for the rest of his life, waiting on street corners and in cafeterias for the connection, the mediator between man and junk. Gains was a mere parish priest in the hierarchy of junk. He would speak of the higher-ups in a voice of sepulchral awe. "The connections say . . ."

His veins were mostly gone, retreated back to the bone to escape the probing needle. For a while he used arteries, which are deeper than veins and harder to hit, and for this procedure he bought special long needles. He rotated from his arms and hands to the veins of his feet. A vein will come back in time. Even so, he had to shoot in the skin about half the time. But he only gave up and "skinned" a shot after an agonizing half-hour of probing and poking and cleaning out the needle, which would stop up with blood.

•

One of my first customers was a Village character named Nick. Nick painted when he did anything. His canvasses were very small and looked as if they had been concentrated, compressed, misshapen by a tremendous pressure. "The product of a depraved mind," a narcotics agent pronounced solemnly, after viewing one of Nick's pictures.

Nick was always half sick, his large, plaintive brown eyes watering slightly and his thin nose running. He slept on couches in the apartments of friends, existing on the precarious indulgence of neurotic, unstable, stupidly suspicious individuals who would suddenly throw him out without reason or warning. For these people he also scored, hoping that he would receive in return at least the head off a cap to take the edge off his constant junk-hunger. Often, he got nothing but a casual thanks, the purchaser having convinced himself that Nick had somehow got his on the other end. As a result, Nick began stealing a small amount from each cap, loosening up the junk so that it filled the cap.

There was not much left of Nick. His constant, unsatisfied hunger had burned out all other concerns. He talked vaguely about going to Lexington for the cure, or shipping out in the merchant marine, or buying paregoric in Connecticut and tapering off on it.

Nick introduced me to Tony, who tended bar in a Village bar and restaurant. Tony had been pushing and nearly got nailed when the Federals rushed into his apartment. He barely had time to throw a $^1/_{16}$-ounce packet of H under the piano. The Federals found nothing but his works and they let him go. Tony was scared and quit pushing. He was a young Italian who obviously knew his way around. He looked capable of keeping his mouth shut. A good type customer.

I went to Tony's bar every day and ordered a Coca-Cola. Tony would tell me how many caps he wanted, and I would go into the phone booth or the W.C. and wrap his caps up in silver paper. When I got back to my Coke, the money for the caps was there on the bar like change. I dropped the caps into an ashtray on the bar and Tony emptied the ashtray under the bar, taking out his caps. This routine was necessary because the owner knew Tony had been a user and told him to stay off stuff or get another job. In fact, the owner's son was a user—at this time in a sanitarium taking the cure. When he got out, he came straight to me to buy stuff. He said he couldn't stay off.

A young Italian hipster named Ray used to come to this bar every day. He seemed O.K. so I took care of him, too, dropping his caps in the ashtray with Tony's. This bar where Tony worked was a small place down several steps from street level. There was only one door. I always felt trapped when I went in there. The place gave me such a feeling of depression and danger that I could hardly bring myself to go through the door.

After taking care of Tony and Ray, I generally met Nick in a cafeteria on Sixth Avenue. He always had the price of a few caps on him. I knew, of course, that he was scoring for other people, but I did not know who they were. I should have known better than to have dealings with anybody like Nick, who was sick and broke all the time and therefore liable to pick up anybody's money. Some people need an intermediary to score for them because they are strangers in town, or because they have not been on junk long enough to get acquainted. But the pusher has reason to be wary of people who send someone else to score. By and large, the reason a man can't score is because he is known to be "wrong." So he sends someone else to score who may not be "wrong" himself, but simply desperate for junk. To score for a pigeon is definitely not ethical. Often a man goes on from scoring for pigeons to become a pigeon himself.

I was not in a position to turn money down. I had no margin. Every day I had to sell enough caps to buy the next ¼-ounce, and I was never more than a few dollars ahead. So I took whatever money Nick had and asked no questions. I knew Nick was a bad security risk, but I could not afford to pack him in.

●

I went into pushing with Bill Gains, who handled the uptown business. I met Bill in an Eighth Avenue cafeteria after I finished up in the Village. He had a few good customers. Izzy, probably his best, had a job as cook on a tugboat in New York harbor. He was one of the 103rd Street boys. Izzy had done time for pushing, was known as a thoroughly right guy, and he had a steady source of income. This is a perfect customer.

Sometimes Izzy showed up with his partner, Goldie, who worked on the same boat. Goldie was a thin, hook-nosed man with the skin drawn tight over his face and a spot of color on each cheekbone. Another of Izzy's friends was a young ex-paratrooper named Matty, a husky, handsome, hard-faced young man who bore none of the marks of a drug addict. There were also two whores that Bill took care of. Generally, whores are not a good deal at all. They attract heat, and most of them will talk. But Bill insisted that these particular whores were O.K.

Another of our customers was Old Bart. He took a few caps every day which he sold on commission. I didn't know his customers, but I didn't worry about it. Bart was O.K. If there was a beef, he would take the rap without talking. Anyway, he had thirty years' experience in junk and he knew what he was doing.

When I arrived at the cafeteria where we had our meet, there was Bill sitting at a table, his skinny frame huddled in someone else's overcoat. Old Bart, shabby and inconspicuous, was dunking a doughnut in his coffee. Bill told me he had already taken care of Izzy so I gave Bart ten caps to sell, and Bill and I took a cab to my apartment. There we had a shot and checked over the stock, setting aside ninety dollars for the next ¼-ounce.

After Bill got his shot, a little color crept into his face and he would become almost coy. It was a gruesome sight. I remember once he told me how he'd been propositioned by a queer who offered him twenty dollars. Bill declined, saying, "I don't think you would be very well satisfied." Bill twitched his fleshless hips. "You should see me in the nude," he said. "I'm really cute."

One of Bill's most distasteful conversation routines consisted of detailed bulletins on the state of his bowels. "Sometimes it gets so I have to reach my fingers in and pull it out. Hard as porcelain, you understand. The pain is terrible."

"Listen," I said, "this connection keeps giving us a short count. I only got eighty caps out of the last batch after it was cut."

"Well, you can't expect too much. If I could go to a hospital and get a good enema! But they won't do a thing for you unless you check into the hospital and, of course, I can't do that. They keep you at least twenty-four hours. I told them, 'You're supposed to be a hospital. I'm in pain and I need treatment. Why can't you just call an attendant and . . .'"

There was no stopping him. When people start talking about their bowel movements they are as inexorable as the processes of which they speak.

●

Things went on like this for several weeks. One by one, Nick's contacts located me. They were tired of scoring through Nick and having him steal the head off their caps. What a crew! Mooches, fags, four-flushers, stool pigeons, bums—unwilling to work, unable to steal, always short of money, always whining for credit. In the whole lot there was not one who wouldn't wilt and spill as soon as someone belted him in the mouth and said "Where did you get it?" The worst of the lot was Gene Doolie, a scrawny little Irishman with a manner between fag and pimp. Gene was informer to the bone. He probably pulled out dirty lists of people—his hands were always dirty—and read them off to the law. You could see him bustling into Black and Tan headquarters during the Irish Trouble, in a dirty gray toga turning in Christians, giving information to the Gestapo, the GPU, sitting in a cafeteria talking to a narcotics agent. Always the same thin, ratty face, shabby, out-of-date clothes, whiny, penetrating voice.

The most unbearable thing about Gene was his voice. It went all through you. This voice was my first knowledge of his existence. Nick had just arrived at my apartment with some score money when I was called to the hall phone by the buzzer.

"I'm Gene Doolie," said the voice. "I'm waiting for Nick, and I've been waiting a long time." His voice went up on "long time" to a shrill, grating whine.

I said, "Well, he's here now. I expect you will see him directly," and I hung up.

Next day, Doolie called me again. "I'm just around the corner from your place. Do you mind if I come on over? It's cooler for me to meet you alone."

He hung up before I could say anything, and ten minutes later he was standing in the door.

When one personality meets another for the first time, there is a period of mutual examination on the intuitive level of empathy and identification. But it was impossible to relate one's self to Doolie in any way. He was simply the focal point for a hostile intrusive force. You could feel him walk right into your psyche and look around to see if anything was there he could make use of. I stepped back a little from the door to avoid contact with him. He squeezed himself into the room and immediately sat down on the couch and lit a cigarette.

"It's better to meet alone like this." His smile was ambiguously sexual. "Nick is a very un-cool guy." He stood up and handed me four dollars. "Do you mind if I take off here?" he asked, pulling off his coat.

I had never heard anyone else use this expression. For an insane moment I thought he was making advances. He dropped his coat on the couch and rolled up his sleeve. I brought him two caps and a glass of water. He had his own works, for which I was grateful. I watched him as he hit a vein, pressed the dropper and rolled down his sleeve.

When you are hooked, the effects of a shot are not dramatic. But the observer who knows what to look for can see the immediate working of junk in the blood and cells of another user. I could detect no change whatever in Doolie. He put on his coat and picked up the cigarette which had been smoldering in an ashtray. He looked at me with his pale blue eyes that seemed to have no depth at all. They looked artificial.

"Let me tell you something," he said. "You're making a big mistake to trust Nick. A few nights ago I was in Thompson's Cafeteria and I ran into Rogers, the agent. He told me, 'I know Nick is scoring for all you Goddamned junkies here in the Village. You're getting good stuff, too—between sixteen and twenty percent. Well, you can tell Nick this: We can take him any time we want, and when we do catch up to him he's going to work with us. He opened up for me once. He'll do it again. We're going to find out where this stuff is coming from.'"

Doolie looked at me and sucked on his cigarette. "When they get Nick, they'll get you. You'd better let Nick know that if he talks you'll have him poured into a barrel of concrete and dumped in the East River. I don't need to tell you any more. You can see what the situation is."

He looked at me, trying to gauge the effect of his words. It was impossible to tell just how much of this story I was expected to believe. Perhaps it was just a roundabout way of saying, "How will you ever know who fingered you? With Nick such an obvious suspect, if I talked you could never be sure, could you now?"

"Could you let me have one cap on credit?" he asked. "What I've just told you should be worth something."

I gave him a cap and he pocketed it without comment.

He stood up. "Well, I'll be seeing you. I'll call at this same time tomorrow."

I put out a grapevine to see what I could find out about Doolie, and to check his story. No one knew anything definitive about him. Tony the bartender said, "Doolie will fink if he has to." But he couldn't give me a definite instance. Yes, Nick was known to have talked once. But the facts of this case, in which Doolie was also involved, indicated the tip could just as well have come from Doolie.

Several days after the Gene Doolie episode, I was coming out of the subway at Washington Square when a thin, blond kid walked up to me. "Bill," he said, "I guess you don't know who I am. I've been scoring off you through Nick and I'm tired of having him steal the head off all my caps. Can't you take care of me directly?"

I thought, *What the hell? After Gene Doolie, why get particular?* "O.K., kid," I said. "How many do you want?"

He gave me four dollars.

"Let's take a walk," I said, and started towards Sixth Avenue. I had two caps in my hand and waited for one of the empty spaces you run into in a city. "Get ready to cop," I said, and dropped the caps into his hands. I made a meet with him for the next day in the Washington Square Bickford's.

This blond kid's name was Chris. I heard from Nick that his folks had money and that he lived on an allowance from home. When I met him the next day in Bickford's, he immediately began to give me the let-me-warn-you-about-Nick routine. "Nick is followed all the time now. You know yourself when a guy is yenning, he doesn't look behind him. He's running. So you see who you picked out to give your address and phone number to."

"I know all about that," I said.

Chris pretended to be hurt. "Well, I hope you know what you're doing. Now listen, this is not a routine. I'm positively getting a check from my aunt this afternoon. Look at this."

He pulled a telegram from his pocket. I glanced at it. There was some vague reference to a check. He went on explaining about the check. As he talked, he kept putting his hand on my arm and gazing earnestly into my face. I felt I could not stand any more of this sweet con. To cut him short, I handed him one cap before he could put it on me for two or three.

Next day he showed up with a dollar-eighty. He didn't say anything about the check. And so it went. He came up short, or not at all. He was always about to get money from his aunt, or mother-in-law, or somebody. These stories he documented with letters and telegrams. He got to be almost as much of a drag as Gene Doolie.

Another prize customer was Marvin, part-time waiter in a Village nightclub. He was always unshaved and dirty-looking. He had only one shirt, which he washed every week or so and dried out on the radiator. The final touch was that he wore no socks. I used to deliver stuff to his room, a dirty, furnished room in a red brick house on Jane Street. I figured it was better to deliver to his place than to meet him anywhere else.

Some people are allergic to junk. One time I delivered a cap to Marvin and he took a shot. I was looking out the window—it is nerve-racking to watch someone probe for a vein—and when I turned around I noticed his dropper was full of blood. He had passed out and the blood had run back into the dropper. I called to Nick and he pulled the needle out and slapped Marvin with a wet towel. He came around partly and muttered something.

"I guess he's O.K.," I said. "Let's cut."

He looked like a corpse slumped there on the dirty, unmade bed, his limp arm stretched out, a drop of blood slowly gathering at the elbow.

As we walked downstairs, Nick told me that Marvin had been after him for my address.

"Listen," I said, "if you give it to him, you can find yourself a new connection. One thing I don't need is somebody dying in my apartment."

Nick looked hurt. "Of course I won't give him your address."

"What about Doolie?"

"I don't know how he got the address. I swear I don't."

•

Along with these bums, I picked up a couple of good customers. One day, I ran into Bert, a character I knew from the Angle Bar. Bert was known as a muscle man. He was a heavy-set, round-faced, deceptively soft-looking young man who specialized in strong-arm routines and "shakes." I never knew him to use anything but weed, and I was surprised when he asked me if I was holding any junk. I told him, yes, I was pushing junk, and he bought ten caps. I found out he had been hooked for about six months.

Through Bert, I met another customer. This was Louis, a very handsome type with a waxy complexion, delicate features, and a silky black moustache. He looked like an 1890 portrait. Louis was a pretty fair thief and was generally well-heeled. When he asked for credit, which was seldom, he always made good the next day. Sometimes he brought around a watch, or a suit, instead of cash, which was all right with me. I picked up a fifty-dollar watch from him for five caps.

Pushing junk is a constant strain on the nerves. Sooner or later you get the "copper jitters," and everybody looks like a cop. People moving about in the subway seem to be edging closer so they can grab you before you have a chance to throw away the junk. Doolie came around every day, impudent, demanding, insufferable. Usually he had some new bulletin on the Nick-Rogers situation. He didn't mind letting me know that he was in constant touch with Rogers.

"Rogers is shrewd, but he's corny," Doolie told me. "He keeps saying, 'I don't care about you damned junkies. I'm after the guys who make money out of it. When we find Nick, he's going to fink. He opened up for me once. He'll do it again.'"

Chris kept hounding me for credit, whining and pawing at me and talking about the money he was going to have for sure in a few days, or a few hours.

Nick looked harried and desperate. I guess he didn't waste any money on food. He looked like the terminal stages of some wasting disease.

When I delivered to Marvin, I left before he took his shot. I knew he would die from junk sooner or later and I didn't want to be around when it happened.

On top of all this, I was just barely scraping by. The short counts we kept getting from the wholesaler, the constant nibbles of credit, and customers coming up twenty-five, fifty, or even a dollar short, plus my own habit, cut profits to bare subsistence.

When I complained about the wholesaler, Bill Gains got snappish and said I ought to cut the stuff more. "You're giving a better cap than anybody in New York City. Nobody sells sixteen percent stuff on the street. If your customers don't like it, they can take their business to Walgreen's."

We kept moving our uptown meets from one cafeteria to another. It doesn't take the manager long to spot a bookie or a junk pusher. There were about six regular uptown customers now, and that means quite a bit of traffic. So we kept moving.

Tony's bar still gave me the horrors. One day it was raining very hard, and I was on my way to Tony's about a half hour late. Ray, the young Italian hipster, stuck his head out of the door of a restaurant and called me over. It was a lunch counter with booths along one wall. We sat down at a booth and I ordered tea.

"There's an agent outside in a white trenchcoat," Ray told me. "He followed me over here from Tony's and I'm afraid to go out."

The table was made of tube metal, and Ray showed me, guiding my hand under the table, where there was an open end to one of the tubes. I sold him two caps. He wrapped them in a paper napkin and stuffed the napkin into the tube.

"I'm going out clean first in case I get a shake," he said.

I drank my cup of tea, thanked him for the information, and left ahead of him. I had the stuff in a package of cigarettes and was ready to throw it in the water-filled gutter. Sure enough, there was a burly young man in a white trenchcoat standing in a doorway. When he saw me he started sauntering up the street ahead of me. Then he turned a corner, waiting for me to walk past so he could fall in behind. I turned and ran back in the opposite direction. When I reached Sixth Avenue, he was about fifty feet behind me. I vaulted the subway turnstile and shoved the cigarette package into the space at the side of a gum machine. I ran down one level and got a train up to the Square.

Bill Gains was sitting at a table in the cafeteria. He was wearing one stolen overcoat, and another lay on his lap. He looked sly and satisfied. Old Bart was there and an unemployed cab driver named Kelly, who hung around 42nd Street and sometimes picked up a few dollars peddling condoms and with a routine of hitting commuters for fifty cents, which is one variety of the "short con." I told them about the agent, and Old Bart went down to pick up the stuff.

Gains looked annoyed and said pettishly, "For God's sake, watch whose money you pick up."

"If I hadn't picked up Ray's money, I'd be on my way to the Federal building."

"Well, be careful."

We waited around for Bart, and Kelly began telling a long story about how he told off a guard in the Tombs.

Bart was back soon with the stuff. He reported that a guy in a white trenchcoat was still walking around on the station platform. I gave Bart two caps under the table.

Gains and I walked over to his room to take a shot. "Really," he said, "I'm going to have to tell Bart I can't carry him any longer." Gains lived in a cheap rooming house in the West Forties. He opened the door to his room. "You wait here," he said. "I'm going to get my works." Like most junkies, he kept his "works" and caps stashed somewhere outside his room. He came back with the works and we both took a shot.

Gains was aware of his talent for invisibility, and at times he felt the need for holding himself together so he would at least have enough flesh to put a needle in. At these times he would assemble all his claims to reality. Now he began rummaging around in the bureau and brought out a worn manila envelope. He showed me a discharge from Annapolis "for the good of the service," an old, dirty letter from "my friend, the captain," a card to the Masons and a card to the Knights of Columbus.

"Every little bit helps," he said, indicating these credentials. He sat for a few minutes, silent and reflective. Then he smiled. "Just a victim of circumstances," he said. He stood up and carefully put away his envelope. "I've about burned down all the pawnshops in New York. You don't mind pawning these coats for me, do you?"

•

After that, things got worse and worse. One day, the hotel clerk stopped me in the lobby. "I don't know how to say this," he said, "but there's something wrong about the people who come up to your room. I used to be in illegitimate business myself years ago. I just wanted to warn you to be careful. You know, all calls come through the office. I heard one this morning and it was pretty obvious. If someone else had been at the switchboard . . . So be careful and tell these people to watch what they say over the phone."

The call he referred to was Doolie's. That morning he had called me up. "I want to see you," he yelled. "I'm sick. I'll be over right away."

I could feel the Federals moving steadily closer. It was a question of time. I did not trust any of the Village customers, and I was convinced that at least one of them was a rank stool pigeon. Doolie was my number one suspect, with Nick running a very close second, and Chris trailing in third place. Of course, there was always the possibility that Marvin might take the easy way of raising money to buy a pair of socks.

Nick also scored for some respectable working people in the Village who indulged in an occasional "joy bang." This type person is a bad security risk because of timidity. They are afraid of the police, they are afraid of losing their responsible jobs. It does not occur to them that there is anything wrong about giving information to the law. Of course, they will not come forward with information because of their fear of being "involved." But they will generally spill under police questioning.

Narcotics agents operate largely with the aid of informers. The usual routine is to grab someone with junk on him, and let him stew in jail until he is good and sick. Then comes the spiel:

"We can get you five years for possession. On the other hand, you can walk out of here right now. The decision is up to you. If you work with us, we can give you a good deal. For one thing, you'll have plenty of junk and pocket money. That is, if you deliver. Take a few minutes to think it over."

The agent takes out a few caps and puts them on the table. This is like pouring a glass of ice water in front of a man dying of thirst. "Why don't you pick them up? Now you're being sensible. The first man we want to get is—"

Some of them don't need to be pressured. Junk and pocket money is all they want, and they don't care how they get it. The new pigeon is given marked money and sent out to make a buy. When the pigeon makes a buy with this money, the agents close in right away to make the arrest. It is essential to make the arrest before the peddler has a chance to change the marked money. The agents have the marked money that bought the junk, and the junk it bought. If the case is important enough, the pigeon may be called upon to testify. Of course, once he appears in court and testifies, the pigeon is known to the trade and no one will serve him. Unless the agents want to send him to another town (some especially able pigeons go on tour), his informing career is finished.

Sooner or later, the peddlers get wise to a pigeon and the pigeon can't score. When this happens, his usefulness to the agents is at an end, and they usually turn him in. Often he ends up doing more time than anybody he sent up.

In the case of young kids who would be no use as full-time pigeons, the procedure is different. The agent may come on with the old cop con: "I hate to send a young kid like you away. Sure you made a mistake. That can happen to anybody. Now listen. I'm going to give you a break, but you'll have to cooperate with us. Otherwise I won't be able to help you." Or else they just belt him in the mouth and say, "Where did you get it?" With lots of people that's all it takes. You could find an example of every type informer, overt or potential, among my customers.

After the hotel clerk spoke to me, I moved to another hotel and registered under another name. I stopped going to the Village and shifted all the Village customers to uptown meets.

When I told Gains what the hotel clerk said to me and how lucky we were he happened to be a right guy, he said, "We've got to pack in. We can't last with this crowd."

"Well," I said, "they're up there now, waiting for us in front of the automat. The whole lot of them. Shall we go today?"

"Yes. I'm going to Lexington for the cure and I need bus fare. I'm leaving tonight."

As soon as we got in sight of the meet, Doolie broke from the others and ran up to us at full speed, pulling off a two-tone sports jacket. He was wearing some sort of sandals, or slippers.

"Give me four caps for this coat," he said. "I've been in the can twenty-four hours."

Doolie sick was an unnerving sight. The envelope of personality was gone, dissolved by his junk-hungry cells. Viscera and cells, galvanized into a loathsome insect-like activity, seemed on the point of breaking through the surface. His face was blurred, unrecognizable, at the same time shrunken and tumescent.

Gains gave Doolie two caps and took the coat.

"I'll give you two more tonight," he said. "Right here at nine o'clock."

Izzy, who'd been standing by, silent, had been looking at Doolie with amazed disgust. "Holy Jesus!" he said. "Sandals!"

The others swarmed around, holding out their hands like a crowd of Asiatic beggars. None of them had any money.

I said, "No credit," and we started walking down the street. They followed us, whining and clutching at our sleeves. "Just one cap."

I said no and kept on walking. One after the other, they fell away. We walked down into the subway and told Izzy we were packing in.

"Jeez," he said, "I don't blame you. Sandals!"

Izzy bought six caps and we gave two caps to Old Bart, who was going out to Riker's for the thirty-day cure.

Bill Gains was examining the sports coat with a practiced eye. "It should bring ten dollars easy," he said. "I know a tailor who will sew up this rip for me." One pocket was slightly torn. "Where did he get it?"

"He claims from Brooks Brothers. But he's the kind of guy who would say anything he stole came from Brooks Brothers or Abercrombie & Fitch."

"It's too bad," said Gains, smiling. "My bus leaves at six. I won't be able to give him the other two caps I promised."

"Don't worry about it. He's into us for a double sawski."

"He is? Well, then, it doesn't make any difference."

●

Bill Gains left for Lexington, and I started for Texas in my car. I had $1/16$-ounce of junk with me. I figured this was enough to taper off, and I had a reduction schedule carefully worked out. It was supposed to take twelve days. I had the junk in solution, and in another bottle distilled water. Every time I took a dropper of solution out to use it, I put the same amount of distilled water in the junk solution bottle. Eventually I would be shooting plain water. This method is well known to all junkies. A variation of it is known as the Chinese cure, which is carried out with hop and Wampole's Tonic. After a few weeks, you find yourself drinking plain Wampole's Tonic.

Four days later in Cincinnati, I was out of junk and immobilized. I have never known one of these self-administered reduction cures to work. You find reasons to make each shot an exception that calls for a little extra junk. Finally, the junk is all gone and you still have your habit.

I left the car in storage and took a train to Lexington. I did not have the papers that are required for admittance, but I was relying on my Army discharge to get me in. When I got to Lexington I took a taxi out to the hospital, which is several miles from the town. The taxi took me to the gate-house of the hospital. In the gate-house was an old Irish guard. He looked at my Army discharge.

"Are you addicted to the use of habit-forming drugs?"

I said yes.

"Well, sit down." He pointed to a bench.

He called the main building. "No, no papers. . . . Got an Army discharge." He looked over from the phone. "You ever been here before?" he asked.

I said no.

"Says he hasn't been here before." The guard hung up. "A car will be down for you in a few minutes," he told me. "Have you got any drugs or needles or droppers on your person? You can surrender them here, but if you take them up to the main building you are liable to prosecution for introducing contraband articles into a Government reservation."

"I've got nothing."

After a short wait, a car came down to the gate and drove me up to the main building. A heavy, barred, iron door opened automatically to let the car in, then closed after it. A polite guard took my addiction history.

"You're doing a sensible thing to come here," he told me. "There's one man in here now who's spent every Christmas for the past twenty-five years locked up somewhere."

I checked my clothes into a basket and took a shower. The next step was a physical examination. I had to wait about fifteen minutes for the doctor. The doctor apologized for keeping me waiting, gave me a physical examination and took my addiction history. His manner was courteous and efficient. He listened to my addiction history, interrupting with an occasional comment or question. When I mentioned buying junk by the ¼-ounce, he smiled and said, "Selling some of it to keep up the habit, eh?"

Finally he leaned back in his chair. "As you know," he said, "you can leave here on twenty-four hours' notice. Some people leave after ten days, and stay off permanently. Some stay six months and go back two days after they get out. But, statistically speaking, the longer you stay the better chance you have of staying off. The procedure here is more or less impersonal. The cure lasts about eight or ten days, depending on severity of addiction. You can put on that dressing gown now."

He pointed to pajamas and dressing gown and slippers that were laid out for me. The doctor was speaking rapidly into a dictaphone. He gave a brief account of my physical condition and addiction history. "Patient seems secure and states his reason for seeking cure is necessity of providing for his family."

A guard took me to my ward.

"If you want to get off drugs," he said, "this is the place to do it."

The ward attendant asked me if I really wanted to get off drugs. I said yes. He assigned me to a private room.

About fifteen minutes later the attendant called, "Shot line!" Everyone in the ward lined up. As our names were called, we put an arm through a window in the door of the ward dispensary, and the attendant gave the shots. Sick as I was, the shot fixed me. Right away, I began to get hungry.

I walked up to the middle of the ward, where there were benches, chairs and a radio, and got in conversation with a thuggish-looking young Italian. He asked if I had much of a record. I said no.

"You ought to be up with the Do-Rights," he said. "You get a longer cure there and better rooms."

The Do-Rights were people in Lexington for the first time, who were considered to be especially good prospects for a permanent cure. Evidently, the doctors in Reception didn't think too much of my prospects.

Others drifted out and joined the conversation. The shot had made them feel sociable. First came a Negro from Ohio.

"How much time you bringing with you?" the Italian asked him.

"Three years," the Negro said. He was in for forging and selling scripts. He began telling about a stretch he did in Ohio State. "That's a fuck of a place to do time. A bunch of kids in there, rough little bastards. You get your stuff at the commissary and some punk comes up to you and says, 'Give it to me.' If you don't give it to him, he belts you one in the kisser. Then they all gang up on you. You ain't going to whip all of them."

A gambling-house dealer from East St. Louis was describing a method for cooking the carbolic acid out of a phenol, sweet oil and tincture of opium script.

"I tell the croaker I've got an aged mother and she uses this prescription for piles. After you get the sweet oil drained off, you put the stuff in a tablespoon and hold it over a gas flame. That burns the phenol right out. It'll hold you twenty-four hours."

A handsome, powerfully built man of forty or so, with a tan complexion and iron-gray hair, was telling how his girl smuggled stuff to him in an orange. "So there we were in County. Goddamn both of us shitting in our pants like a goose. Hell, when I bit into that orange it was so bitter. Must have been fifteen or twenty grains in it, shot in with a hypo. I didn't know she had that much sense."

"The guard says to me, 'Drug addict! Why you sonofabitch, you mean you're a dope fiend! Well, you'll get no medicine in here!'"

"Sweet oil and tincture. The oil floats to the top and you can draw it off with a dropper. Cooks up black as tar."

"So I hit Philly sick as a sonofabitch."

"Well, the croaker says, 'Okay, how much do you use?'"

"Ever used powdered Dilaudid? Lots of guys killed themselves with it. About as much as you can put on the end of a toothpick. The big end, that is, no more."

"Cook it up and shoot it."

"On the nod."

"Loaded."

"That was back in '33. Twenty-eight dollars an ounce."

"We used to make a pipe out of a bottle and a rubber tube. When we got through smoking, we'd break the bottle."

"Cook it up and shoot it."

"On the nod."

"Sure you can shoot cocaine in the skin. It hits you right in the stomach."

"H and coke. You can *smell* it going in."

Like hungry men who can talk about nothing but food. After a while the shot began to wear off. Conversation slackened. People drifted off to lie down, read or play cards. Lunch was served in the ward room and was an excellent meal.

There were three shots a day. One at seven a.m., when we got up, one at one p.m., and one at nine p.m. Two old acquaintances had come in during the afternoon, Matty and Louis. I ran into Louis as we were lining up for the evening shot.

"Did they get you?" he asked me.

"No. Just here for the cure. How about you?"

"Same with me," he answered.

With the evening shot, they gave me some chloral hydrate in a glass. Five new arrivals were brought to the ward during the night. The ward attendant threw up his hands. "I don't know where I'm going to put them. I've got thirty-one dope fiends in here now."

Among the new arrivals was a dignified, white-haired man of seventy named Bob Riordan, an old-time con man, junk pusher, and pickpocket. He looked the way bankers looked around 1910. He had come with two friends in a car. On the way to Lexington, they had called the Surgeon General in Washington and asked him to wire ahead to the gate that they were coming and should be let right in. They referred to the Surgeon General as Felix and seemed to know him from 'way back. But only Riordan got in that night. The other two drove to a town near Lexington, where they knew a croaker, to get fixed before they were immobilized for lack of junk.

They both came in about noon the next day. Sol Bloom was a fat man with a heavy Jewish face. Con man stuck out all over him. With him was a little thin man called Bunky. Bunky might have been an old farmer or any dried-up skinny old man except for his gray eyes, serene and cold behind steel-rimmed spectacles. These were Riordan's two friends. All of them had done a lot of time, mostly Federal time for pushing junk. They were affable, but maintained a certain reserve. The story they put down was that they really wanted to get off junk because the Federals bothered them all the time.

As Sol said, "Hell, I love junk and I can get a room full of it. But if I can't use without I get static all the time from the law, I'll get off junk and stay off." He went on talking about some old acquaintances who got their start in junk and later turned respectable. "Now they say, 'Don't have anything to do with Sol. He's a *shmecker*.'"

I don't think they expected anyone to believe the getting-off-junk routine. It was just a way of saying, "Why we came here is our own business."

Another new arrival was Abe Green, a long-nosed Jew with one leg. He was almost a ringer for Jimmy Durante. He had pale blue birdlike eyes. Even junk sick, he radiated a fierce vitality. His first night in the ward, he was so sick a doctor came down to examine him and gave him an extra ½ grain of morphine. In a few days he was stumping around the ward, talking and playing cards. Green was a well-known pusher from Brooklyn, one of the few independent operators in the business. Most pushers have to work for the syndicate or quit, but Green had so many connections he could stay in business on his own. At the time, he was out on bail, but expected to beat the rap on the grounds of illegal seizure. "He (the agent) wakes me up in the middle of the night and starts beating me over the head with his gun. Wants me to give him my connection. I told him, 'I'm fifty-four years old and I've never given you guys anything yet. I'll be dead first.'"

Telling about a stretch in Atlanta, where he kicked a habit cold: "Fourteen days I was beating my head against the wall and blood came out of my eyes and nose. When the screw came, I'd spit in his face." Coming from him, these narratives had an epic quality.

Benny was another oldtime Jewish shmecker from New York. He had been in Lexington eleven times and was in on the Blue Grass this trip. According to the Blue Grass Law of Kentucky, any "known user of narcotic drugs can be sentenced to the county jail for one year, with the alternative of taking the cure in Lexington." He was a short, fat, little Jew with a round face. I would never have made Benny for junk. He had a fair singing voice in a loud way, and his best number was "April Showers."

One day Benny came into the day-room all excited.

"Moishe just checked in," he said. "He's a panhandler *and* a fruit. A disgrace to the Jewish race."

"But, Benny," someone said, "he's got a wife and kids."

"I don't care if he's got ten kids," Benny said. "He's still a fruit."

Moishe showed about an hour later. He was a pretty obvious fruit and strictly on the mooch. He was a man of about sixty, with a smooth, pink face and white hair.

Matty was all over the ward, talking to everybody, asking crude, blunt questions, describing his withdrawal symptoms in detail. He never complained. I don't think he was capable of self-pity. Bob Riordan asked him what he did to get by and Matty replied, "I'm just a dumb fucking thief." He told a story about a drunk asleep on a subway platform bench. "I knew he had a roll in his side pocket, but every time I got within ten feet of him, he'd wake up and say,

'What do you want?'" It was easy to see how Matty's vigorous, intrusive emanations would wake up the lush. "So I went and found a guy I knew. Some old goof-ball bum. He sat right down by the drunk, and in twenty seconds he had it. He cut the pocket."

"Why didn't you shove him back against the wall and take the money?" said Riordan in his good-natured, condescending way.

Matty had unlimited brass and there was no uncertainty behind it. He looked completely unlike a drug addict. If a drugstore refused to sell him a needle, he would say, "Why won't you sell it to me? Do I look like a dope fiend?" A doctor had got Matty on stuff. "The Jew bastard," Matty said, "he used to say to me, 'Matty, you need a little shot. There's no color.' But I made him wish he'd never seen me."

I could see a fat old Jewish doctor trying to refuse Matty a shot on credit. Characters like Matty constitute one of the hazards of pushing. They usually have money. When they don't, they expect credit. If you refuse, they will try to strong-arm you. They won't listen to no when they want junk.

The cure at Lexington is not designed to keep the addicts comfortable. It starts at one-quarter of a grain of M three times a day and lasts eight days—the preparation now used is a synthetic morphine called dolophine. After eight days, you get a send-off shot and go over in "population." There you receive barbiturates for three nights and that is the end of medication.

For a man with a heavy habit, this is a very rough schedule. I was lucky, in that I came in sick, so the amount given in the cure was sufficient to fix me. The sicker you are and the longer you have been without junk, the smaller the amount necessary to fix you.

When the time came for my send-off shot, I was assigned to Ward B—"Skid Row," it was called. There was nothing wrong with the accommodations, but the inmates were a sorry-looking lot. In my section, there were a bunch of old bums with the spit running out of their mouths.

You are allowed seven days to rest in population after medication stops. Then you have to choose a job and go to work. Lexington has a complete farm and dairy. There is a cannery to put up the fruits and vegetables raised on the farm. The inmates run a dental laboratory where they make false teeth, a radio repair service, a library. They serve as janitors, they cook and serve food, and they act as assistants to the ward attendants. So there is a wide variety of jobs to select from.

I did not figure to stay around long enough to work. After my send-off shot began to wear off, I got sick. Just a shadow of the way I felt when I came in, but bad enough. Even with the sedative, I did not sleep that night. Next day I was worse. I couldn't eat anything, and it was an effort for me to move around. The dolophine suspends the sickness, but when the medication stops the sickness returns. "You don't kick your habit in the shooting gallery," an inmate told me. "You kick it over here in population." When the night medication stopped, I checked out still sick. On a cold windy afternoon, five of us took a cab into Lexington.

"The thing to do is get right out of Lexington," my companions told me. "Go right to the bus station and stay there until your bus leaves. Otherwise you're liable to get the Blue Grass." This law was devised to protect the doctors and druggists of Kentucky against the importunities of addicts on their way to and from the Lexington Narcotics Farm. It is also intended to discourage addicts from lingering in the town of Lexington.

In Cincinnati, I went around to several drugstores buying one-ounce bottles of paregoric. Two ounces of paregoric will fix an addict when his habit is reduced, as mine was at that time. I drank three ounces of paregoric, followed with a little warm water. In about ten minutes I could feel the junk take hold, and the sickness was gone. I felt hungry right away and went out of the hotel to eat.

●

Eventually, I got to Texas and stayed off junk for about four months. Then I went to New Orleans. New Orleans presents a stratified series of ruins. Along Bourbon Street are ruins of the 1920s. Down where the French Quarter blends into Skid Row are ruins of an earlier stratum: chili joints, decaying hotels, oldtime saloons with mahogany bars, spittoons, and crystal chandeliers. The ruins of 1900.

There are people in New Orleans who have never been outside the city limits. The New Orleans accent is exactly similar to the accent of Brooklyn. The French Quarter is always crowded. Tourists, servicemen, merchant seamen, gamblers, perverts, drifters, and lamsters from every State in the Union. People wander around, unrelated, purposeless, most of them looking vaguely sullen and hostile. This is a place where you enjoy yourself. Even the criminals have come here to cool off and relax.

But a complex pattern of tensions, like the electrical mazes devised by psychologists to unhinge the nervous systems of white rats and guinea pigs, keeps the unhappy pleasure-seekers in a condition of unconsummated alertness. For one thing, New Orleans is inordinately noisy. The drivers orient themselves largely by the use of their horns, like bats. The residents are surly. The transient population is completely miscellaneous and unrelated, so that you never know what sort of behavior to expect from anybody.

New Orleans was a strange town to me and I had no way of making a junk connection. Walking around the city, I spotted several junk neighborhoods: St. Charles and Poydras, the area around and above Lee Circle, Canal and Exchange Place. I don't spot junk neighborhoods by the way they look, but by the feel, somewhat the same process by which a dowser locates hidden water. I am walking along and suddenly the junk in my cells moves and twitches like the dowser's wand: "Junk here!"

I didn't see anybody around, and besides I wanted to stay off, or at least I thought I wanted to stay off.

•

One night, I was in Frank's Bar off Exchange Place drinking a rum and Coke. It was an equivocal place; seamen and longshoremen, queers, dealers from the all-night poker game next door, and some characters who could not be classified. Standing next to me was a middle-aged man with a long, thin face and gray hair. I asked him if he would join me in a beer.

He said, "I would, but unfortunately . . . unfortunately I am not in a condition to reciprocate." Clearly a man who made his living by physical work, self-educated, a terrific bore once he has spotted you as "a man of intelligence."

I ordered two beers, and he went on telling me how he was accustomed to reciprocate. When the beers came, he said, "Shall we find a table where we can discuss the state of the world and the meaning of life without being disturbed?" We took our glasses to a table. I was preparing an excuse to leave. The man said, suddenly, "Now, for example, I know that you are interested in narcotics."

"How do you know that?" I asked.

"I know," he said, smiling. "I know that you are here to investigate narcotics. I've done a lot of work in that line myself. I've been up to the FBI here fifty times to tell them what I know. You know, of course, how narcotics ties right in with Communism? I shipped out with the C and A line last year. That line is Communist-controlled. The chief engineer was one of them. I spotted him right away. He used to smoke a pipe and light it with a cigarette lighter. He used the lighter to signal." He showed me how the engineer lighted his pipe with a cigarette lighter and covered and uncovered the lighter to signal. "Oh, he was smooth."

"Signal to whom?" I asked.

"I don't know exactly. There was a plane that followed us for a while. I could hear it every time he went out to light his pipe. Let me tell you something that may save you a lot of time. The place to look for the information you want is the Frontier Hotel. The same people that run the Frontier Hotel here control the Standish Hotel in Philadelphia. They are in on narcotics, and they are connected with Communism."

"Isn't it dangerous for you to talk this way? You don't know who I am. Suppose I was on the other side."

"I know who I'm talking to," he said. "If I didn't, I wouldn't be here. I'd be dead. Out of all the people in this bar I picked you, didn't I?"

"Yes, but why?"

"There is something that tells me what to do." He showed me a religious medal he wore around his neck. "If I didn't carry this I would have stopped a knife or a bullet long ago."

"Why are you concerned about narcotics?"

"Because I don't like what it does to people. I had a shipmate who used it."

"Tell me," I said, "exactly what is the tie-up between narcotics and Communism?"

"You know the answer to that one a lot better than I do. I see you are trying to find out how much I know. All right. The same people are in both narcotics and Communism. Right now they control most of America. I'm a seaman. I've been shipping out for twenty years. Who gets the jobs over there in the NMU Hall? American white men like you and me? No. Dagos and Spiks and Niggers. Why? Because the union controls shipping, and Communists control the union."

"I'll be around if you need me," he said when I got up to leave.

●

In the French Quarter there are several queer bars so full every night the fags spill out on to the sidewalk. A room full of fags gives me the horrors. They jerk around like puppets on invisible strings, galvanized into hideous activity that is the negation of everything living and spontaneous. The live human being has moved out of these bodies long ago. But something moved in when the original tenant moved out. Fags are ventriloquists' dummies who have moved in and taken over the ventriloquist. The dummy sits in a queer bar nursing his beer, and uncontrollably yapping out of a rigid doll face.

Occasionally, you find intact personalities in a queer bar, but fags set the tone of these joints, and it always brings me down to go into a queer bar. The bring-down piles up. After my first week in a new town I have had about all I can take of these joints, so my bar business goes somewhere else, generally to a bar in or near Skid Row.

But I backslide now and then. One night, I got lobotomized drunk in Frank's and went to a queer bar. I must have had more drinks in the queer joint, because there was a lapse of time. It was getting light outside when the bar hit one of those sudden pockets of quiet. Quiet is something that does not often happen in a queer joint. I guess most of the fags had left. I was leaning against the bar with a beer I didn't want in front of me. The noise cleared like smoke and I saw a red-haired kid was looking straight at me and standing about three feet away.

He didn't come on faggish, so I said, "How you making it?" or something like that.

He said: "Do you want to go to bed with me?"

I said, "O.K. Let's go."

As we walked out, he grabbed my bottle of beer off the bar and stuck it under his coat. Outside, it was daylight with the sun just coming up. We staggered through the French Quarter passing the beer bottle back and forth. He was leading the way in the direction of his hotel, so he said. I could feel my stomach knot up like I was about to take a shot after being off the junk a long time. I should have been more alert, of course, but I never could mix vigilance and sex. All this time he was talking on in a sexy Southern voice which was not a New Orleans voice, and in the daylight he still looked good.

We got to a hotel and he put down some routine why he should go in first alone. I pulled some bills out of my pocket. He looked at them and said, "Better give me the ten."

I gave it to him. He went in the hotel and came right out.

"No rooms there," he said. "We'll try the Savoy."

The Savoy was right across the street.

"Wait here," he said.

I waited about an hour and by then it occurred to me what was wrong with the first hotel. It'd had no back or side door he could walk out of. I went back to my apartment and got my gun. I waited around the Savoy and looked for the kid all through the French Quarter. About noon, I got hungry and ate a plate of oysters with a glass of beer, and suddenly felt so tired that when I walked out of the restaurant my legs were folding under me as if someone was clipping me behind the knees.

I took a cab home and fell across the bed without taking off my shoes. I woke up around six in the evening and went to Frank's. After three quick beers I felt better.

There was a man standing by the jukebox and I caught his eye several times. He looked at me with a special recognition, like one queer looks at another. He looked like one of those terra-cotta heads that you plant grass in. A peasant face, with peasant intuition, stupidity, shrewdness and malice. He couldn't have been anything but Irish.

The jukebox wasn't working. I walked over and asked him what was wrong with it. He said he didn't know. I asked him to have a

drink and he ordered Coke. He told me his name was Pat. I told
him I had come up recently from the Mexican border.

He said, "I'd like to get down that way, me. Bring some stuff
in from Mexico."

"The border is pretty hot," I said.

"I hope you won't take offense at what I say," he began, "but
you look like you use stuff yourself."

"Sure I use."

"Do you want to score?" he asked. "I'm due to score in a few
minutes. I've been trying to hustle the dough. If you buy me a cap,
I can score for you."

I said, "O.K."

We walked around the corner past the NMU hall.

"Wait here a minute," he said, disappearing into a bar. I half-
expected to get beat for my four dollars, but he was back in a few
minutes. "O.K.," he said, "I got it."

I asked him to come back to my apartment to take a shot. We
went back to my room, and I got out my outfit that hadn't been
used in five months.

"If you don't have a habit, you'd better go slow with this stuff,"
he cautioned me. "It's pretty strong."

I measured out about two-thirds of a cap.

"Half is plenty," he said. "I tell you it's strong."

"This will be all right," I said. But as soon as I took the needle
out of the vein, I knew it wasn't all right. I felt a soft blow in the
heart. Pat's face began to get black around the edges, the blackness
spreading to cover his face as though it were actually changing color.
I could feel my eyes roll back in their sockets.

I came to several hours later. Pat was gone. I was lying on the
bed with my collar loosened. I stood up and fell to my knees. I
was dizzy and my head ached. Ten dollars were missing from my
watch-pocket. I guess he figured I wasn't going to need it any more.

Several days later I met Pat in the same bar.

"Holy Jesus," he said, "I thought you was dying! I loosened your collar and rubbed ice on your neck. You turned all blue. So I says, 'Holy Jesus, this man is dying! I'm going to get out of here, me!'"

A week later, I was hooked. I asked Pat about the possibilities of pushing in New Orleans.

"The town is et up with pigeons," he said. "It's really tough."

So I drifted along, scoring through Pat. I stopped drinking, stopped going out at night, and fell into a routine schedule: a cap of junk three times per day, and the time in between to be filled somehow. Mostly, I spent my time painting and working around the house. Manual work makes the time pass fast. Of course, it often took me a long time to score.

When I first hit New Orleans, the main pusher—or "the Man," as they say there—was a character called Yellow. Yellow was so named because his complexion was yellow and liverish-looking. He was a thin little man with a dragging limp. He operated out of a bar near the NMU hall and occasionally choked down a beer to justify sitting in the bar several hours a day. He was out on bail at the time, and when his case came to trial he drew two years.

A period of confusion followed, during which it was difficult to find a score. Sometimes I spent six or eight hours riding around in the car with Pat, waiting and looking for different people who might be holding. Finally, Pat ran into a wholesale connection, a dollar-fifty per cap, no less than twenty. This connection was Bob Brandon, one of the few pushers I ever knew who didn't use the stuff himself.

Pat and I began pushing in a small way, just enough to keep up our habits. We only took care of people that Pat knew well and was sure of. Dupré was our best customer. He was a dealer in a gambling joint and always had money. But he was a hog for junk and so couldn't keep his hand out of the till. Eventually, he lost his job. Don, an old neighborhood friend of Pat's, had a city job. He inspected something, but was off half the time sick. He never had money for more than one cap, and most of the money he did have was given him by his sister. Pat told me Don had cancer.

"Well," I said, "I guess he'll die soon."

He did. He took to his bed, vomited for a week, and died.

"Seltzer Willy" owned a seltzer truck, and had a seltzer delivery route. This business brought him two caps a day, but he was not a very enterprising seltzer pusher. He was a thin, red-haired, mild-mannered man, the type described as harmless.

"He's timid," said Pat. "Timid and stupid."

There were a few others who dropped by for an occasional bang. One was called Whitey—I never found out why, because he was dark—a fattish, stupid man who worked as a waiter in one of the big hotels. He figured that if he paid for one cap he was entitled to the next cap on credit. Once, after Pat turned him down, he rushed to the door in a rage and held up a nickel. "See this nickel," he said. "You're going to be sorry you turned me down. I'm going to call 'the People' on you."

I told Pat we'd better stop serving Whitey.

"Yes," said Pat, "but he knows where I live. We ought to find another place."

Another occasional was Lonny the Pimp, who had grown up in his mother's whorehouse. Lonny tried to space his shots so he wouldn't get a habit. He was always beefing how he couldn't clear anything now, he had to put out so much for hotel rooms, and the law kept him on the move. "See what I mean?" he said. "There's no percentage."

Lonny was pure pimp. He was skinny and nervous. He couldn't sit still and he couldn't shut up. As he talked, he moved his thin hands which were covered on the backs with long, greasy, black hairs. You could tell by looking at him that he had a big penis. Pimps always do. Lonny was a sharp dresser and he drove a Buick convertible. But he wouldn't hesitate to hang us up for credit on a two-dollar cap.

After he took the shot he'd say, as he rolled down the sleeve of his striped silk shirt and fastened his cufflinks, "Look, boys, I'm a little short. You don't mind putting this one on the cuff, do you? You know I'm good for it."

Pat would look at him with his little bloodshot eyes. A surly peasant look. "For Chris' sake, Lonny, we have to put out for this stuff. How would you like it if people came in on you, laid your girls and then wanted to put it on the cuff?" Pat shook his head. "You're like all of them. Once they get it in the vein that's all they care. Here I have a cool place where they can come and shoot, and what consideration do I get? Once they get it in the vein that's all they care."

"Well, look, Pat, I don't want to hang you up. Now here's a dollar and I'll bring the rest this afternoon. O.K.?"

Pat took the dollar and put it in his pocket without saying anything. He pursed his lips in disapproval.

Seltzer Willy dropped by around ten o'clock on his route, took a cap and bought a cap for the night. Dupré came in around twelve when he got off work. He was on the night shift. The others came any time they had the inclination.

Bob Brandon, our connection, was out on bail. He was charged in State Court with possession of junk, a felony under Louisiana law. The case against him was based on traces—that is, he got rid of the junk before the cops shook his place down. But he did not wash out the jar in which the junk had been kept. The Federals will not take a "traces" case, so the State took it. This is regular procedure in Louisiana. Any case too shaky for the Federal Courts passes to the State Courts who will prosecute anything. Brandon expected to beat the case. He had good connections with the political machine and in any event the State had a weak case. But the D.A. dragged in Brandon's record, which included a murder conviction, and he drew two to five years.

Pat found another connection right away and we went on pushing. A peddler named Jonkers began selling on the corner of Exchange and Canal. Pat lost a few customers to Jonkers. Actually, Jonkers' stuff was better, and sometimes I scored from Jonkers, or Jonkers' partner, an old one-eyed character named Richter. Pat always found out somehow—he was intuitive as a possessive mother—and then he would sulk for two or three days.

Jonkers and Richter did not last long. Exchange and Canal is one of the hottest spots in New Orleans for junk. One day they were gone and Pat said, "Now you'll see some of those guys come back to me. I told Lonny, 'If you want to score off Jonkers, go ahead, but don't come back here and expect me to serve you.' You'll see what I tell him if he comes back here. Whitey, too. He's been scoring off Jonkers." Pat gave me a long sullen look.

One day the woman who managed Pat's hotel stopped me in the lobby. "I just want to tell you to be careful," she said. "The cops were here yesterday and made a thorough investigation of Pat's room. And they arrested the boy with the seltzer truck. He's in jail now."

I thanked her. A little later Pat came in. He told me the cops had grabbed Seltzer Willy as he left the hotel. They didn't find any junk on him so they took him to the Third Precinct and booked him to "hold for investigation." He was there seventy-two hours, which is the longest period they can hold anyone without placing charges.

The cops searched Pat's room, but he kept his junk stashed in the hall so they didn't find it. Pat said, "They told me, 'We have information you're running a regular shooting gallery up here. You'd better pack in, because next time we're going to come and take you, that's all.'"

"Well," I said, "better pack in except for Dupré. No harm to serve him."

"Dupré lost his job," Pat said. "He's already into me for twenty dollars."

We were back looking for a score every day. We found out that Lonny was "the Man." That is the way it went in New Orleans. You never knew who was going to be "the Man" next.

About this time an anti-narcotics drive hit the town. The chief of police said, "This drive is going to continue as long as there is a single violator left in this city." The State legislators drew up a law making it a crime to be a drug addict. They did not specify where or when or what they meant by drug addict.

The cops began stopping addicts on the street and examining their arms for needle marks. If they found marks, they pressured the addict to sign a statement admitting his condition so he could be charged under the "drug addicts law." The addicts were promised a suspended sentence if they would plead guilty and get the new law started. Addicts ransacked their persons looking for veins to shoot in outside the arm area. If the law could find no marks on a man they usually let him go. If they found marks they would hold him for seventy-two hours and try to make him sign a statement.

Lonny's wholesale connection gave out and a character called Old Sam was "the Man." Old Sam was after doing twelve years in Angola. He operated in the territory directly above Lee Circle, which is another hot spot in New Orleans for junk or anything.

●

One day I was broke and I wrapped up a pistol to take it in town and pawn it. When I got to Pat's room there were two people there. One was Red McKinney, a shriveled-up, crippled junkie; the other was a young merchant seaman named Cole. Cole did not have a habit at this time and he wanted to connect for some weed. He was a real tea head. He told me he could not enjoy himself without weed. I have seen people like that. For them, tea occupies the place usually filled by liquor. They don't have to have it in any physical sense, but they cannot have a really good time without it.

As it happened I had several ounces of weed in my house. Cole agreed to buy four caps in exchange for two ounces of weed. We went out to my place, Cole tried the weed and said it was good. So we started out to score.

Red said he knew a connection on Julia Street. "We should be able to find him there now."

Pat was sitting at the wheel of my car on the nod. We were on the ferry, crossing from Algiers, where I lived, to New Orleans. Suddenly Pat looked up and opened his bloodshot eyes.

"That neighborhood is too hot," he said loudly.

"Where else can we score?" said McKinney. "Old Sam is up that way, too."

"I tell you that neighborhood is too hot," Pat repeated. He looked around resentfully, as though what he saw was unfamiliar and distasteful.

There was, in fact, no place else to score. Without a word, Pat started driving in the direction of Lee Circle. When we came to Julia Street, McKinney said to Cole, "Give me the money because we are subject to see him at any time. He walks around this block. A walking connection."

Cole gave McKinney fifteen dollars. We circled the block three times slowly, but McKinney did not see "the Man."

"Well, I guess we'll have to try Old Sam," McKinney said.

We began looking for Old Sam above Lee Circle. Sam was not in the old frame rooming house where he lived. We drove around slowly. Every now and then Pat would see someone he knew and stop the car. No one had seen Old Sam. Some of the characters Pat called to just shrugged in a disagreeable way and kept walking.

"Those guys wouldn't tell you nothing," Pat said. "It hurts 'em to do anybody a favor."

We parked the car near Sam's rooming house, and McKinney walked down to the corner to buy a package of cigarettes. He came back limping fast and got in the car.

"The law," he said. "Let's get out of here."

We started away from the curb and a prowl car passed us. I saw the cop at the wheel turn around and do a double-take when he saw Pat.

"They've made us, Pat," I said. "Get going!"

Pat didn't need to be told. He gunned the car and turned a corner heading for Corondolet. I turned to Cole, who was in the back seat. "Throw out that weed," I ordered.

"Wait a minute," Cole replied. "We may lose them."

"Are you crazy?" I said. Pat, McKinney and I yelled in chorus "Throw it out!"

We were on Corondolet headed downtown. Cole threw the weed out and it skidded under a parked car. Pat took the first right turn into a one-way street. The prowl car was coming down the same street from the other end, going the wrong way. An old cop trick. We were boxed in. I heard Cole yell, "Oh, Lord, I've got another stick on me!"

The cops jumped out with their hands on their guns, but they did not draw them. They ran up to my car. One of them, the driver who had spotted Pat, had a big smile on his face. "Where did you get the car, Pat?" he asked.

The other cop opened the back door. "Everybody out," he said.

McKinney and Cole were in the back seat. They got out and the cops went through them. Right away the cop who spotted Pat found the stick of weed in Cole's shirt pocket.

"I've got enough here to hold the whole bunch of them," he said. This cop had a smooth red face and he kept smiling all the time. He found my gun in the glove compartment. "This is a foreign gun," he said. "Have you got it registered with the Internal Revenue Department?"

"I thought that only applied to full automatic weapons," I said, "that fire more than one shot with one pull of the trigger."

"No," said the cop smiling, "it applies to all foreign automatics." I knew he was wrong, but there was no percentage in telling him so. He looked at my arms. "You've been hooking that spot so much it's about to get infected," he said, pointing to a needle welt.

The wagon arrived and we all got in. We were taken to the Second Precinct. The cops looked at my car papers. They couldn't believe that the car was mine. I was searched at least six times by different people. Eventually, we were all locked in a cell about six by eight feet. Pat smiled and rubbed his hands together.

"There's going to be some sick fucking dope fiends in here," he said.

A little later the turnkey came and called my name. I was taken to a small room that opened off the reception room of the precinct. In the room were two detectives sitting at a table. One was tall and fat with a deep South frog face. The other was a middle-aged stocky Irish cop. He was missing some front teeth, which gave his face a suggestion of harelip. This type cop could just as well be an oldtime rod-riding thug. There was nothing of the bureaucrat about him.

The frog-faced cop was obviously in charge of the interrogation. He told me to sit down and I sat down at the table opposite him. He pushed a package of cigarettes and a box of matches across the table. "Have a cigarette," he said. The Irish cop was sitting at the end of the table to my left. He was close enough to reach me without getting up. The cop in charge was studying the papers of my car. Everything they had taken out of my pockets was spread on the table in front of him, a glasses case, identification papers, wallet, keys, a letter from a friend in New York, everything but my pocketknife, which the smooth-faced cop from the patrol car had put in his pocket.

Suddenly I remembered about that letter. The friend in New York who'd written it was a tea head and he pushed weed from time to time. He'd written to me asking the price of good weed in New Orleans. I asked Pat, who quoted me a tentative price of forty dollars per pound. In the letter on the table my friend made reference to the forty-dollar per pound price and said he wanted some at that figure.

At first I thought they might pass over the letter. They were Stolen Car Squad and they wanted a stolen car. They kept looking at the papers and asking questions. When I couldn't remember exact dates on the car, that was the clincher. They seemed on the point of getting tough.

Finally, I said, "Well, it's just a question of checking. When you check, you'll find out that I'm telling the truth and the car is mine. But there is no way I can convince you by talking. Of course, if you want me to say I stole the car, I will. But when you check, you will find out that the car is mine."

"We'll check, all right."

The frog-faced cop folded the car papers carefully and put them aside. He picked up the envelope and looked at the address and the postmark. Then he took the letter out. He read the letter to himself. Then he read aloud, skipping where there was no reference to weed. He put the letter down and looked at me.

"Not only do you use weed," he said, "you peddle it, too, and you've got a batch of this weed stashed somewhere." He looked at the letter. "About forty pounds." He looked at me. "You'd better straighten yourself out."

I didn't say anything.

The old Irish cop said, "He's like all these guys. He ain't talking. Till they get their fucking ribs kicked in. Then they'll talk, and be glad to talk."

"We're going out and search your house," the frog-faced cop said. "If we find anything, your wife will be put in jail, too. I don't know what will happen to your children. They'll have to go to some home."

"Why don't you make the man a proposition?" the old Irish cop said.

I knew that if they searched the house they would find the stuff. "Call in the Federals and I'll show you where the stuff is," I said. "But I want your word that the case will be tried in Federal, and that my wife will not be molested."

The frog-faced cop nodded. "All right," he said. "I accept your proposition." He turned to his partner. "Go call Rogers," he said.

A few minutes later the old cop was back. "Rogers is out of town and won't be back until morning, and Williams is sick."

"Well, call Hauser."

We went out and got in the car. The old cop was driving, and the captain was sitting in back with me.

"This is it here," said the captain.

The old cop stopped the car and honked. A man with a pipe came out of a house and got in the back seat. He looked at me and then looked away, puffing on his pipe. The man looked young in the dark, but when we passed under a street light I saw that his face was wrinkled, and he had black circles under the eyes. It was a clean-cut, American Boy face, a face that had aged but could not mature. I assumed that he was a Federal agent.

After smoking in silence for several blocks, the agent turned to me and took out his pipe. "Who are you scoring off now?" he asked.

"It's hard to find a score now," I said. "Most of them have gone away."

He began asking me who I knew, and I mentioned a number of people who had already gone away. He seemed pleased with this worthless information. If you dummy up on cops they will slap you around. They want you to give them something, even if what you give has no conceivable use.

He asked what record I had, and I told him about the script case in New York.

"How much time did you do on that?" he asked.

"None. It's a misdemeanor in New York. Public Health law. Health Law Number 334, as I remember."

"He's pretty well versed," said the old cop.

The captain was explaining to the agent that I seemed to have a particular fear of the State Courts, and that he had made a deal with me to turn the case over to the Federals.

"Well," said the agent, "that's the way the captain is. He'll treat you right if you treat him right." He smoked for a while. We were on the ferry to Algiers. "There's an easy way and a hard way of doing things," he said finally.

When we got to the house the captain grabbed me by the back of the belt. "Who's in there besides your wife?"

I said, "Nobody."

We came to the door, and the guy with the pipe showed my wife his hunk of tin and opened the door. I showed them the weed I had in the house which was not more than a pound, and a few caps of junk. This didn't satisfy the captain. He wanted forty pounds of weed.

"You're not coming up with all of it, Bill," he kept saying. "Come on, now. We've shown you every courtesy."

I told them there wasn't any more.

The man with the pipe looked at me. "We want it all," he said. His eyes did not want anything very much. He was standing under the light. His face had not only aged, it had decayed. He had the look of a man suffering from a fatal illness.

I said, "You've got it all."

He looked vaguely away and began poking about in drawers and closets. He found some old letters which he read sitting on his heels on the floor. I wondered why he didn't sit in a chair. Evidently, he did not want to be comfortable while reading someone else's mail. The two cops from Stolen Cars were getting bored. Finally, they collected the weed, the caps, and a .38 revolver I kept in the house, and got ready to leave.

"He belongs to Uncle, now," said the captain to my wife as they left the house.

They drove back to the Second Precinct and I was locked in. This time I was locked in a different cell. Pat and McKinney were in the next cell over. Pat called to me and asked what happened.

"That's tough," he said when I told him.

Pat had given a wagon-chasing lawyer ten dollars to get him out in the morning.

●

I was in a cell with four strangers, three of them addicts. There was only one bench and that was occupied, so the rest of us stood up or lay down on the floor. I lay down on the floor beside a man named McCarthy. I had seen him around town. He had been in for almost seventy-two hours. Every now and then he would groan slightly. Once he said, "Isn't this hell?"

A junkie runs on junk time. When his junk is cut off, the clock runs down and stops. All he can do is hang on and wait for nonjunk time to start. A sick junkie has no escape from external time, no place to go. He can only wait.

Cole was talking about Yokohama. "All that good Henry and Charly. When you shoot Henry and Charly, you can smell it going in."

McCarthy groaned hollowly from the floor. "Man," he said, "don't talk about that stuff."

Next morning, we were taken to line-up. A kid with epilepsy was ahead of us on the stage. The cops took a long time wisecracking with this subnormal character.

"How long you been in New Orleans?"

"Thirty-five days."

"What have you been doing all that time?"

"I've been in jail thirty-three days."

They thought that was funny and batted it around for another five minutes or so.

When our turn came, the cop who ran the line-up read off the circumstances of the case.

"How many times you been here?" they asked Pat.

Some cop laughed and said, "About forty times."

They asked each of us how many times arrested and how much time done. When they came to me, they asked how much time I did on the New York script charge. I said, "None. I got a suspended sentence."

"Well," said the cop in charge of the line-up. "You'll get one here, too."

All of a sudden there was a tremendous slobbering and screaming off stage, and I thought for a minute the cops were working over the epileptic. But when I walked off the stage, I saw that he was flopping around on the floor in a fit while two detectives were hovering around trying to talk to him. Someone went for a doctor.

We were locked in a cell. A fat dick who seemed to know Pat came and stood at the door. "The guy's a psycho," he said. "He's saying now, 'Take me to my captain.' A psycho. I sent for the doctor."

After two hours or so, they took us back to the precinct where we waited some more hours. About noon, the guy with the pipe and another man came to the precinct and drove a bunch of us over to the Federal Building. The new man was young and fattish. He was chewing on a cigar. Cole, McCarthy, I and two Negroes piled into the back seat. The guy with the cigar was driving. He took his cigar out and turned to me.

"What is it you do, Mr. Lee?" he asked politely, in the accents of an educated man.

"Farm," I answered.

The man with the pipe laughed.

"Corn with weed between the rows, eh?" he said.

The man with the cigar shook his head. "No," he said. "It won't grow well in corn. It has to grow by itself." He turned to McCarthy, speaking over his shoulder. "I'm going to send you up to the penitentiary at Angola," he said.

"Why, Mr. Morton?" asked McCarthy.

"Because you're a goddamned drug addict."

"Not me, Mr. Morton."

"What about those needle marks?"

"I have syphilis, Mr. Morton."

"All junkies have syphilis," said Morton. His voice was cool, condescending, amused.

The guy with the pipe was making an unsuccessful attempt to kid one of the Negroes. The Negro was called Clutch because of a deformed hand.

"Old monkey climbing up on your back?" asked the man with the pipe.

"I don't know what you're talking about now," said Clutch. It was just a flat statement. There was no insolence. Clutch did not have a junk habit and he was saying so.

They parked in front of the Federal Building and took us up to the fourth floor. Here we waited around in an outer office and were summoned to the inner office one at a time for questioning. When my turn came I walked in and the man with the cigar was sitting at a table. He motioned me to a chair.

"I'm Mr. Morton," he said. "A Federal narcotics agent. Do you want to make a statement? As you know, you have a Constitutional right to refuse. Of course, it takes more time for you to be charged in the event you do not make a statement."

I said I would make a statement.

The man with the pipe was there.

"Bill isn't feeling very well today," he said. "Maybe a little shot of heroin would help."

"Maybe," I said. He began asking me questions, some of them so pointless that I could hardly believe what I heard. Clearly, he had no cop intuition. No way of knowing what was important and what was not.

"Who are your connections in Texas?"

"I don't have any." This was true.

"Do you want to see your wife in jail?"

I wiped the sweat off my face with a handkerchief. "No," I said.

"Well, she's going to be in jail. She uses this benzedrine. That's worse than junk. Are you and your wife legally married?"

"Common law."

"I asked are you and your wife legally married?"

"No."

"Have you studied psychiatry?"

"What?"

"I asked, have you studied psychiatry?"

He had read a letter from a friend of mine who is a psychiatrist. In fact, he had taken all my old letters away with him after he searched the house.

"No, I have not studied psychiatry. Just a hobby, you might say."

"You have some peculiar hobbies."

Morton leaned back in his chair and yawned.

The man with the pipe suddenly doubled his fist and hit himself in the chest. "I'm a cop, see?" he said. "Wherever I go I associate with cops. Your business is narcotics. It stands to reason you know the other people in your line of business. We don't deal with people like you once a month. We deal with them every day. You weren't alone in this. You have connections in New York, Texas, and here in New Orleans. Now, you had some deal lined up, something was about to materialize."

"I think we'll let this farmer do his farming up at Angola if he can't give us any information," said Morton.

"What about this hot-car ring?" said the man with the pipe, turning his back to me and walking across the room.

"What hot-car ring?" I asked, really surprised. It was sometime later I remembered a letter five years old that contained a reference to stolen cars. He went on and on. He mopped his brow and stalked around the room. Finally, Morton cut him short.

"As I see it, Mr. Lee," he said, "you are prepared to admit your own guilt, but not to involve anybody else, is that correct?"

"That's correct," I said.

He shifted his cigar. "Well," he said, "that's all for the present. How many more out there?" he called.

A cop stuck his head in. "About five."

Morton made a movement of exasperation. "There's no time. I have to be in court at one o'clock. Bring them all in."

All the others came in and stood around in front of the table. Morton leafed through a stack of papers. He looked at McCarthy and turned to a young agent with a crewcut.

"Have you got anything on him?" he asked.

The agent shook his head and smiled. He raised one foot. "See this foot?" he said to McCarthy. "I'm going to put it right down your throat."

"I'm not fooling with stuff, Mr. Morton," said McCarthy, "because I don't want to go to the penitentiary."

"What were you doing standing on the corner with those other junkies?"

"I just walked by. I was Regaling up, Mr. Morton." (The reference is to Regal Beer, a New Orleans product.) "I Regal up every chance I get. Look here." He took some cards out of his wallet and showed them around like a magician about to do a card trick. Nobody looked at the cards. "I work as a waiter, and here's my union card. I can get on at the Roosevelt over the weekend. There's a convention stopping there. It's a good deal if you guys will let me go."

He walked over to Morton and held out his hand. "Give me a dime, Mr. Morton, for carfare."

Morton slapped a coin into his hand.

"Get your cotton-picking ass out of here," he said.

"We'll get you next time," the agents shouted in chorus, but McCarthy was out the door.

The young agent with the crewcut laughed. "I'll bet he took the stairs."

Morton was gathering up his papers and shoving them into a briefcase. "I'm sorry," he said, "but I can't take any more statements now. I have to go to court. If I possibly can, I'll take statements from the rest of you this afternoon."

"I sent for the wagon," said the guy with the pipe. "We'll take them over to the Third Precinct and put them on ice."

At the Third Precinct, Cole and I had a cell to ourselves. I lay down on the bench. There was a raw ache through my lungs. People vary in the way junk sickness affects them. Some suffer mostly from vomiting and diarrhea. The asthmatic type, with narrow and deep chest, is liable to violent fits of sneezing, watering at eyes and nose, in some cases spasms of the bronchial tubes that shut off the breathing. In my case, the worst thing is lowering of blood pressure with consequent loss of body liquid, and extreme weakness, as in shock. It is a feeling as if the life energy has been shut off so that all the cells in the body are suffocating. As I lay there on the bench, I felt like I was subsiding into a pile of bones.

We were in the Third Precinct about three hours and then the laws put us in the wagon and took us to Parish Prison, for no reason that I could see. The man with the pipe met us at Parish and took us to the Federal Building.

A middle-aged, faceless bureaucrat told me he was head of the New Orleans office. Did I want to make a statement?

"Yes," I said. "You write it and I'll sign it."

His face wasn't blank or expressionless. It simply wasn't there. The only thing I remember about his face is that he wore glasses. He called in a stenographer and got ready to dictate a statement. He turned to the man with the pipe who was sitting there on a desk, and asked if there was anything special he wanted to put in the statement.

The man with the pipe said, "Well, no, that's the whole story."

The head bureaucrat seemed to think of something. "Wait a minute," he said. He led the man with the pipe into another office. They came back after a few minutes and the bureaucrat went on with his statement. The statement admitted possession of the weed and heroin found in my house.

He asked how I acquired the heroin.

I said I went to Exchange and Canal and contacted a street peddler.

"What did you do then?" he asked.

"I drove home."

"In your own car?"

I saw what he was getting at, but did not have the energy to say, "I changed my mind. I don't want to make any statement." Besides, I was afraid of spending another day sick in the precinct. So I said, "Yes."

Finally, I signed a separate statement to the effect that it was my intention to plead guilty to these charges in Federal Court. I was taken back to the Second Precinct. The agents assured me I would be charged first thing the next morning.

Cole said, "You'll feel better in five days. Only time, or a shot, will take away the bad feeling."

I knew this, of course. No one will stand still for junk sickness unless he is in jail or otherwise cut off from junk. The reason it is practically impossible to stop using and cure yourself is that the sickness lasts five to eight days. Twelve hours of it would be easy, twenty-four possible, but five to eight days is too long.

I lay on the narrow wood bench, twisting from one side to the other. My body was raw, twitching, tumescent, the junk-frozen flesh in agonizing thaw. I turned over on my stomach and one leg slipped off the bench. I pitched forward and the rounded edge of the bench, polished smooth by the friction of cloth, slid along my crotch. There was a sudden rush of blood to the genitals at the slippery contact. Sparks exploded behind my eyes; my legs twitched—the orgasm of a hanged man when the neck snaps.

The turnkey opened the door of my cell. "Your lawyer is here to see you, Lee," he said.

The lawyer looked at me quite a while before he introduced himself. He had been recommended to my wife, and I had not seen him before. The turnkey led the way to a large room above the cell block where there were benches.

"I can see you don't feel much like talking now," the lawyer began. "We'll go into the details later on. Did you sign anything?"

I told him about the statement.

"That was to get your car," he said. "You're charged in State. I talked to the Federal D.A. an hour ago on the phone and asked if he was going to take the case. He said, 'Absolutely no. There's an illegal seizure involved, and under no circumstances will this office prosecute the case.' I think I can get you over to the hospital for a shot," he said, after a pause. "The man at the desk now is a good friend of mine. I'll go down and talk to him."

The turnkey took me back to my cell. A few minutes later he opened the door again and said, "Lee, do you want to go to the hospital?"

Two cops took me over to Charity Hospital in the wagon. The nurse at the receiving desk wanted to know what was wrong with me.

"Emergency case," said one of the cops. "He fell off a building."

The cop walked away and came back with a heavy-set young doctor with reddish hair and gold-rimmed glasses. The doctor asked a few questions and looked at my arms. Another doctor with a long nose and hairy arms walked up to put in his two cents.

"After all, doctor," he said to his colleague, "there is the moral question. This man should have thought of all this before he started using narcotics."

"Yes, there is the moral question, but there is also a physical question. This man is sick." He turned to a nurse and ordered half a grain of morphine.

As the wagon jolted along on the way back to the precinct, I felt the morphine spread through all my cells. My stomach moved and rumbled. A shot when you are very sick always starts the stomach moving. Normal strength came back to all my muscles. I was hungry and sleepy.

●

About eleven the next morning, a bondsman came around so I could sign the bond. He had the embalmed look of all bondsmen; as though paraffin had been injected under the skin. My lawyer, Tige, showed up around twelve to check me out. He had made arrangements for me to go directly to a sanitarium to take a cure. He told me the cure was necessary from a legal point of view. We drove to a sanitarium in a police car with two detectives. This was part of the lawyer's plan, and the detectives fitted in as possible witnesses.

When we stopped in front of the sanitarium, the lawyer pulled some bills out of his pocket and turned to one of the cops. "Put this on that horse for me, will you?" he said.

The dick's frog-eyes bugged out with indignation. He made no move to take the money. "I'm not going to put any money on a horse," he said.

The lawyer laughed and tossed the money onto the seat of the car. "Mack will," he said.

This apparent tactlessness in paying off the cops in front of me was deliberate. When they asked him later what was the idea, he said, "Why, that boy was too sick to notice anything." So if these two cops were called as witnesses they would say I seemed in very bad shape. The point was, the lawyer wanted witnesses who would testify I was in bad shape at the time I signed the statement.

An attendant took my clothes and I lay down on the bed waiting for a shot. My wife came to see me and reported that the management did not know anything about junk or junkies.

"When I told them you were sick, they said, 'What's the matter with him?' I told them you were sick and that you needed a shot of morphine, and they said, 'Oh, we thought it was just a question of a marijuana habit.'"

"A marijuana habit!" I said. "What in hell is that? Find out what they plan to give me," I told her. "I need a reduction cure. If they aren't going to give me one, check me out of here right now."

She came back shortly and told me she finally got a doctor on the phone who seemed to know what the score was. This was the lawyer's doctor who was not connected with the sanitarium.

"He seemed surprised when I told him you hadn't had anything. He said he would call the hospital right away and see that you were taken care of."

A few minutes later a nurse came in with a hypo. It was demerol. Demerol helps some, but it is not nearly as effective as codeine in relieving junk sickness. A doctor came that evening to give me a physical examination. My blood was thick and concentrated by loss of body fluid. During the forty-eight hours I had been without junk, I lost ten pounds. It took the doctor twenty minutes to draw a tube of blood for a blood test because the thick blood kept clotting in the needle.

At nine p.m., I got another shot of demerol. This shot had no effect. The third day and night of junk sickness are generally the worst. After the third day, the sickness begins to recede. I felt a cold burn over the whole surface of my body as though the skin was one solid hive. It seemed like ants were crawling around under the skin.

It is possible to detach yourself from most pain—injury to teeth, eyes, and genitals present special difficulties—so that the pain is experienced as neutral excitation. From junk sickness there seems to be no escape. Junk sickness is the reverse side of junk kick. The kick of junk *is* that you have to have it. Junkies run on junk time and junk metabolism. They are subject to junk climate. They are warmed and chilled by junk. The kick of junk is living under junk conditions. You cannot escape from junk sickness any more than you can escape from junk kick after a shot.

I was too weak to get out of bed. I could not lie still. In junk sickness, any conceivable line of action or inaction seems intolerable. A man might die simply because he could not stand to stay in his body.

At six o'clock in the morning I got another shot, which seemed to have some effect. As I learned later, this shot was not demerol. I was even able to eat a little toast and drink some coffee.

When my wife came to see me later in the day, she told me that they were using a new treatment in my case. The treatment had started with my morning shot.

"I noticed a difference. I thought the morning shot was M."

"I talked to Dr. Moore on the phone. He told me this is the wonder drug they have been looking for to treat drug addiction. It relieves withdrawal symptoms without forming a new habit. It isn't a narcotic at all. It is one of the antihistamines. Thephorin, I believe he said."

"Then it would seem withdrawal symptoms are an allergic reaction."

"That's what Dr. Moore says."

The doctor who recommended this treatment was my lawyer's doctor. He was not connected with the sanitarium and he was not a psychiatrist. In two days I could eat a full meal. The antihistamine shots lasted three to five hours and then the sickness came back. The shots felt like junk.

When I was up and walking around, a psychiatrist came to interview me. He was very tall. He had long legs and a heavy body shaped like a pear with the narrow end up. He smiled when he talked and his voice was whiny. He was not effeminate. He simply had none of whatever it is that makes a man a man. This was Dr. Fredericks, head psychiatrist of the hospital.

He asked the question they all ask. "Why do you feel that you need narcotics, Mr. Lee?"

When you hear this question you can be sure that the man who asks it knows nothing about junk.

"I need it to get out of bed in the morning, to shave and eat breakfast."

"I mean psychically."

I shrugged. Might as well give him his diagnosis so he will go. "It's a good kick."

Junk is not a "good kick." The point of junk to a user is that it forms the habit. No one knows what junk is until he is junk sick.

The doctor nodded. *Psychopathic personality.* He stood up. Suddenly he moved his face into a smile that was obviously intended to be understanding and to dissolve my reticence. The smile took over and ended up an insane leer. He leaned forward and brought his smile close to my face.

"Is your sex life satisfactory?" he asked. "Do you and your wife have satisfactory relations?"

"Oh yes," I said, "when I'm not on the junk."

He straightened up. He didn't like my answer at all.

"Well, I'll see you again." He blushed and lunged awkwardly for the door. I had made him for a faker when he walked in the room—obviously he was putting down a self-assured routine for himself and the others—but I had expected a deeper and tougher front.

The doctor told my wife I had a very bad prognosis. My attitude towards junk was "so what?" A relapse was to be expected because the psychic determinants of my condition remained in operation. He could not help me unless I agreed to cooperate. Given cooperation, he apparently was ready to take down my psyche and reassemble it in eight days.

●

The other patients were a pretty square and sorry lot. Not another junkie in the place. The only patient in my ward who knew the score was a drunk who came in with a broken jaw and other injuries of the face. He told me all the public hospitals turned him away. At Charity they told him: "Get out of here. You're dripping blood all over the floor." So he came to this sanitarium where he had been before and they knew he was good for the bill.

The others were a beat, nowhere bunch of people. The type psychiatrists like. The type Dr. Fredericks could impress. There was a thin, pale, little man with bloodless, almost transparent, flesh. He looked like a cold and enfeebled lizard. This character complained of nerves and spent most of the day wandering up and down the halls, saying, "Lord, Lord, I don't even feel like a human." He did not have the concentration of energy necessary to hold himself together and his organism was always on the point of disintegrating into its component parts.

Most of the patients were old. They looked at you with the puzzled, resentful, stupid look of a moribund cow. A few never left their rooms. One young schizophrenic had both hands fastened in front with a bandage so he could not bother the other patients. A depressing place and depressing people.

I was feeling the shots less all the time and after eight days I began to pass them up. When I had passed the shots for twenty-four hours, I decided it was time to leave.

My wife went to see Dr. Fredericks and caught him in the hall outside his office. He said I should stay four or five days longer. "He doesn't know it yet," the doctor said, "but his shots are stopped from now on."

"He's already passed up the shots for twenty-four hours," my wife told him.

The doctor got very red in the face. When he could talk, he said, "Anyway, he might develop withdrawal symptoms."

"It isn't likely after ten days, is it?"

"He might," said the doctor, and walked away before she could say anything else.

"To hell with him," I told her. "We don't need his testimony. Tige wants to use his own doctor as a witness to my condition. No telling what this jerk might say on the stand."

Dr. Fredericks had to sign my discharge from the hospital. He stayed in his office and a nurse took the paper in so he could sign it. Of course, he wrote "against medical advice" on the discharge.

●

It was five in the afternoon when we left the hospital and took a cab to Canal Street. I went into a bar and drank four whisky sodas and got a good lush kick. I was cured.

As I walked across the porch of my house and opened the door, I had the feel of returning after a long absence. I was coming back to the point in time I left a year ago when I took that first "joy bang" with Pat.

After a junk cure is complete, you generally feel fine for a few days. You can drink, you can feel real hunger and pleasure in food, and your sex desire comes back on you. Everything looks different, sharper. Then you hit a snag. It is an effort to dress, get out of a chair, pick up a fork. You don't want to do anything or go anywhere. You don't even want junk. The junk craving is gone, but there isn't anything else. You have to sit this period out. Or work it out. Farm work is the best cure.

Pat came around as soon as he heard I was out. Did I want to "pick up"? Just one wouldn't hurt any. He could get a good price on ten or more. I said no. You don't need will power to say no to junk when you are off. You don't want it.

Besides, I was charged in State, and State junk raps pile up like any other felony. Two junk raps can draw you seven years, or you can be charged in State on one and Federal on the other so that when you walk out of the State joint the Federals meet you at the door. If you do your Federal time first, then the State is waiting for you at the door of the Federal joint.

I knew the law was out to hang another on me because they had messed up the deal by coming on like Federals and by searching the house without a warrant. I had a free hand to arrange my account of what happened since there was no statement with my signature on it to tie me down. The State could not introduce the statement I had signed for the Federals without bringing up the deal I had made with that fair-play artist, the fat captain. But if they could hang another charge on me, they would have a sure thing.

Usually, a junkie makes straight for a connection as soon as he leaves any place of confinement. The law would expect me to do this and they would be watching Pat. So I told Pat I was staying off until the case was settled. He borrowed two dollars and went away.

A few days later I was drinking in the bars around Canal Street. When a junkie off junk gets drunk to a certain point, his thoughts turn to junk. I went into the toilet in one bar, and there was a wallet on the toilet-paper box. There is a dream feeling when you find money. I opened the wallet and took out a twenty, a ten and a five.

I decided to use some other toilet in some other bar and walked out leaving a full martini.

I went up to Pat's room.

Pat opened the door and said, "Hello, old buddy, I'm glad to see you."

There was another man sitting on the bed who turned his face to the door as I came in. "Hello, Bill," he said.

I looked at him a long three seconds before I recognized Dupré. He looked older and younger. The deadness had gone from his eyes and he was twenty pounds thinner. His face twitched at intervals like dead matter coming alive, still jerky and mechanical. When he was getting plenty of junk, Dupré looked anonymous and dead, so you could not pick him out of a crowd or recognize him at a distance. Now, his image was clear and sharp. If you walked fast down a crowded street and passed Dupré, his face would be forced on your memory—like in the card trick where the operator fans the cards rapidly, saying, "Take a card, any card," as he forces a certain card into your hand.

When he was getting plenty of junk, Dupré was silent. Now he was garrulous. He told me how he finally got so deep in the till, he lost his job. Now he had no money for junk. He couldn't even raise the price of P.G. and goof balls to taper off. He talked on and on.

"It used to be, all the cops knew me before the War. Many's the seventy-two hours I put in right over in the Third Precinct. It was the First Precinct then. You know how it is when you start to come off the stuff." He indicated his genitals, pointing with all his fingers, then turning the hand palm up. A concrete gesture as though he had picked up what he wanted to talk about and was holding it in his palm to show you. "You get a hard-on and shoot off right in your pants. It doesn't even have to get hard. I remember one time I was in with Larry. You know that kid Larry. He was pushing a while back. I said, 'Larry, you got to do it for me.' So he took down his pants. You know he had to do that for me."

Pat was looking for a vein. He pursed his lips in disapproval. "You guys talk like degenerates."

"What the matter, Pat?" I said. "Can't you hit it?"

"No," he said. He moved the tie-up down to his wrist to hit a vein in his hand.

Later, I stopped by my lawyer's office to talk about the case and to ask whether I could leave the State and go to the Rio Grande Valley in Texas, where I owned farm property.

"You're hot as a firecracker in this town," Tige told me. "I have permission from the judge for you to leave the State. So you can go on to Texas any time you like."

"I might want to take a trip to Mexico," I said. "Would that be okay?"

"So long as you are back here when your case comes up. There are no restrictions on you. One client of mine went to Venezuela. So far as I know, he's still there. He didn't come back."

Tige was a hard man to figure. Was he telling me not to come back? When he seemed to come on clumsy or irrelevant, he was often following a plan. Some of his plans extended far into the future. Often he would take up a plan, see that it was nowhere, and drop it. For an intelligent man, he could get some amazingly silly ideas. For example, when I told him I had studied medicine in Vienna (six months), he said:

"That's fine. Now suppose we say this. That you, having studied medicine yourself, had confidence that with your medical knowledge you could administer a cure to yourself, and that it was for this purpose of giving yourself a cure that you acquired the drugs that were found in your possession."

I thought this was too thick for anyone to swallow. "Not a good idea to come on too educated. Juries don't like people who study in Europe."

"Well, you could easily loosen your tie and lapse into a broad Southern accent."

I could see myself coming on like plain folks in a phony Southern accent. I gave up trying to be one of the boys twenty years ago. I told him this sort of act wasn't in my line at all, and he never mentioned the idea again.

Criminal law is one of the few professions where the client buys someone else's luck. The luck of most people is strictly nontransferable. But a good criminal lawyer can sell all his luck to a client, and the more luck he sells the more he has to sell.

●

I left New Orleans several days later and went to the Rio Grande Valley. The Rio Grande River runs into the Gulf of Mexico at Brownsville. Sixty miles up river from Brownsville is the town of Mission. The Valley runs from Brownsville to Mission, a strip of ground sixty miles long and twenty miles wide. The area is irrigated from the Rio Grande River. Before irrigation, nothing grew here but mesquite and cactus. Now it is one of the richest farm areas in the U.S.

A three-lane highway runs from Brownsville to Mission, and the towns of the Valley string out along this highway. There are no cities in the Valley, and no country. The area is a vast suburb of flimsy houses. The Valley is flat as a table. Nothing grows there but crops, citrus and palms brought from California. A hot dry wind starts every afternoon and blows until sundown. The Valley is citrus country. Pink and red grapefruit grow there that will not grow anywhere else. Citrus country is real-estate-promoted country, country of flimsy houses, "Bide-A-Wee" tourist courts and old people waiting around to die. The whole Valley has the impermanent look of a camp, or carnival. Soon the suckers will all be dead and the pitchmen will go somewhere else.

During the Twenties, real estate operators brought trainloads of prospects down to the Valley and let them pick grapefruit right off the trees and eat it. One of these pioneer promoters is said to have constructed a large artificial lake and sold plots all around it. "The lake will sub-irrigate your groves." As soon as the last sale closed, he turned off the water and disappeared with his lake, leaving the prospects sitting there in a desert.

As put down by the realtor, citrus is a flawless set-up for old people who want to retire and take life easy. The grove owner does nothing. A citrus association cares for the grove and markets the fruit, and hands the owner a check. Actually, citrus is a risky deal for the small investor. Over a period of time the average return is high, especially on the pink and ruby red fruit. But a small operator cannot ride out the years when the prices are low, or the yield of fruit small.

A premonition of doom hangs over the Valley. You have to make it now before something happens, before the black fly ruins the citrus, before support prices are taken off the cotton, before the flood, the hurricane, the freeze, the long dry spell when there is no water to irrigate, before the Border Patrol shuts off your wetbacks. The threat of disaster is always there, persistent and disquieting as the afternoon wind. The Valley was desert, and it will be desert again. Meanwhile you try to make yours while there is still time.

Old men sitting in real estate offices say, "Well, this is nothing new. I've seen all this before. I remember back in '28 . . ."

But a new factor, something that nobody has seen before, is changing the familiar aspect of disaster like the slow beginnings of a disease, so that no one can say just when it began.

Death is absence of life. Wherever life withdraws, death and rot move in. Whatever it is—orgones, life force—that we all have to score for all the time, there is not much of it in the Valley. Your food rots before you can get it home. Milk sours before you can finish the meal. The Valley is a place where the new anti-life force is breaking through.

Death hangs over the Valley like an invisible smog. The place exerts a curious magnetism on the moribund. The dying cell gravitates to the Valley:

Gary West came from Minneapolis. He had saved up twenty thousand dollars from operating a dairy farm during the War. With this money he bought a house and grove in the Valley. The place was on the far side of Mission, where irrigation stops and the desert begins. Five acres of Ruby Reds and a house in 1920 Spanish style. There he sat with his mother, his wife, and two children. In his eyes you could see the baffled, frightened, resentful looks of a man who feels the stirring in his cells of a fatal disease process. He was not sick at that time, but his cells were looking for death and West knew it. He wanted to sell out and leave the Valley.

"I feel closed in here. You have to go so far to get out of the Valley," he would say.

He began running from one project to another. A plantation in Mississippi, a winter vegetable set-up in Mexico. He went back to Minnesota and bought into a cow-feed company. He did this with the down payment on the sale of his Valley property. But he couldn't keep away from the Valley. He would run like a hooked fish until the drag of his dying cells tired him out, and the Valley reeled him in. He tried out various illnesses. A throat infection settled in his heart. He lay in the McAllen Hospital and tried to see himself as a man of business impatient to get up and back to work. His projects became more and more preposterous.

"That man is crazy," said Roy, the real estate man. "He don't know what he wants."

Only the Valley was real to West now. There was no other place for him to go. The other places were fantasy. Listening to him talk, you got the uncanny feeling that places like Milwaukee didn't exist. West rallied and went to look over a fifteen-dollar-per-acre sheep-raising set-up in Arkansas. He came back to the Valley and started building a house on credit. Something went wrong with his kidneys, and his body swelled up with urine. You could smell urine on his breath and through his skin. "This is uremic poisoning," exclaimed the doctor as the smell of urine filled the room. West went into convulsions and died. He left his wife a tangle of exchange notes between Milwaukee and the Valley that she will be ten years untangling.

All the worst features of America have drained down to the Valley and concentrated there. In the whole area, there is not one good restaurant. The food situation could only be tolerated by people who do not taste what they eat. In the Valley, restaurants are not operated by people who *are* cookers and purveyors of food. They are opened by somebody who decides that "people always eat" so a restaurant is a "good deal." His place will have a glass front so people can see in, and chromium fixtures. The food is bad U.S. restaurant food. So there he sits in his restaurant and looks at his customers with puzzled, resentful eyes. He didn't much want to run a restaurant anyway. Now he isn't even making money.

A lot of people made quick easy money during the War and for several years after. Any business was good, just as any stock is good on a rising market. People thought they were sharp operators, when actually they were just riding a lucky streak. Now the Valley is in a losing streak and only the big operators can ride it out. In the Valley economic laws work out like a formula in high school algebra, since there is no human element to interfere. The very rich are getting richer and all the others are going broke. The Big Holders are not shrewd or ruthless or enterprising. They don't have to say or think anything. All they have to do is sit and the money comes pouring in. You have to get up with the Big Holders or drop out and take any job they hand you. The middle class is getting the squeeze, and only one in a thousand will go up. The Big Holders are the house, and the small farmers are the players.

The player goes broke if he keeps on playing, and the farmer has to play or lose to the Government by default. The Big Holders own all the Valley banks, and when the farmer goes broke the bank takes over. Soon the Big Holders will own the Valley.

The Valley is like an honest dice table where the players do not have the vitality to influence the dice and they win or lose by pure chance. You never hear anyone say, "It had to happen that way," or when they do say it they are talking about a death. An event that "had to happen that way" may be good or bad, but there it is, and you cannot regret it or rehash it. Since everything that happens in the Valley—except death—happens by chance, the inhabitants are always tampering with the past like the two-dollar bettor on the return train from the track: "I should have hung on to that hundred acres on the lower lift; I should have took up them oil leases; I should have planted cotton instead of tomatoes." A nasal whine goes up from the Valley, a vast muttering of banal regret and despair.

When I arrived in the Valley, I was still in the post-cure drag. I had no appetite and no energy. All I wanted to do was sleep, and I slept twelve to fourteen hours a day. Occasionally I bought two ounces of paregoric, drank it with two goof balls and felt normal for several hours. You have to sign for P.G. when you buy it, and I did not want to burn down the drugstores. You can only buy P.G. so often, or the druggist gets wise. Then he packs in, or ups the price.

I had gone into partnership with a friend named Evans to buy machinery, hire a farmer and raise a cotton crop. We had a hundred and fifty acres in cotton. Good cotton land will pick a bale to an acre, and the U.S. support price guaranteed us a hundred and fifty dollars to a bale. So we stood to gross about $22,000. The farmer did all the actual work. Evans and I would drive around every few days to see how the cotton was looking. It took us about an hour to look at all our cotton because the fields were scattered around from Edingburg to the lower lift, almost on the river. There was no particular point in looking at the cotton since neither of us knew the first thing about it. We just drove around to pass the time until five p.m., when we started drinking.

There were five or six regulars who gathered every afternoon at Evans' house. Exactly at five, someone would bang a tin pan and yell "Drinking time!" and the others would jump up like fighters coming out at the bell. We made our own gin from Mexican alcohol as a measure of economy. Martinis mixed with this gin had a terrible taste, and you had to fill the cocktail with pieces of ice or it would be warm before you could get it down. I cannot drink even good martinis in hot weather, so I made myself a long drink with sugar and lime and seltzer and a tiny pinch of quinine to approximate gin and tonic. No one in the Valley had ever heard of quinine water.

All that summer was perfect cotton weather. Hot and dry, day after day. We started picking after the Fourth of July and all our cotton was off by the September 1st deadline. We broke a little better than even. High operating costs and the high cost of living— I figured it was costing me about seven hundred a month to live in that valley without a maid or a car—took most of the profit. I decided it was time to pull out of the Valley.

Early in October, I got a letter from the bonding company saying my case was coming up in four days. I called Tige and he said, "Pay no attention. I will get a continuance." A few days later I got a letter from Tige saying that he had scored for a three-week continuance, but was doubtful of getting the trial put off again.

I called him on the phone and told him I was taking a trip to Mexico. He said, "Fine. You just have as good a time as you can in three weeks and be back here for the trial."

I asked him how were the chances of another continuance.

He said, "Frankly, not good. I can't do a thing with this judge. His ulcers are bothering him."

I decided to take steps to remain in Mexico when I got there.

•

As soon as I hit Mexico City, I started looking for junk. At least, I always had one eye open for it. As I said before, I can spot junk neighborhoods. My first night in town I walked down Dolores Street and saw a group of Chinese junkies standing in front of an Exquisito Chop Suey joint. Chinamen are hard to make. They will only do business with another Chinaman. So I knew it would be a waste of time trying to score with these characters.

One day I was walking down San Juan Létran and passed a cafeteria that had colored tile set in the stucco around the entrance, and the floor was covered with the same tile. The cafeteria was unmistakably Near Eastern. As I walked by, someone came out of the cafeteria. It was a type character you see only on the fringes of a junk neighborhood.

As the geologist looking for oil is guided by certain outcroppings of rock, so certain signs indicate the near presence of junk. Junk is often found adjacent to ambiguous or transitional districts: East Fourteenth near Third in New York; Poydras and St. Charles in New Orleans; San Juan Létran in Mexico City. Stores selling artificial limbs, wig-makers, dental mechanics, loft manufacturers of perfumes, pomades, novelties, essential oils. A point where dubious business enterprise touches Skid Row.

There is a type person occasionally seen in these neighborhoods who has connections with junk, though he is neither a user nor a seller. But when you see him the dowser wand twitches. Junk is close. His place of origin is the Near East, probably Egypt. He has a large straight nose. His lips are thin and purple-blue like the lips of a penis. The skin is tight and smooth over his face. He is basically obscene beyond any possible vile act or practice. He has the mark of a certain trade or occupation that no longer exists. If junk were gone from the earth, there might still be junkies standing around in junk neighborhoods feeling the lack, vague and persistent, a pale ghost of junk sickness.

So this man walks around in the places where he once exercised his obsolete and unthinkable trade. But he is unperturbed. His eyes are black with an insect's unseeing calm. He looks as if he nourished himself on honey and Levantine syrups that he sucks up through a sort of proboscis.

What is his lost trade? Definitely of a servant class and something to do with the dead, though he is not an embalmer. Perhaps he stores something in his body—a substance to prolong life—of which he is periodically milked by his masters. He is as specialized as an insect, for the performance of some inconceivably vile function.

●

The Chimu Bar looks like any cantina from the outside, but as soon as you walk in you know you are in a queer bar.

I ordered a drink at the bar and looked around. Three Mexican fags were posturing in front of the jukebox. One of them slithered over to where I was standing, with the stylized gestures of a temple dancer, and asked for a cigarette. There was something archaic in the stylized movements, a depraved animal grace at once beautiful and repulsive. I could see him moving in the light of campfires, the ambiguous gestures fading out into the dark. Sodomy is as old as the human species. One of the fags was sitting in a booth by the jukebox, perfectly immobile with a stupid animal serenity.

I turned to get a closer look at the boy who had moved over. Not bad. "*¿Por qué triste?*" I asked. ("Why sad?") Not much of a gambit, but I wasn't there to converse.

The boy smiled, revealing very red gums and sharp teeth far apart. He shrugged and said something to the effect that he wasn't sad or not especially so. I looked around the room.

"*Vámonos a otro lugar*," I said. ("Let's go some place else.")

The boy nodded. We walked down the street into an all-night restaurant, and sat down in a booth. The boy dropped his hand onto my leg under the table. I felt my stomach knot with excitement. I gulped my coffee and waited impatiently while the boy finished a beer and smoked a cigarette.

The boy knew a hotel. I pushed five pesos through a grill. An old man unlocked the door of a room and dropped a ragged towel on the chair. "*¿Llevas pistola?*"—("You carry a pistol?")—asked the boy. He had caught sight of my gun. I said yes.

I folded my pants and dropped them over a chair, placing the pistol on my pants. I dropped my shirt and shorts on the pistol. I sat down naked on the edge of the bed and watched the boy undress. He folded his worn blue suit carefully. He took off his shirt and placed it around his coat on the back of a chair. His skin was smooth and copper-colored. The boy stepped out of his shorts and turned around and smiled at me. Then he came and sat beside me on the bed. I ran one hand slowly over the boy's back, following with the other hand the curve of the chest down over the flat brown stomach. The boy smiled and lay down on the bed.

Later we smoked a cigarette, our shoulders touching under the covers. The boy said he had to go. We both dressed. I wondered if he expected money. I decided not. Outside, we separated at a corner, shaking hands.

●

Some time later I ran into a boy named Angelo in the same bar. I saw Angelo off and on for two years. When I was on junk I wouldn't meet Angelo for months, but when I got off I always ran into him on the street somewhere. In Mexico your wishes have a dream power. When you want to see someone, he turns up.

Once I had been looking for a boy and I was tired and sat down on a stone bench in the Alameda. I could feel the smooth stone through my pants, and the ache in my loins like a toothache when the pain is light and different from any other pain. Sitting there looking across the park, I suddenly felt calm and happy, seeing myself in a dream relationship with The City, and knew I was going to score for a boy that night. I did.

Angelo's face was Oriental, Japanese-looking, except for his copper skin. He was not queer, and I gave him money; always the same amount, twenty pesos. Sometimes I didn't have that much and he would say: "*No importa.*" ("It does not matter.") He insisted on sweeping the apartment out whenever he spent the night there.

Once I connected with Angelo, I did not go back to the Chimu. Mexico or Stateside, queer bars brought me down.

●

The meaning of "*mañana*" is "Wait until the signs are right." If you are in a hurry to score for junk and go around cracking to strangers, you will get beat for your money and likely have trouble with the law. But if you wait, junk will come to you if you want it.

I had been in Mexico City several months. One day I went to see the lawyer I had hired to get working and residence papers for me. A shabby middle-aged man was standing in front of the office.

"He ain't come yet," the man said. I looked at the man. He was an old-time junkie, no doubt about it. And I knew he didn't have any doubts about me either. A user may be ten years off the junk, but you can still make him for a junkie. The mark of junk is indelible.

We stood around talking until the lawyer came. The junkie was there to sell some religious medals. The lawyer had told him to bring a dozen up to his office.

After I had seen the lawyer, I asked the junkie if he would join me for supper and we went to a restaurant on San Juan Létran.

The junkie asked me what my story was and I told him. He flipped back his coat lapel and showed me a spike stuck in the underside of the lapel.

"I've been on junk for twenty-eight years," he said. "Do you want to score?"

•

There is only one pusher in Mexico City, and that is Lupita. She has been in the business twenty years. Lupita got her start with one gram of junk and built up from there to a monopoly of the junk business in Mexico City. She weighed three hundred pounds, so she started using junk to reduce, but only her face got thin and the result is no improvement. Every month or so she hires a new lover, gives him shirts and suits and wrist watches, and then packs him in when she has enough.

Lupita pays off to operate wide open, like she was running a grocery store. She doesn't have to worry about stool pigeons because every law in the Federal District knows that Lupita sells junk. She keeps outfits in glasses of alcohol so the junkies can fix in the joint and walk out clean. Whenever a law needs money for a quick beer, he goes over by Lupita and waits for someone to walk out on the chance he may be holding a paper. For ten pesos ($1.25) the cop lets him go. For twenty pesos, he gets his junk back. Now and then, some ill-advised citizen starts pushing better papers for less money, but he doesn't push long. Lupita has a standing offer: ten free papers to anybody who tells her about another pusher in the Federal District. Then Lupita calls one of her friends on the narcotics squad and the pusher is busted.

Lupita fences on the side. If anyone makes a good score, she puts out a grapevine to find out who was in on the job. Thieves sell to her at her price or she tips the law. Lupita knows everything that happens in the lower-bracket underworld of Mexico City. She sits there doling out her papers like an Aztec goddess.

Lupita sells her stuff in papers. It is supposed to be heroin. Actually, it is pantopon cut with milk sugar and some other crap that looks like sand and remains undissolved in the spoon after you cook up.

I started scoring for Lupita's papers through Ike, the old-time junkie I met in the lawyer's office. I had been off junk three months at this time. It took me just three days to get back on.

An addict may be ten years off the junk, but he can get a new habit in less than a week; whereas someone who has never been addicted would have to take two shots per day for two months to get any habit at all. I took a shot daily for four months before I could notice withdrawal symptoms. You can list the symptoms of junk sickness, but the feel of it is like no other feeling and you can not put it into words. I did not experience this junk sick feeling until my second habit.

Why does an addict get a new habit so much quicker than a junk virgin, even after the addict has been clean for years? I do not accept the theory that junk is lurking in the body all that time— the spine is where it supposedly holes up—and I disagree with all psychological answers. I think the use of junk causes permanent cellular alteration. Once a junkie, always a junkie. You can stop using junk, but you are never off after the first habit.

When my wife saw I was getting the habit again, she did something she had never done before. I was cooking up a shot two days after I'd connected with Old Ike. My wife grabbed the spoon and threw the junk on the floor. I slapped her twice across the face and she threw herself on the bed, sobbing, then turned around and said to me: "Don't you want to do anything at all? You know how bored you get when you have a habit. It's like all the lights went out. Oh well, do what you want. I guess you have some stashed, anyway."

I did have some stashed.

Lupita's papers cost fifteen pesos each—about two dollars. They are half the strength of a two-dollar Stateside cap. If you have any habit at all, it takes two papers to fix you, and I mean just fix. To get really loaded, you would need four papers. I thought this was an outrageous price considering everything is cheaper in Mexico and I was expecting bargain prices on junk. And here I was, paying above-U.S. prices for junk of lower quality. Ike told me, "She has to charge high because she pays off to the law."

So I asked Ike, "What about scripts?"

He told me the croakers could only prescribe M in solution. The most they were allowed to prescribe in one script was fifteen centogramos, or about two and a half grains. I figured it would work out a lot cheaper than Lupita, so we started hitting the croakers. We located several who would write the script for five pesos, and five more would get it filled.

One script will last a day if you keep the habit down. The trouble is, scripts are easier to get than to fill, and when you do find a drugstore that will fill the script, like as not the druggist steals all the junk and gives you distilled water. Or he doesn't have any M and puts anything on the shelf in the bottle. I have cashed scripts that came back full of undissolved powder. I could have killed myself trying to shoot this crap.

Mexican croakers are not like Stateside croakers. They never pull that professional man act on you. A croaker who will write at all will write without hearing a story. In Mexico City, there are so many doctors that a lot of them have a hard time making it. I know croakers who would starve to death if they didn't write morphine scripts. They don't have patient one, unless you call junkies patients.

I was keeping up Ike's habit as well as my own and it ran into money.

I asked Ike what the score was on pushing in Mexico City. He said it was impossible.

"You wouldn't last a week. Sure, you can get plenty customers that would pay you fifteen pesos for a shot of good M like we get with the scripts. But first time they wake up sick with no money, they go right to Lupita and tell her for a few papers. Or if the law grabs them, they open their mouth right away. Some of them don't even have to be asked. Right away they say, 'Turn me loose and I'll tell you somebody pushing junk.' So the law sends them up to make a buy with the marked money, and that's it. You're fucked right there. It's eight years for selling this stuff and there's no bail.

"I have 'em come to me: 'Ike, we know you get stuff on the scripts. Here's fifty pesos. Get me one script.' Sometimes they got good watches or a suit of clothes. I tell 'em I'm off. Sure, I could make two hundred pesos a day, but I wouldn't last a week."

"But can't you find like five or six good customers?"

"I know every hip in Mexico City. And I wouldn't trust one of 'em. Not one."

●

At first we filled the scripts without too much trouble. But after a few weeks the scripts had piled up in the drugstores that would fill M scripts and they began packing in. It looked like we would be back with Lupita. Once or twice we got caught short and had to score with Lupita. Using that good drugstore M had run up our habits, and it took two of Lupita's fifteen-peso papers to fix us. Now, thirty pesos in one shot was a lot more than I could afford to pay. I had to quit, cut down to where I could make it on two of Lupita's papers per day, or find another source of supply.

One of the script-writing doctors suggested to Ike that he apply for a government permit. Ike explained to me that the Mexican government issued permits to hips allowing them a definite quantity of morphine per month at wholesale prices. The doctor would put in an application for Ike for one hundred pesos. I said, "Go ahead and apply," and gave him the money. I did not expect the deal to go through, but it did. Ten days later, he had a government permit to buy fifteen grams of morphine every month. The permit had to be signed by his doctor and the head doctor at the Board of Health. Then he would take it to a drugstore and have it filled.

The price was about two dollars per gram. I remember the first time he filled the permit. A whole boxful of cubes of morphine. Like a junkie's dream. I had never seen so much morphine before all at once. I put out the money and we split the stuff. Seven grams per month allowed me about three grains per day, which was more than I ever had in the States. So I was supplied with plenty of junk for a cost of thirty dollars per month as compared with about three hundred per month in the U.S.

●

During this time I did not get acquainted with the other junkies in Mexico City. Most of them make their junk money by stealing. They are always hot. They are all pigeons. Not one of them can be trusted with the price of a paper. No good can come from associating with these characters.

Ike didn't steal. He made out selling bracelets and medals that looked like silver. He had to keep ahead of his customers because this phony silver turned black in a matter of hours. Once or twice, he was arrested and charged with fraud, but I always bought him out. I told him to find some routine that was strictly legitimate, and he started selling crucifixes.

Ike had been a booster in the States and claimed to have scored for a hundred dollars per day in Chicago with a spring suitcase he shoved suits into and the side sprang back in place. All the money went for coke and M.

But Ike would not steal in Mexico. He said even the best thieves spend most of their time in the joint. In Mexico, known thieves can be sent to the Tres Marias penal colony without trial. There are no middle-class, white-collar thieves who make good livings, like you find in the States. There are big operators with political connections, and there are bums who spend half their time in jail. The big operators are usually police chiefs or other high officials. That is the set-up in Mexico, and Ike did not have connections to operate.

One junkie I did see from time to time was a dark-skinned Yucatecan whom Ike referred to as "the Black Bastard." The Black Bastard worked the crucifix routine. He was, in fact, extremely religious and made the pilgrimage to Chalma every year, going the last quarter mile on his knees over rocks with two people holding him up. After that, he was fixed for a year.

Our Lady of Chalma seems to be the patron saint of junkies and cheap thieves because all Lupita's customers make the pilgrimage once a year. The Black Bastard rents a cubicle in the church and pushes papers of junk outrageously cut with milk sugar.

I used to see the Black Bastard around from time to time, and I heard a great deal about him from Ike. Ike hated the Black Bastard only as one junkie can hate another. "The Black Bastard burned down that drugstore. Going up there saying I sent him. Now the druggist won't fill no more scripts."

So I drifted along from month to month. We were always a little short at the end of the month and had to fill a few scripts. I always had an insecure feeling when I was out of stuff and a comfortable feeling of security when I had those seven gramos stashed safely away.

Once, Ike got fifteen days in the city prison—the Carmen, they call it—for vagrancy. I was short and could not pay the fine, and it was three days before I got in to see him. His body had shrunk;

all the bones stuck out in his face; his brown eyes were bright with pain. I had a piece of hop covered with cellophane in my mouth. I spit the hop on half an orange and handed it to Ike. In twenty minutes, he was loaded.

I looked around and noticed how the hips stood out as a special group, like the fags who were posturing and screeching in one corner of the yard. The junkies were grouped together, talking and passing the junkie gesture back and forth, the arm swinging out from the elbow palm up, a gesture of separateness and special communion like the limp wrist of the fag.

Junkies all wear hats, if they have hats. They all look alike, as if wearing a costume identical in some curious way that escapes exact tabulation. Junk has marked them all with its indelible brand.

Ike told me that the prisoners often steal the pants off a newcomer. "Such a lousy people they got in here." I did see several men walking around in their underwear. The Commandante would catch wives and relatives bringing junk to the prisoners, and shake them down for all they had.

He caught one woman bringing a paper to her husband, but she only had five pesos. So he took her dress and sold it for fifteen pesos and she went home wrapped in an old lousy sheet.

The place was crawling with pigeons. Ike was afraid to hold any of the hop I brought him for fear the other prisoners would take it or turn him over to the Commandante.

●

I fell into a routine of staying home with three or four shots a day. For something to do, I enrolled in Mexico City College. The students impressed me as a sorry-looking lot, with a few exceptions— but then, I wasn't looking at them very hard.

When you look back over a year on the junk, it seems like no time at all. Only the periods when you were sick stand out. You remember the first few shots of a habit and the shots when you were really sick.

(Even in Mexico there is always the day when everything goes wrong. The drugstore is closed or your boy is off duty, the croaker is out of town at some fiesta, and you can't score.)

Aside from junk itself, what you experience during a habit is flat, almost two-dimensional. You can remember what happened if you take the trouble, but no memories come back spontaneously from a habit period—except for the intervals of sickness.

The end of the month. I was out of junk and sick. Waiting for Old Ike to show with a morphine script. A junkie spends half his life waiting. There was a cat in the house we had been feeding, an ugly-looking gray cat. I picked the animal up and held it on my lap, petting it, and tightened my hold when it tried to jump down. The cat began to mew, looking for a way to escape.

I brought my face down to touch the cat's cold nose with mine, and the cat scratched at my face. It was a half-assed scratch, and it did not land. But it was all I needed. I held the cat out at arm's length, slapping it back and forth across the face with my free hand. The cat screamed and clawed me, then started spraying piss all over my pants. I went on hitting the cat, my hands bloody from scratches. The animal twisted loose and ran into the closet, where I could hear it groaning and whimpering with terror.

"Now I'll finish the bastard off," I said, picking up a heavy painted cane. Sweat was running down my face. I was trembling with excitement. I licked my lips and started toward the closet, alert to block any escape attempt.

At this point my old lady intervened, and I put down the cane. The cat scrabbled out of the closet and ran down the stairs.

My old lady looked at me, smiling. "Bill," she said. "Aren't you ashamed of yourself? Sometimes I don't know. Sometimes I just don't know," she said, shaking her head.

•

Ike brought me cocaine when he could score for it. C is hard to find in Mexico. I had never used any good coke before. Coke is pure kick. It lifts you straight up, a mechanical lift that starts leaving you as soon as you feel it. I don't know anything like C for a lift, but the lift only lasts ten minutes or so. Then you want another shot. You can't stop shooting C—as long as it is there you shoot it. When you are shooting C, you shoot more M to level the C kick and smooth out the rough edges. Without M, C makes you too nervous, and M is an antidote for an overdose. There is no tolerance with C, and not much margin between a regular and a toxic dose. Several times I got too much and everything went black and my heart began turning over. Luckily I always had plenty of M on hand, and a shot of M fixed me right up.

Junk is a biological necessity when you have a habit, an invisible mouth. When you take a shot of junk you are satisfied, just like you ate a big meal. You don't want another shot right away. But using C you want another shot as soon as the effect wears off. If you have C in the house, you will not go out to a movie or go out at all until the C is all gone. One shot creates an urgent desire for another shot to maintain the high. But once the C is out of your system, you forget about it. There is no habit to C.

•

Junk short-circuits sex. The drive to non-sexual sociability comes from the same place sex comes from, so when I have an H or M shooting habit I am non-sociable. If someone wants to talk, O.K. But there is no drive to get acquainted. When I come off the junk, I often run through a period of uncontrolled sociability and talk to anyone who will listen.

Junk takes everything and gives nothing but insurance against junk sickness. Every now and then I took a good look at the deal I was giving myself and decided to take the cure. When you are getting plenty of junk, kicking looks easy. You say, "I'm not getting any kick from the shots any more. I might as well quit." But when you cut down into junk sickness, the picture looks different.

During the year or so I was on the junk in Mexico, I started the cure five times. I tried reducing the shots, I tried the Chinese cure with a solution of hop and Wampole's medicine. Every time you take some of the hop solution you add an equal amount of Wampole's medicine. In ten days or so you are drinking plain Wampole's Tonic, and the reduction was so slow you never noticed.

That is the theory of the Chinese cure. What generally happens is this: You start taking a little more hop solution than your schedule allows and that means you put in more Wampole's and dilute the hop that much quicker. After a few days you don't know how much is in there and you take it all to be sure. So you wind up with a worse habit than you had before the Chinese cure.

An eating habit is the worst habit you can contract. It takes longer to break than a needle habit, and the withdrawal symptoms are considerably more severe. In fact, it is not uncommon for a junkie with an eating habit to die if he is cut off cold turkey in jail. A junkie with an eating habit suffers from excruciating stomach cramps when he is cut off. And the symptoms last up to three weeks as compared to eight days on a needle habit.

When you kick the spike you get worse until you hit the third day and you think, this is it: You *couldn't* feel worse. But the fourth day is worse. After the fourth day relief is dramatic. And on the sixth day there is only a pale shadow of junk sickness.

But with an eating habit you can look forward to at least ten days of horrible suffering. So when you are taking a cure with hop you have to be careful not to get an eating habit. If you can't make it on schedule, best go back to the needle.

After my Chinese fiasco, I made up some papers and gave them to my wife to hide and dole out according to a schedule. I had Ike help me make up the papers, but he had an inaccurate mind, and his schedule was all top-heavy on the beginning and suddenly ended with no reduction. So I made up my own schedule. For a while I stayed with the schedule, but I didn't have any real push. I got stuff from Ike on the side and made excuses for the extra shots.

I knew that I did not want to go on taking junk. If I could have made a single decision, I would have decided no more junk ever. But when it came to the process of quitting, I did not have the drive. It gave me a terrible feeling of helplessness to watch myself break every schedule I set up as though I did not have control over my actions.

●

One morning in April, I woke up a little sick. I lay there looking at shadows on the white plaster ceiling. I remembered a long time ago when I lay in bed beside my mother, watching lights from the street move across the ceiling and down the walls. I felt the sharp nostalgia of train whistles, piano music down a city street, burning leaves.

A mild degree of junk sickness always brought me the magic of childhood. "It never fails," I thought. "Just like a shot. I wonder if all junkies score for this wonderful stuff."

I went into the bathroom to take a shot. I was a long time hitting a vein. The needle clogged twice. Blood ran down my arm. The junk spread through my body, an injection of death. The dream was gone. I looked down at the blood that ran from elbow to wrist. I felt a sudden pity for the violated veins and tissue. Tenderly I wiped the blood off my arm.

"I'm going to quit," I said aloud.

I made up a solution of hop and told Ike to stay away for a few days. He said, "I hope you make it, kid. I hope you get off. May I fall down and be paralyzed if I don't mean it."

In forty-eight hours the backlog of morphine in my body ran out. The solution barely cut the sickness. I drank it all with two nembutals and slept several hours. When I woke up, my clothes were soaked through with sweat. My eyes were watering and smarting. My whole body felt itchy and irritable. I twisted about on the bed, arching my back and stretching my arms and legs. I drew my knees up, my hands clasped between the thighs. The pressure of my hands set off the hair trigger orgasm of junk sickness. I got up and changed my underwear.

There was a little hop left in the bottle. I drank that, went out and bought four tubes of codeine tablets. I took the codeine with hot tea and felt better.

Ike told me, "You're taking it too fast. Let me mix up a solution for you." I could hear him out in the kitchen crooning over the mixture: "A little cinnamon in case he starts to puke . . . a little sage for the shits . . . some cloves to clean the blood . . ."

I never tasted anything so awful, but the mixture leveled off my sickness at a bearable point, so I felt a little high all the time. I wasn't high on the hop; I was high on withdrawal tone-up. Junk is an inoculation of death that keeps the body in a condition of emergency. When the junk is cut off, emergency reactions continue. Sensations sharpen, the addict is aware of his visceral processes to an uncomfortable degree, peristalsis and secretion go unchecked. No matter what his actual age, the kicking addict is liable to the emotional excesses of a child or an adolescent.

About the third day of using Ike's mixture, I started drinking. I had never been able to drink before when I was on the junk, or junk sick. But eating hop is different from shooting the white stuff. You can mix hop and lush.

At first I started drinking at five in the afternoon. After a week, I started drinking at eight in the morning, stayed drunk all day and all night, and woke up drunk the next morning.

Every morning when I woke up, I washed down benzedrine, sanicin, and a piece of hop with black coffee and a shot of tequila. Then I lay back and closed my eyes and tried to piece together the night before and yesterday. Often, I drew a blank from noon on. You sometimes wake up from a dream and think, "Thank God, I didn't really do that!" Reconstructing a period of blackout you think, "My God, did I really do it?" The line between saying and thinking is blurred. Did you say it or just think it?

A junkie does not ordinarily kick of his own choice. I had never kicked before until I couldn't score for junk in any form and had to throw in the towel. No one can hit the skids harder or quicker than a self cured junkie.

After ten days of the cure I had deteriorated shockingly. My clothes were spotted and stiff from the drinks I had spilled all over myself. I never bathed. I had lost weight, my hands shook, I was always spilling things, knocking over chairs, and falling down. But I seemed to have unlimited energy and a capacity for liquor I never had before. My emotions spilled out everywhere. I was uncontrollably sociable and would talk to anybody I could pin down. I forced distastefully intimate confidences on perfect strangers. Several times I made the crudest sexual propositions to people who had given no hint of reciprocity.

Ike was around every few days. "I'm glad to see you getting off, Bill. May I fall down and be paralyzed if I don't mean it. But if you get too sick and start to puke—here's five centogramos of M."

Ike took a severe view of my drinking. "You're drinking, Bill. You're drinking and getting crazy. You look terrible. You look terrible in your face. Better you should go back to stuff than drink like this."

●

I was in a cheap cantina off Dolores Street, Mexico City. I had been drinking for about two weeks. I was sitting in a booth with three Mexicans, drinking tequila. The Mexicans were fairly well dressed. One of them spoke English. A middle-aged, heavy-set Mexican with a sad, sweet face sang songs and played the guitar. He was sitting at the end of a booth in a chair. I was glad the singing made conversation impossible.

Five cops came in. I figured I might get a shake, so I slipped the gun and holster out of my belt and dropped them under the table with a piece of hop I had stashed in a cigarette package. The cops had a quick beer and took off.

When I reached under the table, my gun was gone but the holster was there.

I was sitting in another bar with the Mexican who spoke English. The singer and the other two Mexicans were gone. The place was suffused with a dim yellow light. A moldy-looking bullhead mounted on a plaque hung over the mahogany bar. Pictures of bullfighters, some autographed, decorated the walls. The word "saloon" was etched in the frosted-glass swinging door. I found myself reading the word "saloon" over and over. I had the feeling of coming into the middle of a conversation.

I inferred from the expression of the other man that I was in mid-sentence, but did not know what I had said or what I was going to say or what the discussion was about. I thought we must be talking about the gun. "I am probably trying to buy it back." I noticed the man had the piece of hop in his hand, and was turning it over.

"So you think I look like a junkie?" he said.

I looked at him. The man had a thin face with high cheekbones. The eyes were a gray-brown color often seen in mixed Indian and European stock. He was wearing a light gray suit and a tie. His mouth was thin, twisted down at the corners. A junkie mouth, for sure. There are people who look like junkies and aren't, just as some people look queer and aren't. It's a type that causes trouble.

"I'm going to call a cop," he said, starting for a phone attached to a support pillar.

I jerked the telephone out of the man's hand and pushed him against the bar so hard he bounced off it. The man smiled at me. His teeth were covered by a brown film. He turned his back and called the bartender over and showed him the piece of hop. I walked out and got a cab.

I remember going back to my apartment to get another gun— a heavy-caliber revolver. I was in a hysterical rage, though exactly why I cannot, in retrospect, understand.

I got out of a taxi and walked down the street and into the bar. The man was leaning against the bar, his gray coat pulled tight over his thin back and shoulders. He turned an expressionless face to me.

I said, "Walk outside ahead of me."

"Why, Bill?" he asked.

"Go on, walk."

I flipped the heavy revolver out of my waistband, cocking it as I drew, and stuck the muzzle in the man's stomach. With my left hand, I took hold of the man's coat lapel and shoved him back against the bar. It did not occur to me until later that the man had used my correct first name and that the bartender probably knew it too.

The man was perfectly relaxed, his face blank with controlled fear. I saw someone approaching from behind on my right side, and half turned my head. The bartender was closing in with a cop. I turned around, irritated at the interruption. I shoved the gun in the cop's stomach.

"Who asked you to put in your two cents?" I asked in English. I was not talking to a solid three-dimensional cop. I was talking to the recurrent cop of my dreams—an irritating, nondescript, darkish man who would rush in when I was about to take a shot or go to bed with a boy.

The bartender grabbed my arm, twisting it to one side out of the cop's stomach. The cop stolidly hauled out his battered .45 automatic, placing it firmly against my body. I could feel the coldness of the muzzle through my thin cotton shirt. The cop's stomach stuck out. He had not sucked it in or leaned forward. I relaxed my hold on the gun and felt it leave my hand. I half-raised my hands, palm out in a gesture of surrender.

"All right, all right," I said, and then added, "*bueno.*"

The cop put away his .45. The bartender was leaning against the bar examining the gun. The man in the gray suit stood there without any expression at all.

"*Esta cargado,*"—("It's loaded")—said the bartender, without looking up from the gun.

I intended to say, "Of course—what good is an unloaded gun?" but I did not say anything. The scene was unreal and flat and pointless, as though I had forced my way into someone else's dream, the drunk wandering out on to the stage.

And I was unreal to the others, the stranger from another country. The bartender looked at me with curiosity. He gave a little shrug of puzzled disgust and slipped the gun into his waistband. There was no hate in the room. Perhaps they would have hated me if I had been closer to them.

The cop took me firmly by the arm. "*Vámanos gringo,*" he said.

I walked out with the cop. I felt limp and had difficulty controlling my legs. Once I stumbled, and the cop steadied me. I was trying to convey the idea that, while I had no money on my person, I could borrow some "*de amigos.*" My brain was numb. I mixed Spanish and English and the word for borrow was hidden in some filing cabinet of the mind cut off from my use by the mechanical barrier of alcohol-numbed connections. The cop shook his head. I was making an effort to reform the concept. Suddenly the cop stopped walking.

"*Ándale, gringo,*" he said, giving me a slight push on the shoulder. The cop stood there for a minute, watching as I walked on down the street. I waved. The cop did not respond. He turned and walked back the way he had come.

I had one peso left. I walked into a cantina and ordered a beer. There was no draft beer and bottle beer cost a peso. There was a group of young Mexicans at the end of the bar, and I got talking to them. One of them showed me a Secret Service badge. Probably a phony, I decided. There's a phony cop in every Mexican bar. I found myself drinking a tequila. The last thing I remembered was the sharp taste of the lemon I sucked with the glass of tequila.

I woke up next morning in a strange room. I looked around. Cheap joint. Five pesos. A wardrobe, a chair, a table. I could see people passing outside, through the drawn curtains. Ground floor. Some of my clothes were heaped on the chair. My coat and shirt lay on the table.

I swung my legs out of the bed, and sat there trying to remember what happened after that last glass of tequila. I drew a blank. I got out of bed and took inventory of my effects. "Fountain pen gone. It leaked anyway . . . never had one that didn't . . . pocketknife gone . . . no loss either . . ." I began putting on my clothes. I had the shakes bad. "Need a few quick beers . . . maybe I can catch Rollins home now."

It was a long walk. Rollins was in front of his apartment, walking his Norwegian elk-hound. He was a solidly built man of my age, with strong, handsome features and wiry, black hair a little gray at the temples. He was wearing an expensive sports shirt, whipcord slacks, and a suede leather jacket. We had known each other for thirty years.

Rollins listened to my account of the previous evening. "You're going to get your head blown off carrying that gun," he said. "What do you carry it for? You wouldn't know what you were shooting at. You bumped into trees twice there on Insurgentes.

You walked right in front of a car. I pulled you back and you threatened me. I left you there to find your own way home, and I don't know how you ever made it. Everyone is fed up with the way you've been acting lately. If there's one thing I don't want to be around, and I think no one else particularly wants to be around, it's a drunk with a gun."

"You're right, of course," I said.

"Well, I want to help you in any way I can. But the first thing you have to do is cut down on the sauce and build up your health. You look terrible. Then you'd better think about making some money. Speaking of money, I guess you're broke, as usual." Rollins took out his wallet. "Here's fifty pesos. That's the best I can do for you."

I got drunk on the fifty pesos. About nine that night, I ran out of money and went back to my apartment. I lay down and tried to sleep. When I closed my eyes I saw an Oriental face, the lips and nose eaten away by disease. The disease spread, melting the face into an amoeboid mass in which the eyes floated, dull crustacean eyes. Slowly, a new face formed around the eyes. A series of faces, hieroglyphs, distorted and leading to the final place where the human road ends, where the human form can no longer contain the crustacean horror that has grown inside it.

I watched curiously. "I got the horrors," I thought matter of factly.

I woke up with a start of fear. I lay there, my heart beating fast, trying to find out what had scared me. I thought I heard a slight noise downstairs. "There is someone in the apartment," I said aloud, and immediately I knew that there was.

I took my 30-30 carbine out of the closet. My hands were shaking; I could barely load the rifle. I dropped several cartridges on the floor before I got two in the loading slot. My legs kept folding under me. I went downstairs and turned on all the lights. Nobody. Nothing.

I had the shakes bad, and on top of that I was junk sick! "How long since I've had a shot?" I asked myself. I couldn't remember. I began ransacking the apartment for junk. Some time before, I had stashed a piece of hop in a hole in one corner of the room. The hop had slid under the floorboards, out of reach. I had made several abortive attempts to recover it.

"I'll get it this time," I said grimly. With shaking hands, I made a hook out of a coat-hanger and began fishing for the hop. The sweat ran down my nose. I skinned my hands on the jagged wood edges of the hole. "If I can't get to it one way, I will another," I said grimly, and began looking for the saw.

I couldn't find it. I rushed from one room to the other, throwing things around and emptying drawers on the floor in a mounting frenzy. Sobbing with rage, I tried to rip the boards up with my hands. Finally, I gave up and lay on the floor panting and whimpering.

I remembered there was some dionin in the medicine chest. I got up to look. Only one tablet left. The tablet cooked up milky and I was afraid to shoot it in the vein. A sudden involuntary jerk of my hand pulled the needle out of my arm and the shot sprayed over my skin. I sat there looking at my arm.

I finally slept a little and woke up next morning with a terrific alcohol depression. Junk sickness, suspended by codeine and hop, numbed by weeks of constant drinking, came back on me full force. "I have to have some codeine," I thought.

I looked through my clothes. Nothing, not a cigarette, not a centavo. I went into the living room and reached into the sofa, where the sofa back joined the seat. I ran my hand along it. A comb, a piece of chalk, a broken pencil, one ten-centavo piece, one five. I felt a sickening shock of pain and pulled my hand out. I was bleeding from a deep cut in my finger. A razor blade, evidently. I tore off a piece of towel and wrapped it around my finger. The blood soaked through and dripped on the floor. I sent my wife out to try and borrow some money. She said, "We have about burned everybody down. But I will try." I went back to bed. I couldn't sleep. I couldn't read. I lay there looking at the ceiling, with the cellular stoicism that junk bestows on the user.

A matchbox sailed past the door into the bathroom. I sat up, my heart pounding. "Old Ike, the pusher!" Ike often sneaked into the house and manifested his presence like a poltergeist, throwing something or knocking on the walls. Old Ike appeared in the doorway.

"How you getting along?" he asked.

"Not so good. I got the shakes. I need a shot."

Ike nodded. "Yeah," he began, "M is the thing for the shakes. I remember once in Minneapolis—"

"Never mind Minneapolis. Have you got any?"

"I got it, but not with me. Take me about twenty minutes to get it." Old Ike was sitting down, leafing through a magazine. He looked up. "Why? You want some?"

"Yes."

"I'll get it right away." Ike was gone two hours.

"I had to wait for the guy to get back from lunch to open the safe in the hotel. I keep my stuff in the safe so nobody makes me for it. I tell 'em at the hotel it's gold dust I use—"

"But you got it?"

"Yes, I got it. Where is your works?"

"In the bathroom."

Ike came back from the bathroom with the works and began cooking up a shot. He kept talking. "You're drinking and you're getting crazy. I hate to see you get off this stuff and on something worse. I know so many that quit the junk. A lot of them can't make it with Lupita. Fifteen pesos for a paper and it takes three to fix you. Right away they start in drinking and they don't last more than two or three years."

"Let's have that shot," I said.

"Yes. Just a minute. The needle is stopped." Ike began feeling along the edge of his coat lapel, looking for a horsehair to clean out the needle. He went on talking: "I remember once out by Mary Island. We was on the boat and the Colonel got drunk and fell in the water and come near drowning with his two pistolas. We had a hell of a time to get him out." Ike blew through the needle. "Clear now. I see a guy used to be a hip down by Lupita's. They called him *El Sombrero* because he makes it grabbing people's hats and running. Comes up by a streetcar just when it starts. Reaches in and grabs a hat and *pfut*—he's gone. You should see him now. His legs all swelled up and covered with sores and dirty, oh my God! The people walk around him like this." Ike was standing with the dropper in one hand and the needle in the other.

I said, "How about that shot?"

"O.K. How much you want? About five centogramos? Better make it five."

The shot was a long time taking effect. It hit slowly at first, then with mounting force. I lay back on the bed like I was in a warm bath.

●

I kept on drinking. Several days later, I passed out in the Ship Ahoy after drinking tequila for eight hours steadily. Some friends carried me home. Next morning I had the worst hangover of my life. I began vomiting at ten-minute intervals until I brought up green bile.

Then Old Ike was around. "You got to quit drinking, Bill. You're getting crazy."

I had never been so sick. Nausea wracked my body like a convulsion. Old Ike was holding me up as I vomited a few spoonfuls of bile into the toilet. He put an arm around my shoulder and hugged me and helped me back to bed. About five in the afternoon, I stopped vomiting and managed to keep a bottle of grape juice and a glass of milk down.

"It stinks like piss in here," I said. "One of them cats must have pissed under the bed."

Ike began sniffing around the bed. "No, nothing there." He sniffed some more near the head of the bed, where I was lying propped up on pillows. "Bill, it's you smells like piss!"

"Huh?" I began smelling my hands, with mounting horror, as if I was discovering leprosy. "Good Lord!" I said, my stomach cold with fear. "I got uremic poisoning! Ike, go out and get me a croaker."

"O.K., Bill, I'll get you one right away."

"And don't come back with one of them five-peso script-writing bums!"

"O.K., Bill."

I lay there trying to control the fear. I did not know much about uremic poisoning. A woman I knew slightly in Texas died of it after drinking a bottle of beer every hour, night and day, for two weeks. Rollins had told me about it. "She swelled up and turned sorta black and went into convulsions and died. The whole house smelled like piss!"

I relaxed, trying to tune in on my viscera and find out what the score was. I did not feel death or indication of grave illness. I felt tired, battered, languid. I lay there with my eyes closed in the darkening room.

Old Ike came in with the doctor and turned on the light. A Chinese doctor—one of Ike's script-writers. He said there was no uremia since I could piss and did not have a headache.

I asked, "How come I stink like this?"

The doctor shrugged. Ike said, "He says it's nothing serious. He says you have to stop drinking. He says better you go back to the other than drink like this." The doctor nodded. I could hear Ike out in the hall, hitting the croaker for a morphine script.

"Ike, I don't think that doctor knows a thing. I want you to do this. Go to my friend Rollins—I'll write down his address—and ask him to send me over a good doctor. He will know because his wife has been sick."

"Well, all right," said Ike. "But I think you're wasting your money. This doctor is pretty good."

"Yeah, he's got a good writing arm."

Ike laughed and shrugged. "All right."

He was back in an hour with Rollins and another doctor. When they walked into the apartment, the doctor sniffed and smiled and, turning to Rollins, nodded. He had a round, smiling, Oriental face. He made a quick examination and asked if I could urinate. Then, turning to Ike, he asked if I was subject to fits.

Ike told me, "He ask if you are ever crazy. I tell him, no, you just play with the cat some time."

Rollins spoke in his halting Spanish, looking for each word. "*Esto señor huele muy malo and quiere saber por qué.*" ("This man smells very bad and he wants to know why.")

The doctor explained it was an incipient uremia, but the danger was now past. I would have to stop drinking for a month. The doctor picked up an empty tequila bottle. "One more of these and you were dead." He was putting away his instruments. He wrote out a prescription for an anti-acid preparation to take every few hours, shook hands with me and Ike and left.

Next day I had the chucks and ate everything in sight. I stayed in bed three days. The metabolic set-up of alcoholism had ceased operating. When I started drinking again, I drank normally and never before the late afternoon. I stayed off the junk.

●

At that time, the G.I. students patronized Lola's during the day-time and the Ship Ahoy at night. Lola's was not exactly a bar. It was a small beer and soda joint. There was a boxful of beer and soda and ice at the left of the door as you came in. A counter with tube metal stools, covered in yellow glazed leather, ran down one side of the room as far as the jukebox. Tables were lined along the wall opposite the counter. The stools had long since lost the rubber caps for the legs and made a horrible screeching noise when the maid pushed them around to sweep. There was a kitchen in back, where a slovenly cook fried everything in rancid fat. There was neither past nor future in Lola's. The place was a waiting room.

I was sitting in Lola's reading the papers. After a while I put the paper down and looked around. At the next table somebody was talking about lobotomy. "They sever the nerves." At another table two young men were trying to make time with some Mexican girls. "*Mi amigo es muy, muy . . .*" He was looking for a word. The girls giggled. The conversations had a nightmare flatness, talking dice spilled in the tube metal chairs, human aggregates disintegrating in cosmic inanity, random events in a dying universe where every-thing is exactly what it appears to be, and no other relation than juxtaposition is possible.

I had been off junk two months. When you quit junk, every-thing seems flat, but you remember the shot schedule, the static horror of junk, your life draining into your arm three times a day. Every time exactly that much less.

I picked up a comic section from the next table. It was two days old. I put it down. Nothing to do. No place to go. My wife was in Acapulco with the children. I started back to my apartment, and spotted Old Ike a block away.

Some people you can spot as far as you can see; others you can't be sure of until you are close enough to touch them. Junkies are mostly in sharp focus. There had been a time when my blood pressure rose with pleasure at the sight of Old Ike. When you are on the junk, the pusher is like the loved one to the lover. You wait for his special step in the hall, his special knock, you scan the approaching faces on a city street. You can hallucinate every detail of his appearance as though he were standing there in the doorway, going into the old pusher joke: "Sorry to disappoint you, but I couldn't score." Watching the play of hope and anxiety on the other's face, savoring the feel of benevolent power, the power to give or withhold. Pat in New Orleans always pulled that routine. Bill Gains in New York. Old Ike would swear he didn't have anything, then slip the paper in my pocket and say, "Look, you had some all the time."

But I was off the junk now. Still a shot of morphine would be nice later when I was ready to sleep, or, better, a speedball, half cocaine, half morphine. I overtook Ike at the door of the apartment. I dropped a hand on his shoulder and he turned, his toothless, old-woman, junkie face breaking into a smile as he recognized me.

"Hello," he said.

"Haven't seen you in a dog's age," I said. "Where you been?"

He laughed. "I was in the can," he said. "Anyway, I didn't want to come around because I knew you was off. You off completely?"

"Yeah, I'm off."

"You wouldn't want a shot, then?" Old Ike was smiling.

"Well . . ." I felt a touch of the old excitement like meeting someone you used to go to bed with and suddenly the excitement is there and you both know that you are going to go to bed again.

Ike made a deprecatory gesture. "I got about ten centogramos here. Not enough to do me any good. Got a little coke, too."

"Come on in," I said.

I opened the door. The apartment was dark and musty. Clothes, books, newspapers, dirty plates and glasses were scattered around on chairs and tables and on the dirty floor. I pushed a stack of magazines off a ratty-looking couch.

"Sit down," I said. "You got the stuff on you?"

"Yeah, I got it planted." He opened his fly and extracted a rectangular paper packet—the junkie fold, with one end fitting into another. Inside the packet were two smaller packets, each similarly folded. He placed the papers on the table. Ike watched me with his bright brown eyes. His mouth, toothless and tightly closed, gave the impression of being sewed together.

I went into the bathroom to get my works. Needle, dropper, and a piece of cotton. I fished a teaspoon out of a pile of dirty dishes in the kitchen sink. Old Ike tore a long strip of paper and wet it with his mouth and wrapped it around the end of the dropper. He fitted the needle on over the wet paper collar. He opened one of the papers, with care not to flip the contents out by a spring motion of the waxed paper.

"This is the coke," he said. "Be careful, it's strong stuff."

I emptied the morphine paper into the spoon, adding a little water. About half a grain, I figured. Nearer four centogramos than ten. I held a match under the spoon until the morphine dissolved. You never heat coke. I added a little coke on the end of a knife blade and the coke dissolved instantly, like snow hitting water. I wrapped a frayed tie around my arm. My breath was short with excitement and my hands shook.

"Hit me, will you, Ike?"

Old Ike poked a gentle finger along the vein, holding the dropper poised between thumb and fingers. Ike was good. I hardly felt the needle slide in the vein. Dark, red blood spurted into the dropper.

"O.K.," he said. "Let it go."

I loosened the tie, and the dropper emptied into my vein. Coke hit my head, a pleasant dizziness and tension, while the morphine spread through my body in relaxing waves.

"Was that all right?" asked Ike, smiling.

"If God made anything better, he kept it for Himself," I said.

Ike was cleaning out the needle, squirting water through it. "Well," he said inanely, "when the roll is called up yonder we'll be there, right?"

I sat down on the couch and lit a cigarette. Old Ike went out into the kitchen to make a cup of tea. He began another installment in the endless saga of the Black Bastard. "The Black Bastard is putting out to three guys now. Pickpockets, all three of them, and they make pretty good in the market. Pay off the cops. He gives about four centogramos in a shot for fifteen pesos. He don't want to talk to me now he's doing good, the dirty bastard. He won't last a month, you wait and see. First time one of those guys gets caught he's going to stool like that!" Ike came to the kitchen door and snapped his fingers. "He won't last a month." His toothless mouth was twisted with hate.

●

When I jumped bail and left the States, the heat on junk already looked like something new and special. Initial symptoms of nation-wide hysteria were clear. Louisiana passed a law making it a crime to be a drug addict. Since no place or time is specified and the term "addict" is not clearly defined, no proof is necessary or even relevant under a law so formulated. No proof, and consequently, no trial. This is police-state legislation penalizing a state of being. Other states were emulating Louisiana. I saw my chance of escaping conviction dwindle daily as the anti-junk feeling mounted to a paranoid obsession, like anti-Semitism under the Nazis. So I decided to jump bail and live permanently outside the United States.

Safe in Mexico, I watched the anti-junk campaign. I read about child addicts and Senators demanding the death penalty for dope peddlers. It didn't sound right to me. Who wants kids for customers? They never have enough money and they always spill under questioning. Parents find out the kid is on junk and go to the law. I figured that either Stateside peddlers have gone simpleminded or the whole child-addict set-up is a propaganda routine to stir up anti-junk sentiment and pass some new laws.

Refugee hipsters trickled down into Mexico. "Six months for needle marks under the vag-addict law in California." "Eight years for a dropper in Washington." "Two to ten for selling in New York." A group of young hipsters dropped by my place every day to smoke weed.

There was Cash, a musician who played trumpet. There was Pete, a heavy-set blond, who could have modeled for a clean-cut American Boy poster. There was Johnny White, who had a wife and three children and looked like any average young American. There was Martin, a dark, good-looking kid of Italian stock. No zoot-suiters. The hipster has gone underground.

I learned the new hipster vocabulary: "pot" for weed, "twisted" for busted, "cool," an all-purpose word indicating anything you like or any situation that is not hot with the law. Conversely, anything you don't like is "uncool." From listening to these characters I got a picture of the situation in the U.S. A state of complete chaos where you never know who is who or where you stand. Old-time junkies told me: "If you ever see a man take a shot in the arm, you know he is not a Federal agent."

This is no longer true. Martin told me: "This cat fell in and says he's sick. He had the names of some friends of ours in 'Frisco. So these two other cats turned him on H and he was fixing right with them for over a week. And then they got busted. I wasn't along when it happened because I didn't dig this cat and I wasn't on H at the time. So the lawyer for these two cats that got twisted found out the cat was a Federal narcotics agent. An *agent*, not a pigeon. Even found out his name."

And Cash told me of cases where two hips take a fix together and then one pulls out his badge.

"How can you beat it?" Cash said. "I mean these guys are hips themselves. Guys just like you and me with one small difference—they work for Uncle."

Now that the Narcotics Bureau has taken it upon itself to incarcerate every addict in the U.S., they need more agents to do the work. Not only more agents, but a different type agent. Like during prohibition, when bums and hoodlums flooded the Internal Revenue Department, now addict-agents join the department for free junk and immunity. It is difficult to fake addiction. An addict knows an addict. The addict-agents manage to conceal their addiction, or, perhaps, they are tolerated because they get results. An agent who has to connect or go sick will bring a special zeal to his work.

Cash, the trumpet player, who did six months on the vag-addict rap, was a tall, skinny young man with a ragged goatee and dark glasses. He wore shoes with thick crepe leather soles, expensive camel-hair shirts, and a leather jacket you tie with a belt in front. You could see he had about a hundred dollars in haberdashery on his person. His old lady had the money and Cash was spending it. When I met him, the money was about gone. Cash told me: "Women come to me. I don't care about women. The only thing gives me a real kick is playing trumpet."

Cash was a junk mooch on wheels. He made it difficult to refuse. He would lend me small amounts of money—never enough to cover the junk he used—and then say he had given me all his money and had no money left to buy codeine pills. He told me he was getting off the junk. When he arrived in Mexico, I gave him half a grain of M and he went on the nod. I guess the stuff they sell now Stateside is cut right down to the paper.

After that, he would drop around every day and ask me for "half a fix." Or he would mooch junk off Old Ike, who couldn't turn down anyone sick. I told Old Ike to pack him in, and explained to Cash I wasn't in the junk business. I kept a little on hand for emergencies like when out of town friends dropped in sick, and Old Ike wasn't really in the business either. Certainly he wasn't in the business for nothing. In short, we were not the junkies' benevolent society. From then on, I didn't see much of Cash.

●

Peyote is a new kick in the States. It isn't under the Harrison Act, and you can buy it from herb dealers through the mail. I had never tried peyote, and I asked Johnny White if he could score for peyote in Mexico.

He said, "Yes. An herb dealer here sells it. He invited all of us to come to his place and eat peyote with him. You can come along if you like. I want to see if he has anything I can take back to the States and sell there."

"Why not take back peyote?"

"It doesn't keep. It rots or dries up in a few days and loses its kick." We went to the herb dealer's house and he brought out a bowl of peyote, a grater and a pot of tea.

Peyote is a small cactus and only the top part that appears above the ground is eaten. This is called a button. The buttons are prepared by peeling off the bark and fuzz and running the button through a grater until it looks like avocado salad. Four buttons is the average dose for a beginner.

We washed down the peyote with tea. I came near gagging on it several times. Finally I got it all down and sat there waiting for something to happen. The herb dealer brought out some bark he claimed was like opium. Johnny rolled a cigarette of the stuff and passed it around. Pete and Johnny said, "Crazy! This is the greatest."

I smoked some and felt a little dizzy and my throat hurt. But Johnny bought some of that awful-smelling bark with the intention of selling it to desperate hipsters in the U.S.

After ten minutes I began to feel sick from the peyote. Everyone told me, "Keep it down, man." I held out ten minutes more, then headed for the W.C. ready to throw in the towel, but I couldn't vomit. My whole body contracted in a convulsive spasm, but the peyote wouldn't come up. It wouldn't stay down either.

Finally, the peyote came up solid like a ball of hair, solid all the way up, clogging my throat. As horrible a sensation as I ever stood still for. After that, the high came on slow.

Peyote high is something like benzedrine high. You can't sleep and your pupils are dilated. Everything looks like a peyote plant. I was driving in the car with the Whites and Cash and Pete. We were going out to Cash's place in the Lomas. Johnny said, "Look at the bank along the road. It looks like a peyote plant."

I turned around to look, and was thinking, "What a damn silly idea. People can talk themselves into anything." But it did look like a peyote plant. Everything I saw looked like a peyote plant.

Our faces swelled under the eyes and our lips got thicker through some glandular action of the drug. We actually looked like Indians. The others claimed they felt primitive and were laying around on the grass and acting the way they figured Indians act. I didn't feel any different from ordinary except high like on benny.

We sat up all night talking and listening to Cash's records. Cash told me about several cats from 'Frisco who had kicked junk habits with peyote. "It seems like they didn't want junk when they started using peyote." One of these junkies came down to Mexico and started taking peyote with the Indians. He was using it all the time in large quantities: up to twelve buttons in one dose. He died of a condition that was diagnosed as polio.

I understand, however, that the symptoms of peyote poisoning and polio are identical.

I couldn't sleep until the next morning at dawn, and then I had a nightmare every time I dozed off. In one dream, I was coming down with rabies. I looked in the mirror and my face changed and I began howling. In another dream, I had a chlorophyll habit. Me and about five other chlorophyll addicts are waiting to score on the landing of a cheap Mexican hotel. We turn green and no one can kick a chlorophyll habit. One shot and you're hung for life. We are turning into plants.

●

The young hipsters seem lacking in energy and spontaneous enjoyment of life. The mention of pot or junk will galvanize them like a shot of coke. They jump around and say, "Too much! Crazy! Man, let's pick up! Let's get loaded." But after a shot, they slump into a chair like a resigned baby waiting for life to bring the bottle again.

I found that their interests were very limited. Particularly, I noticed they seemed less interested in sex than my generation. Some of them expressed themselves as not getting any kick out of sex at all. I have frequently been misled to believe a young man was queer after observing his indifference to women, and found out subsequently he was not at all homosexual, but simply disinterested in the whole subject.

●

Bill Gains threw in the towel and moved to Mexico. I met him at the airport. He was loaded on H and goof balls. His pants were spotted with blood where he had been fixing on the plane with a safety pin. You make a hole with the pin, and put the dropper over (not in) the hole, and the solution goes right in. With this method, you don't need a needle, but it takes an old-time junkie to make it work. You have to use exactly the right degree of pressure feeding in the solution. I tried it once and the junk squirted out to the side and I lost it all. But when Gains made a hole in his flesh, the hole stayed open waiting for junk.

Bill was an old-timer. He knew everybody in the business. He had an excellent reputation and he could score as long as anyone sold junk. I figured the situation must be desperate when Bill packed in and left the States.

"Sure, I can score," he told me. "But if I stay in the States I'll wind up doing about ten years."

I took a shot with him, and the what-happened-to-so-and-so routine set in.

"Old Bart died on the Island. Louie the Bellhop went wrong. Tony and Nick went wrong. Herman didn't make parole. The Gimp got five to ten. Marvin the waiter died from an overdose."

I remembered the way Marvin used to pass out every time he took a shot. I could see him lying on the bed in some cheap hotel, the dropper full of blood hanging to his vein like a glass leech, his face turning blue around the lips.

"What about Roy?" I asked.

"Didn't you hear about him? He went wrong and hanged himself in the Tombs." It seems the law had Roy on three counts, two larceny, one narcotics. They promised to drop all charges if Roy would set up Eddie Crump, an old-time pusher. Eddie only served people he knew well, and he knew Roy. The law double-crossed Roy after they got Eddie. They dropped the narcotics charge, but not the two larceny charges. So Roy was slated to follow Eddie up to Riker's Island, where Eddie was doing pen indefinite, which is maximum in City Prison. Three years, five months, and six days.

Roy hanged himself in the Tombs, where he was awaiting transfer to Riker's.

Roy had always taken an intolerant and puritanical view of pigeons. "I don't see how a pigeon can live with himself," he said to me once.

I asked Bill about child addicts. He nodded and smiled, a sly gloating smile. "Yes, Lexington is full of young kids now."

●

One day I was in the Opera Bar in Mexico City and ran into a politician I knew. He was standing at the bar with a napkin tucked in his collar, eating a steak. Between mouthfuls he asked me did I know anyone who might be interested to buy an ounce of heroin.

I said, "Maybe. How much?"

He said, "They want five hundred dollars."

I talked to Bill Gains and he said, "All right. If it's anywhere near pure I'll take it. But no sight unseen. I have to try the stuff first."

So I arranged it with the politician and we went down to his office. He brought the stuff out of a drawer in a finger stall and laid it on the desk beside a .45 automatic.

"I don't know anything about this stuff," he said. "All I use is cocaine."

I poured some out on a piece of paper. It didn't look right to me. Sort of gray-black. I guess "they" had cooked it up some place on a kitchen stove.

Gains took a shot, but he was so loaded already on goof balls and M he couldn't tell one way or the other. So I took a shot and told him. "It's H, but there's something not exactly right about it."

People meanwhile were walking in and out the office. Nobody paid us any mind sitting there on the couch with our sleeves rolled up, probing for veins with the needle. Anything can happen in the office of a Mexican politician.

Anyway Bill bought the H and I went somewhere and didn't see him until next day, eleven o'clock on a bright Mexican morning, standing by my bed, cadaverous in his blue-black overcoat, midnight blue, his eyes brighter than I ever saw them, gleaming in the darkness of the curtained room. He stood there with the impurities of amateur H in his brain like spirochetes.

"You just going to lie there on your bed?" he asked. "With all these shipments coming in?"

"Why not?" I said, annoyed. "This isn't any fuckin' farm . . . shipments of what?"

"Good, pure M," he said. Then shoes, overcoat and all, he got right in bed with me.

"What's the matter with you?" I asked. "You crazy?" And looking into his bright blank eyes I saw that he was.

I got him back to his room and confiscated what was left of the piece of H.

Old Ike showed, and we poured ten centimeters of laudanum down Bill's gullet. After that he stopped raving about "shipments of good, pure M" and went to sleep.

"Maybe he die," Old Ike said, "and they blame it onto me."

"If he dies, you clear out," I said. "Listen. He's got six hundred dollars cash in his wallet. Why leave it for some Mexican cop to steal?"

We shook the place down looking for the wallet, but could not find it. We looked everywhere except under the mattress where Bill was lying.

Next day Bill was good as new, but he couldn't find his money.

"You must have stashed it," I said. "Look under the mattress."

He turned up the mattress and the wallet sprung open, it was so full of crisp money.

•

At this time, I was not on junk, but I was a long way from being clean in the event of an unforeseen shake. There was always some weed around, and people were using my place as a shooting gallery. I was taking chances and not making centavo one. I decided it was about time to move out from under and head south.

When you give up junk, you give up a way of life. I have seen junkies kick and hit the lush and wind up dead in a few years. Suicide is frequent among ex-junkies. Why does a junkie quit junk of his own will? You never know the answer to that question. No conscious tabulation of the disadvantages and horrors of junk gives you the emotional drive to kick. The decision to quit junk is a cellular decision, and once you have decided to quit you cannot go back to junk permanently any more than you could stay away from it before. Like a man who has been away a long time, you see things different when you return from junk.

I read about a drug called *yage*, used by Indians in the headwaters of the Amazon. Yage is supposed to increase telepathic sensitivity. A Colombian scientist isolated from yage a drug he called *telepathine*.

I know from my own experience that telepathy is a fact. I have no interest in proving telepathy or anything to anybody. I do want usable knowledge of telepathy. What I look for in any relationship is contact on the nonverbal level of intuition and feeling, that is, telepathic contact.

Apparently, I am not the only one interested in yage. The Russians are using this drug in experiments on slave labor. They want to induce states of automatic obedience and literal thought control. The basic con. No build-up, no routine, just move in on someone's psyche and give orders. The deal is certain to backfire because telepathy is not of its nature a one-way set-up, or a set-up of sender and receiver at all.

I decided to go down to Colombia and score for yage. Bill Gains is squared away with Old Ike. My wife and I are separated. I am ready to move on south and look for the uncut kick that opens out instead of narrowing down like junk.

Kick is seeing things from a special angle. Kick is momentary freedom from the claims of the aging, cautious, nagging, frightened flesh. Maybe I will find in yage what I was looking for in junk and weed and coke. Yage may be the final fix.

# GLOSSARY

"Jive talk" is used more in connection with marijuana than with junk. In the past few years, however, the use of junk has spread into "hip," or "jive talking" circles, and junk lingo has, to some extent, merged with "jive talk." For example, "Are you anywhere?" can mean "Do you have any junk or weed on your person?" Jive talk always refers to more than one level of fact. "Are you anywhere?" can also refer to your psychic condition: "Are you holding psychically?"

**Are you anywhere? Are you holding?**   Do you have any junk or weed on you?

**Beat**   To take someone's money. For example, addict A says he will buy junk for addict B but keeps the money instead. Addict A has "beat" addict B for the money.

**Benny**   Benzedrine. It can also mean overcoat.

**Bring down, Drag**   The opposite of high. Depressing.

**Brown Stuff, or Mud**   Opium.

**Burn Down**   To overdo or run into the ground. Certain restaurants are used so much by junkies as meeting-places that the restaurant gets known to the police. Then the restaurant is "burned down."

**Burning Down Habit, an Oil Burner Habit**   A heavy habit.

**C, Coke, Charge, Charly**   Cocaine.

**Caps**   Capsules of heroin.

**Cat**   A man.

**Chick**   A woman.

**Chucks**   Excessive hunger, often for sweets. This comes on an addict when he has kicked his habit far enough so that he starts to eat. When an addict is cut off the junk, he can't eat for several days. I have seen addicts who did not eat for a month. Then he gets the "chucks" and eats everything in sight.

**Clean**   A user is clean if he does not have any junk on his person or premises in the event of a search by the law.

**Cold Turkey**   To quit using suddenly and completely with no gradual reduction of the dose. Almost always involuntary.

**Collar**   Strip of paper wrapped around a dropper to make a tight fit with a needle.

**Come on**   The way someone acts, his general manner and way of approaching others.

**Come up**   A lush waking up while he is being robbed.

**Cook**   To dissolve junk in water heated in a spoon or other container.

**Cop**   To pass a cap of junk to someone; to hold out a hand for a cap.

**Copper Jitters**   Exaggerated fear of cops. When you have the Copper Jitters, everybody looks like a cop.

**Croaker**   A doctor.

**Dig**   To size up, to understand, to like, or enjoy.

**Fey**   White.

**Five-Twenty-Nine**   Five months and twenty-nine days. This is the term in the workhouse that a lush-worker receives for "jostling." If a detective sees a lush-worker approach or touch a lush, he places a "jostling" charge.

**Flop**   Drunk passed out on a subway station bench.

**G**   One grain. Morphine is the standard for junk measurement. One-half grain of morphine is one "fix." A capsule of heroin should contain at least the equivalent of ½ grain of morphine. Heroin is seven times as strong as morphine.

**Gold**   Money.

**H, Horse, Henry**   Heroin.

**Habit**   A junk habit. It takes at least a month of daily use to get a needle habit, two months for a smoking habit, four months for an eating habit.

**Heat, Fuzz**   Law, cops, the police.

**Heavy**   Junk, as opposed to marijuana.

**Hep or Hip**   Someone who knows the score. Someone who understands "jive talk." Someone who is "with it." The expression is not subject to definition because, if you don't "dig" what it means, no one can ever tell you.

**High**   Feeling good, in a state of euphoria. You can be "high" on benny, weed, lush, nutmeg, ammonia (The Scrubwoman's Kick). You can be high without any chemical boot, just feeling good.

**Hog**   Anyone who uses more junk than you do. To use over five grains per day puts a user in the hog class.

**Hook**   Lush-workers usually work in pairs. One lush-worker covers his partner with a newspaper, while the other goes through the lush's pockets. The one who covers the other is the "hook."

**Hooked**   To get a habit.

**Hot, Uncool**   Somebody liable to attract attention from the law. A place watched by the law.

**Hot Shot**   Poison, usually strychnine, passed to an addict as junk. The peddler sometimes slips a hot shot to an addict because the addict is giving information to the law.

**The Hype, The Bill**   A short-change racket.

**John**   Someone who keeps a woman and spends money on her.

**Joy Bang**   An occasional shot by someone who does not have a habit.

**Kick**   A word with several meanings. It can mean the effect of a drug or a mood brought on by some place, or person. "This bar gives me bad kicks." "This bar depresses me." You can also be on "good kicks." A kick is also a special way of looking at things so that the man who is "on kicks" sees things from a special angle.

**Kick a Habit**   To quit using junk and get over a habit.

**Lay on**   Give.

**Loaded, On the Nod**   Full of junk.

**Lush-worker**   A thief who specializes in robbing drunks on the subway.

**M, M.S.**   Morphine. M.S. stands for Morphine Sulphate, which is the morphine salt most commonly used in the U.S.

**Main Line**   Vein, a vein injection.

**Making Cars**   Breaking into parked cars and stealing the contents.

**Mark**   Someone easy to rob, like a drunk with a roll of money.

**Meet**   An appointment, usually between peddler and customer.

**Nembies, Goof Balls, Yellow Jackets**   Nembutal capsules. Nembutal is a barbiturate used by junkies "to take the edge off" when they can't get junk.

**P.G.**   Paregoric. A weak, camphorated tincture of opium, two grains to the ounce. Two ounces will fix a sick addict. It can be bought without prescription in some states. P.G. can be injected intravenously after burning out the alcohol and straining out the camphor.

**The People**   Narcotics agents. A New Orleans expression.

**Pickup**   To use. Generally refers to weed. But you can "pickup" on nembies, lush, or junk.

**Piece**   Gun.

**Pigeon, Fink, Rat**   Informer.

**Plant, Stash**   To hide something, usually junk, or an "outfit."

**Poke**   Wallet.

**Pop, Bang, Shot, Fix**   Injection of junk.

**Pop Corn**   Someone with a legitimate job, as opposed to a "hustler" or thief.

**Pusher, Peddler, "The Man"**   Junk seller. "The Man" is another New Orleans expression, and can also refer to a Narcotics Agent.

**Put Down a Hype or Routine**   To give someone a story, to persuade, or con someone.

**Put Your Hand Out**   To go through a lush's pockets.

**Score**   To buy junk or marijuana.

**Serve, Take Care Of**   To sell junk to a user.

**Shake, Rumble**   Search by the law.

**Skin**   Skin injection.

**Sick, Gaping, Yenning**   Sickness caused by lack of junk.

**Smash**   Change, money, coins.

**Square**   The opposite of hip. Someone who does not understand the jive.

**Spade**   A Negro.

**Speed Ball**   Cocaine mixed with morphine or heroin.

**Spike**   Needle.

**Stuff, Junk**   General terms for opium and all derivatives of opium: morphine, heroin, Dilaudid, pantopon, codeine, dionine.

**Take a Fall**   To get arrested.

**Tea head, Head, Viper**   User of marijuana.

**Tie-up**   Tie, or handkerchief, used as a tourniquet for a vein shot.

**User, Hyp, Junkie, Junker, Shmecker**   Junk addict.

**Weed, Tea, Gage, Grass, Greefa, Muggles, Pot, Hash**   Marijuana, hashish.

**White stuff**   Morphine, or heroin, as opposed to "brown stuff."

**Working the Hole**   Lush-working.

**Works, Outfit, Joint**   A user's outfit for injecting junk. Consists of an eyedropper, hypodermic needle, strip of paper to fit the dropper tight into the needle, and a spoon or other container in which to dissolve the junk.

**Write**   To write a narcotic prescription. To "make a Croaker for a Script" means to persuade a doctor to write a prescription for junk.

**Wrong**   Term used to describe an informer.

**Yen Pox**   Ash of opium after the opium has been smoked. Yen Pox contains about the same morphine content as opium before smoking. It can be eaten with hot coffee, or dissolved in water and injected intravenously.

It should be understood that the meanings of these words are subject to rapid changes, and that a word that has one hip meaning one year may have another the next. The hip sensibility mutates. For example, "Fey" means not only white, but fated or demoniac. Not only do the words change meanings but meanings vary locally at the same time. A final glossary, therefore, cannot be made of words whose intentions are fugitive.

# APPENDIX 1

## CHAPTER 28 OF
## THE ORIGINAL "JUNK" MANUSCRIPT

At this time I read *The Cancer Biopathy* by Wilhelm Reich. Reich says that Life is a charge, and the charged particles on which life depends he calls "orgones." When your "orgone" charge gives out, you die. Orgones are everywhere in the atmosphere, and in all living and dead matter. An orgone envelope surrounds the earth, and orgones charge the sunlight. Orgones give off a blue color.

Philosophers have been talking for a long time about "life-force" and "cosmic energy." But Reich's orgones are a definite force that can be measured, concentrated and used. He claims clinical results in treating with orgone therapy cancer and other "biopathies." By a "cancer biopathy," Reich means the whole cancer set-up which is established long before the symptoms of cancer appear. Reich devised a method for concentrating orgones based on the experimental finding that orgones are absorbed and retained by organic matter, but pass freely through metal. He built a box with organic material on the outside and a lining of sheet iron inside. The orgones are caught and absorbed by the outer layer of organic matter and pass freely through the sheet iron to the inside of the box. The passage of orgones from the inside of the box out is retarded by a layer of organic matter behind the sheet metal lining. So orgones are coming into the box faster than they can get out and the result is a concentration of orgones inside the box. Reich calls this box an accumulator. The accumulators designed for orgone therapy are constructed with several organic-metal layers to increase the concentration of orgones, and shaped like a steam cabinet so the patient can sit down inside the box.

Cancer is rot of tissue in a living organism. In junk sickness the junk-dependent cells die and are replaced. Cancer is a premature death process. The cancer patient shrinks. A sick junkie shrinks— I have lost up to fifteen pounds in three days. So I figured if the accumulator is therapy for cancer, it should be therapy for the after-effects of junk sickness.

Accumulators are manufactured by the Orgone Institute in New York. They do not sell or rent accumulators. They allow you to use one if you contribute ten dollars per month to the Orgone Institute. I sent three months' contribution in advance and asked them to express collect me an accumulator. They sent back three forms to be filled out and signed. One was a we-are-not-responsible-for-anything affidavit. There was a pledge for me to sign that I would not let anyone else use my accumulator and would report to the Institute if I saw anyone building an accumulator, and a questionnaire to be filled out by my physician what was wrong with me and why did I need an accumulator. I did not want to explain about orgones to some croaker who would take me for a lunatic. Besides, I did not like the way the Orgone people were coming on. Why say "contributions" when you mean rent? And the pledge was ridiculous. So I wrote them to send my money back and here are your forms.

I bought sheet metal, wood and a roll of rock wool, and built an accumulator about the size and shape of a small outhouse. I located it outside (it was not movable), so it would get all the orgones available. Constant use of junk over a period of years has given me the habit of directing attention inward. When I went into the accumulator and sat down I noticed a special silence that you sometimes feel in deep woods, sometimes on a city street, a hum that is more a rhythmic vibration than a sound. My skin prickled and I experienced an aphrodisiac effect similar to good strong weed. No doubt about it, orgones are as definite a force as electricity. After using the accumulator for several days my energy came back to normal. I began to eat, and could not sleep more than eight hours. I was out of the post cure drag. I bought some books on pharmacology to find out what I could about allergy, shock and the antihistamine drugs.

Withdrawal symptoms are allergic symptoms: sneezing, coughing, running at the eyes and nose, vomiting, diarrhea, hive-like conditions of the skin. Severe withdrawal symptoms are shock symptoms: lowered blood pressure, loss of body fluid and shrinking of the organism as in the death process, weakness, involuntary orgasms, death through collapse of the circulatory system. If an addict dies from junk withdrawal, he dies of allergic shock.

All the symptoms of shock can be produced by an overdose of histamine. Histamine is produced by body tissue wherever injury occurs. Histamine enlarges blood vessels so that extra blood comes to the place of injury. When a blood vessel is enlarged, its walls are stretched thin and porous and so fluid escapes. Loss of blood leads to lowered blood pressure. Excess histamine leads to a lowering of blood pressure and shock, as occurs in serious injury. Adrenaline is the body's defense against excess histamine, and before the specific antihistamine drugs, was the only chemical antidote for histamine poisoning.

Most animals have been addicted to junk under experimental conditions. After receiving the shots for a period of ten days or so, the animal reacts to the hypodermic as if it were a food plate, rushing eagerly forward to get his shot. When junk is withdrawn, the animal shows withdrawal symptoms: No other substance has produced this syndrome in animals—that the animal eagerly seeks the substance as if it were food. When the substance is withdrawn the animal shows definite physical symptoms. It would seem that junk is the only habit-forming drug. Cats cannot be addicted to morphine, as they react to an injection of morphine with acute delirium. Cats have a relatively small quantity of histamine in the blood stream. It would seem that histamine is the defense against morphine, and that cats, lacking this defense, cannot tolerate morphine. Perhaps the mechanism of withdrawal is this: Histamine is produced by the body as a defense against morphine during the period of addiction. When the drug is withdrawn, the body continues to produce histamine.

If you have no histamine-produced symptoms, antihistamine drugs produce no effect. I bought some ampoules of an antihistamine drug and shot a double dose. I experienced nothing but a slight depression (the depressing effects of some antihistamine preparations are "side effects" which chemists intend to eliminate). A shot that felt exactly like morphine when I was sick now produced effects that were barely perceptible. It seems that a user does not get a positive kick from junk. What he gets is relief from withdrawal sickness. Possibly all pleasure is basically relief from a condition of need, or tension. Junk is the medium in which the junk-dependent cells live. When junk is cut off junk cells die, and excess histamine is produced to carry away the dead cells. The function of allergic sneezing, running at the nose and eyes, vomiting and diarrhea, is to get rid of something. During addiction, junk is a biologic necessity, like food, water or sex. There is no other substance that becomes in this way a part of the biologic rhythm of the body. When you are junk sick you dream about junk. A curious fact about junk dreams is that something always happens to prevent you from getting a shot. The cops rush in, the needle stops up, the dropper breaks. Anyway, you never get it. I have talked to other users, and I have never known anyone who ever got fixed in a dream. Junk seems to displace the sex drive. When you are on junk the sex drive virtually disappears. When you start to kick you experience sex feelings of adolescent intensity, often spontaneous orgasms.

Junkies live a long time and often look younger than they are. When you stop growing you start dying. An addict never stops growing. Most users periodically kick the habit, which involves shrinking of the organism and replacement of the junk-dependent cells. Scientists recently experimented with a worm that they were able to shrink by withholding food. By periodically shrinking the worm so that it was in continual growth, its life was prolonged indefinitely. A user is in a continual state of shrinking and growing in his daily cycle of shot-need for junk-shot.

Perhaps the reason for the short life of the American business man is that he experiences no cycle of shrinking and growth. He does not exercise, he is never hungry. His life is a one-way process. When his organism reaches maturity it can only start dying.

Opium is formed in the unripe seed pods of the poppy plant. Its function is to protect the seeds from drying out until the plant is ready to die and the seeds are mature. Junk continues to function in the human organism as it did in the seed pod of the poppy. It protects and cushions the body like a warm blanket while death grows to maturity inside. When a junkie is really loaded with junk he looks dead. Junk turns the user into a plant. Plants do not feel pain since pain has no function in a stationary organism. Junk is a pain killer. A plant has no libido in the human or animal sense. Junk replaces the sex drive. Seeding is the sex of the plant and the function of opium is to delay seeding.

Perhaps the intense discomfort of withdrawal is the transition from plant back to animal, from a painless, sexless, timeless state back to sex and pain and time, from death back to life.

# APPENDIX 2

## "INTRODUCTION" TO
## THE ORIGINAL "JUNK" MANUSCRIPT

In this book I have written what I know about junk and the people who use it. The narrative is fiction, but it is based on facts of my experience.

When I say junk I mean opium or derivatives of opium; morphine, heroin, pantopon, Dilaudid, codeine are the opium derivatives generally used in the States.

I would not write about junk unless I had something special to say on the subject that had not already been said. The action of junk on the user is generically different from the action of any other drug. I think that junk is transitional between living and dead matter, between animal and vegetable life. You cannot avoid the feeling that junk is in some way alive.

I can walk around in a strange town and say, "This is a junk neighborhood." I don't have to see junkies waiting around for the connection to spot junk territory. When I pass a place where junk has changed hands the junk in my cells ticks like a Geiger counter. My junk counter is generally accurate, but sometimes I spot a place that used to be junk territory and is no longer in use. The counter tells me: "Junk here," but does not say when. Why doesn't the counter tick when I pass a drugstore? Junk needs a host before it can take on its special junk qualities, because junk is a parasite that can live only in the blood of a user.

The dependence on junk is not confined to addicts. Many narcotics agents and non-using peddlers are as much hung up on junk as any addict. They may not use it, but they need junk, and not just to make a living. The zeal of some agents derives from a special relation to junk. They are addicts at second-hand, and for that condition there is no cure.

Anyone who has ever been an addict will always look like junk to anyone who can see junk. He may not have used it for ten years, but the junk is still there.

Official propaganda opposes any factual statement about junk, so that almost nothing accurate has been written on the subject. When newspapers, magazines and movies deal with junk they seldom deviate from the officially sponsored myth. I will go over the main points of this myth.

1. *All drugs are more or less similar and all are habit forming.* This myth lumps cocaine, marijuana and junk together. Marijuana is not at all habit forming and its action is almost the direct opposite from junk action. There is no habit to cocaine. You can develop a tremendous craving for cocaine, but you won't be sick if you can't get it. When you have a junk habit, on the other hand, you live in a state of chronic poisoning for which junk itself is the specific antidote. If you don't get the antidote at eight-hour intervals, and enough of it, you develop symptoms of allergic poisoning: yawning, sneezing, watering of the eyes and nose, cramps, vomiting and diarrhea, hot and cold flashes, loss of appetite, insomnia, restlessness and weakness, in some cases circulatory collapse and death from allergic shock.

The junkie needs junk like the diabetic needs insulin. Junk creates a deficiency so that the body cannot function without more junk at regular intervals. It seems that junk takes over the function of certain body chemicals, and that the body does not produce these chemicals during addiction. Withdrawal of junk creates a deficiency condition which continues until the body gets back in production on the chemicals that were replaced by junk. When I say "habit forming drug" I mean a drug that alters the endocrine balance of the body in such a way that the body requires that drug in order to function. So far as I know, junk is the only habit forming drug according to this definition.

2. *A drug habit is formed instantly, on first use, or at most, after three or four shots.* From this notion derive the stories of people becoming addicts after using a few "headache pills" given them by the Sympathetic Stranger. Actually, a non-user would have to take a shot every day for at least a month to get any kind of habit. The Stranger would go broke handing out samples. But a cured addict, even if he has not used it for years, can get a new habit in a few days. He is allergic to junk.

3. *Once the habit is formed escape is almost impossible.* Actually, a habit is easily cured. The usual cure takes from ten days to three weeks. You don't need any "will power." If the cure is done right there is very little discomfort.

4. *Addiction ruins the health and leads to early death.* As I read in a magazine article, "Morphine addicts have numbered days on earth." Who hasn't?

The addict enjoys normal health and lives as long, or longer, than the average. Junk conveys a considerable immunity to respiratory complaints. During the "flu" epidemic of 1918 junkies were found to be immune to flu and some addicts were let out of jail to help care for the sick. On the other hand, all users suffer somewhat from constipation and loss of appetite. Most of them lose weight, often running from ten to twenty pounds below normal weight during addiction.

5. *Addicts never get enough. They have to keep raising the dosage. They need more and more. Finally, I quote from a recent movie called* Johnny Stool Pigeon. *"They tear the clothes off their skinny bodies and die screaming" for more junk.*

This is preposterous. Addicts get enough and they do not have to raise the dosage. I know addicts who have used the same dose for years. Of course, addicts do occasionally die if they are cut off the junk cold. They don't die because they need more and more. They die because they can't get any.

6. *Addicts want to get others on the stuff.* This silly idea seems to be universal. Every time I take a fall the laws say to my wife: "It's a wonder he didn't get you on the junk." Why in hell should I? I have enough trouble keeping up my own habit. Of course, a peddling addict wants to get other people on the stuff so he will have more customers.

7. *There is a clear line between addict and peddler. The authorities pity the addict and are out only to get the peddler.* I have never seen an addict who did not sell, or a street peddler who did not use. There is no line at all. The authorities make no distinction, and the penalty for selling and possession are about the same.

8. *Peddlers try to get high school children on junk, or marijuana. A recent magazine article depicts peddlers slipping laudanum into the Coca-Cola of teenagers.*

This is utterly ridiculous. No peddler wants kids for customers. They never have enough money, they talk too much and they cannot stand up under police questioning. The best customers are the old-timers. They know all the angles and generally have some source of revenue.

9. *There is a connection between junk and insanity. Addicts turn into maniacs when they cannot get junk.*

Actually, I have never seen or heard of an insane addict. For some reason, the two conditions do not occur together.

10. *There is a connection between addiction and crime. Marijuana, especially, is supposed to cause people to commit crimes.*

There is no direct connection between crime and drug intoxication that I have ever seen or heard of. The people who talk about drugs causing crime never seem to follow through and take into account the vast number of crimes committed by drunks. Alcohol is a crime-producing drug that outclasses all others. Of course, a lot of junkies steal to keep up their habit. It isn't easy to get up $10–15 per day, which is what the addict has to pay out for a day's supply of junk in the U.S.

Any anti-narcotic legislation is considered a good thing by the public. For this reason the field of narcotic legislation has become a testing ground for a type of law new to this country but familiar in police states. In the states of Louisiana and Kentucky it is a crime punishable by imprisonment (La., two to five years; Ky., one year) to *be* an addict. This is police-state legislation penalizing a condition or state of being. In the Louisiana law, no time or place is specified, nor is the term "addict" defined.

A cure is now available for addiction in the antihistamine drugs. Withdrawal sickness is an allergy, and the new anti-allergic drugs relieve its symptoms. The old-type reduction cures all use habit forming drugs, and withdrawal symptoms return after the drug is finally cut off. But antihistamine drugs are not habit-forming, and when these drugs are used there is no return of withdrawal symptoms. The antihistamine cure is not in general use. I have seen no mention of it in any medical publication. It would appear that this cure is being deliberately withheld from the public. Federal and state narcotic authorities put every obstacle in the way of addicts who want a cure. No reduction cures are given in city or state institutions. Two hundred dollars is minimum for a ten-day cure in a private sanatorium. Hospitals are forbidden by law to give addicts any junk. I knew an addict who needed an operation for stomach cancer. The hospital could not give him any junk. Sudden withdrawal of junk plus the operation would likely have killed him so he decided to skip the operation. Lexington and Fort Worth are the only two public institutions in the U.S. that give reduction cures. Both are usually full. According to bureaucratic regulations, anyone seeking admission to either hospital must send an application (in triplicate, of course) to Washington and wait several months to be admitted. Then he must stay at least six months. In Louisiana a man could be arrested as a drug addict if he applied for the cure.

I do not intend to correct popular misconceptions about junk by presenting the facts that are already known to anyone informed on the subject. I am using the known facts as a starting point in an attempt to reach facts that are not known.

# APPENDIX 3

## LETTER FROM WILLIAM BURROUGHS
## TO A. A. WYN [1959]

Wyn Publishing Co.
23 West 47 Street
NYC

Reading over a published copy of JUNKIE, I found that a number of alterations and omissions had been made. I am listing alterations that I feel to be unwarranted, to blur or completely obscure the original meaning. I strongly urge that these alterations be omitted in the event of a reprinting as they detract from my book.

I spent a year working on this manuscript. I checked over every word many times. Good or bad the manuscript I submitted was written exactly the way I intended. I have not found one instance of a change that I consider necessary, though I am in agreement with some of the omissions. This list is not complete, but covers only the more flagrant mutilations:

*Preface. Page 8, Line 8:* "Put me down as an out and out con." This does not mean anything. The original phrasing was: They "put down an out and out con." Meaning, they attempted to con (deceive) me. There is no such word as "con" used as a noun applied to a person. A con man is never referred to as "a con." Because the editor is not familiar with an expression he is not justified in assuming it to be meaningless, and altering it in accordance with ill-informed caprice.

*Page 21, Line 1:* "His complexion faded . . ." Original was "was fading." I meant his complexion *had been* brown and now *was* fading to yellow.

*Page 85, Line 22:* "He put me down a routine." This is never said. The original was "He put down a routine." I wrote it like that because that is the way it would be said.

*Page 93, Line 5:* "We'll get to see him any time." Original was "We are subject to see him at any time." "Subject to" means liable to. It is an expression much used in New Orleans. *We are liable to* is not synonymous with *we will get to.*

*Page 120, last line:* "And five more that would get it filled." Original was "and five more would get it filled." I meant five more pesos. Not doctors. Doctors do not fill scripts in Mexico.

This list is incomplete. I am merely enumerating the most pointless changes. As regards omissions, I consider the omission of page 150 in the original M.S. in which I describe my first meeting with Old Ike, to be a definite loss. This is not only my opinion, but is shared by everyone I know who read the original M.S. and the published version.

# APPENDIX 4

## "*JUNKIE:* AN APPRECIATION" (1952)
### BY ALLEN GINSBERG

The reader, after a cursory glance at this book, will discover that the author is no ordinary junkie. He seems to have taken pains to disguise the fact that he is also a man with a background that might astonish many of his readers.

Born just before the twenties, of a respectable middle-class family in a large Midwestern city—a family the name of which is a household word in America for the inventions and commercial exploits of its nineteenth-century forebears—he received a good education at a private school where he was known as an aloof, and presumably shy aristocrat with phenomenal scholarly aptitudes and a startling penchant for wildness. His first literary venture was a history of Rome, done (in true 19th-century manner) from common Latin sources, at the age of 15. Having set a record for scholarship at this school, he was sent to Harvard, where he studied English literature. Little is known of his experiences there, except that he was supposed to have kept a weasel on a chain in his rooms, and a portrait of his family house on the walls. When questioned about the latter, his invariable remark, with an offhand gesture of the palm, was "Yes isn't it hideous?" There remains of his undergraduate days only one literary specimen, a 20-page playlet set on a sinking ship in the middle of the Atlantic, with several of his acquaintances cast in varying roles of hysteria, terror, malice, and last-minute turpitude.

On his graduation in the early thirties, considering he had said all he had to say literarily in the aforementioned charade, he studied anthropology, again at Harvard, specializing in Aztec and Mayan archaeology.

Returning to his home city he found no career to his liking and took to drinking, riding around the river sections with his contemporaries on summer drunks, and studying yoga. Presumably he had no formal instruction in the latter discipline, since on being challenged to prove its efficacy, he announced that he was impervious to pain and demonstrated this by cutting off a finger. This exploit led to his incarceration in a private sanitarium nearby, from which he was soon released, as he seemed composed and cognizant of his surroundings.

His next move, in true American style, was the Grand Tour of Europe. He spent a year in Paris in the early thirties, went on through Germany and Austria (as did his English contemporaries in the Isherwood-Auden group), and ended up in Cairo, looking at the pyramids with the practiced eye of an ex-archaeology student. He spent some time in the cities of the north coast of Africa, earlier and later popularized by Gide and Paul Bowles, and returned then to America.

His favorite reading at this time was a dozen or so books, which comprised his whole permanent library, and which he carried around with him in his travels. They included Pareto and Spengler, Cocteau's *Opium*, a copy of Baudelaire, a paperbacked volume of Shakespeare's tragedies, and (later) W. B. Yeats' *A Vision*.

Returning to America he brought with him a bride, whom he had met during one year's abortive career as a medical student in Middle Europe. Bride and groom separated immediately on landing in New York, the purpose of the marriage having been to obtain citizenship for the Jewish lady, supposed also to have been a baroness.

Then followed a tour of U.S. cities, hotel room to hotel room; from New York, through the South and Midwest, with long stops during the early forties in Chicago and New York. This was of course made possible by a small private income from his family.

It was in Chicago that the author first began to explore the underworld within himself and outside of himself, while working as a professional pest exterminator in that city's slum areas. However, certain other less criminal but nonetheless subterranean vices, treated in the later sections of the book, had already been discovered in his youth in America and travels in North Africa and Europe.

For the latter, and its related emotional causes, the author had long ago sought out psychoanalytic aid. This proved, apparently, to be of no avail. As for the former, association with criminal elements of the population of the cities he visited, and the use of various drugs he encountered: the author's story picks up at that point.

One other important moment of background may be mentioned: the author's wife, who appears briefly in the New Orleans section of the book. The common-law marriage, which began in the late forties, ended with her untimely death as the result of a drinking accident in a South American country several years ago. There remains one child born of the union, who lives with his father, now presumably in Venezuela.

This fact has been related last as it will indicate to the reader an important concern of this book: its title is *Junk*, and its subject is drugs and the drug world; it is not in any sense a complete autobiography, though many personal details relating to the main subject have been included. It is the autobiography of one aspect of the author's career, and obviously cannot be taken as an account of the whole man, as these last pages of the introduction demonstrate.

In that respect, the author has done what he set out to do: to give a fairly representative and accurate picture of the junk world and all it involves; a true picture, given for the first time in America, of that vast underground life which has recently been so publicized. It is a notable accomplishment; there is no sentimentality here, no attempt at self-exculpation but the most candid, no romanticization of the circumstances, the dreariness, the horror, the mechanical beatness and evil of the junk life as lived. It is a true account of its pleasures, such as they are; a relentless and perspicacious account of the characters that inhabit the junk world, with their likeness and unlikeness to the known average of the culture; a systematic history of the events of a habit, the cravings, the jailings, the night errands, the day boredoms.

We are fortunate that we have a historian, however firmly he has taken his position on the other side of the dark wall of normal gratification, who is able to give us these facts in a manner of writing which shows signs of literary maturity; a style which is direct, personal, very characteristic, very literal, highly selective, intense and economical in its imagery. It would be too great a presumption to compare such a localized world of horror as that of junk, with the universal Inferno of Dante; and yet that comparison, for certain spareness of manner and realistic use of simile, is what may happily arise in the mind of the trained reader.

It remains to be said that the publisher presents this book to the public for its originality of style and content in dealing with a highly controversial subject. Very little real information is obtainable on this subject, and most of it is romanticized and hyped up or distorted for mass commercial purposes. This book has the advantage of being both real and readable. It is an important document; an archive of the underground; a true history of the true horrors of a vice. It makes clear what even the most foolish may understand.

# APPENDIX 5

## CARL SOLOMON'S PUBLISHER'S NOTE
## IN *JUNKIE* (1953)

"Junk," writes the author of these brutally frank revelations, "is not just a habit. It is a way of life." A way of life in which "kick" is king, and where drug-dominated starvelings float in a half-lighted world of debased values, overpowering hungers and sudden-flaring violence.

Not since De Quincey's *The Confessions of an English Opium Eater* has the finger of light shone so glaringly on the wasteland of the drug addict. Yet, where De Quincey wrote in the vein of dream-phantasy, *Junkie* is pitilessly factual and hard-boiled. From the very first lines, *Junkie* strips down the addict without shame or self-pity in all his nakedness.

But this is more than the story of a drug addict. The anonymous underworld fills its pages—the moochers, fags, four-flushers, stool pigeons, thieves. We follow them as they slink furtively to their "meets" in dim-lit cafeterias and sleazy bars. We watch their hidden gestures, we see them as they "cop the stuff." We see the veins shrink at the needle's thrust, the "bang" as the stuff takes—and the indescribable horrors of junk sickness. We witness the sordidness of every crevice of their lives. For all are a "beat, nowhere bunch of guys," seemingly without past and no future. There has never been a criminal confession better calculated to discourage imitation by thrill-hungry teen-agers. This is the unadulterated, unglamorous, unthrilling life of the drug addict.

William Lee (the name of the author and of all persons appearing in this book are disguised) is an unrepentant, unredeemed drug addict. His own words tell us that he is a fugitive from the law; that he has been diagnosed as schizophrenic, paranoid; that he is totally without moral values. But his pen has been dipped in an acid of strange lustre, and some of his word pictures are vignettes of compelling artistry.

We realized that here was a document which could forearm the public more effectively than anything yet printed about the drug menace. The picture it paints of a sordid netherworld was all the more horrifying for being so authentic in language and point of view.

For the protection of the reader, we have inserted occasional parenthetical notes to indicate where the author clearly departs from accepted medical fact or makes other unsubstantiated statements in an effort to justify his actions.

# APPENDIX 6

## FOREWORD TO *JUNKIE* (1964)
## BY CARL SOLOMON

*Junkie* by William Seward Burroughs was originally entitled *Junk* and was written under the pseudonym of William Lee. First presented for publication in the early '50s, it aroused some interest among hard-cover publishers but was brought out as one of the earliest paperbacks of the newly emerging Ace Books.

Since that time, Burroughs has become famous here and abroad as an avant-garde novelist and short story writer, writing under his own name. His novel *The Naked Lunch* has been published by Grove Press. *In Search of Yage*, about his adventures on the Amazon River among the headhunters in search of the "mind-expanding" drug *yage*, has been brought out by City Lights. *The Soft Machine* and *The Ticket That Exploded* have been published in Paris by Olympia Press with much attendant scandal. And a new novel *Nova Express*, will soon be brought out by Grove.

In Norman Mailer's *Advertisements for Myself*, Burroughs is referred to as the American Jean Genet. His second novel, *Queer*, remains unpublished in this country and abroad.

Behind the "beat" renaissance in mid-Twentieth Century America, which shocked the sensibilities of some and gave new expression to others, William Burroughs remains a seldom seen but by now legendary figure. In 1964, unlike 1950, he has innumerable imitators and would-be imitators. His early creed of junk as a way of life has seeped into the youth of today to the point of becoming a major national problem.

In *Junkie* he is factual. This is his earlier mode. In his more recent work, he ventures into the surrealistic and imaginative. *The New York Post*, in writing of his subject matter, fantasies (homoerotic), and experiments in technique, finds him verging sometimes on the infantile and the schizoid.

In life, he is a peculiar kind of adventurer, seeking out what is unusual or unexplored in our sensibilities or in our way of living. Pursuing what is increasingly hard to find, the unknown, Burroughs has not yet become redundant and his curiosity is not yet exhausted. In this respect he is unlike many other so-called avant-gardists and poets who once experimented but then reclined on their couches and ruefully admitted that there was nothing new under the sun.

As for his junk habit, he has gone off and gone back and taken a variety of cures with different amounts of success. One cure, in England, under a Dr. Dent, resulted in an article written by Burroughs in a scientific quarterly.

Burroughs is a Harvard graduate, has pursued a variety of occupations, is the father of two children, and is the scion of a wealthy family.

One of the more lurid incidents in his past was the accidental shooting of his wife in a "William Tell" experiment . . . demonstrating his marksmanship by attempting to shoot a champagne glass off her head and killing her in the process. For this, in Mexico City, in about 1950, he was acquitted.

In one form or another, under one guise or another, his character and personality seem to have had reflections in fictional characters in the writings of his protégé, Jack Kerouac. This is particularly evident in the character of Dennison in Kerouac's first novel, *The Town and the City*, and also in that of Bull Balloon in *Dr. Sax*. His politics are a bit hazy. We can seldom make out whether he is fighting against real conspiracies or imaginary ones. In *In Search of Yage*, he appears at times to be a liberal or even a radical, and the reputation he acquired in recent years in Paris seems to situate him more or less on the left. Most of the time, Burroughs appears to be too self-preoccupied to show much sustained interest in any political camp.

# APPENDIX 7

## INTRODUCTION TO *JUNKY* (1977)
## BY ALLEN GINSBERG

Bill Burroughs and I had known each other since Xmas 1944, and at the beginning of the '50s were in deep correspondence. I had always respected him as elder & wiser than myself, and in first years' acquaintance was amazed that he treated me with respect at all. As time wore on & our fortunes altered—me to solitary bughouse for awhile, he to his own tragedies and travels—I became more bold in presuming on his shyness, as I intuited it, and encouraged him to write more prose. By then Kerouac and I considered ourselves poet/writers in Destiny, and Bill was too diffident to make such extravagant theater of self. In any case he responded to my letters with chapters of *Junky*, I think begun as curious sketching but soon conceived on his part—to my thrilled surprise—as continuing workmanlike fragments of a book, narrative on a subject. So the bulk of the Ms. arrived sequentially in the mail, some to Paterson, New Jersey. I thought I was encouraging him. It occurs to me that he may have been encouraging me to keep in active contact with the world, as I was rusticating at my parents' house after 8 months in mental hospital as result of hippie contretemps with law.

This took place over quarter century ago, and I don't remember structure of our correspondence—which continued for years, continent to continent & coast to coast, and was the method whereby we assembled books not only of *Junky* but also *Yage Letters, Queer* (as yet unpublished), and much of *Naked Lunch*. Shamefully, Burroughs has destroyed much of his personal epistles of the mid-'50s which I entrusted to his archival care—letters of a more pronouncedly affectionate nature than he usually displays to public—so, alas, that charming aspect of the otherwise Invisible Inspector Lee has been forever obscured behind the Belles Lettristic Curtain.

Once the manuscript was complete, I began taking it around to various classmates in college or mental hospital who had succeeded in establishing themselves in Publishing—an ambition which was mine also, frustrated; and thus incompetent in worldly matters, I conceived of myself as a secret literary Agent. Jason Epstein read the Ms. of Burroughs' *Junky* (of course he knew Burroughs by legend from Columbia days) and concluded that had it been written by Winston Churchill, it would be interesting; but since Burroughs' prose was "undistinguished" (a point I argued with as much as I could in his Doubleday office, but felt faint surrounded by so much Reality . . . mustard gas of sinister intelligent editors . . . my own paranoia or inexperience with the Great Dumbness of Business Buildings of New York) the book was not of interest to publish. That season I was also carrying around Kerouac's Proustian chapters from *Visions of Cody* that later developed into the vision of *On the Road*. And I carried *On the Road* from one publishing office to another. Louis Simpson, himself recovering from nervous breakdown at Bobbs-Merrill, found no artistic merit in the manuscripts either.

By grand chance, my Companion from N.Y. State Psychiatric Institute, Carl Solomon, was given a job by his uncle, Mr. A. A. Wyn of Ace Books. Solomon had the literary taste & humor for these documents—though on the rebound from his own Dada-ist, Lettriste & Paranoiac-Critical literary extravagances, he, like

Simpson, distrusted the criminal or vagabond romanticism of Burroughs & Kerouac. (I was myself at the time a nice Jewish boy with one foot in middle-class writing careful revised rhymed metaphysical verse—not quite.) Certainly these books indicated we were in the middle of an identity crisis prefiguring nervous breakdown for the whole United States. On the other hand Ace Books' paperback line was mostly commercial schlupp with an occasional French Romance or hardboiled novel nervously slipped into the list by Carl, while Uncle winked his eye.

Editor Solomon felt that we (us guys, Bill, Jack, Myself) didn't care, as he did, about the real Paranoia of such publishing—it was not part of our situation as it was of his—Carl's context of family and psychiatrists, publishing house responsibilities, nervousness at being thought mentally ill by his uncle—so that it took bravery on his part to put out "this type of thing," a book on Junk, and give Kerouac $250 advance for a prose novel. "The damn thing almost gave me a nervous breakdown—buildup of fear and terror, to work with that material."

There was at the time—not unknown to the present with its leftover vibrations of police state paranoia cultivated by Narcotics Bureaus—a very heavy implicit thought-form, or assumption: that if you talked aloud about "tea" (much less Junk) on the bus or subway, you might be arrested—even if you were only discussing a change in the law. It was just about illegal to talk about dope. A decade later you still couldn't get away with national public TV discussion of the laws without the Narcotics Bureau & FCC intruding with canned film clips weeks later denouncing the debate. That's history. But the fear and terror that Solomon refers to was so real that it had been internalized in the schlupp publishing industry, and so, before the book could be printed, all sorts of disclaimers had to be interleaved with the text—lest the publisher be implicated criminally with the author, lest the public be misled by arbitrary opinions of the author which were at variance with "recognized medical authority"—at the time a forcible captive of the Narcotics Bureau (20,000 doctors arraigned for trying to treat junkies, thousands fined & jailed 1935–1953, in what N.Y. County Medical Association called "a war on doctors").

The simple and basic fact is that, in cahoots with organized crime, the Narcotics Bureau were involved in under-the-table peddling of dope, and so had built up myths reinforcing "criminalization" of addicts rather than medical treatment. The motive was pure and simple: greed for money, salaries, blackmail & illegal profits, at the expense of a class of citizens who were classified by press & police as "Fiends." The historic working relationship between Police and Syndicate bureaucracies had by early 1970s been documented by various official reports and books (notably N.Y.'s 1972 Knapp Commission Report and *The Politics of Opium in Indochina* by Al McCoy).

Because the subject—*in medias res*—was considered so outré, Burroughs was asked to contribute a preface explaining that he was from distinguished family background—anonymously William Lee—and giving some hint how some supposedly normal citizen could arrive at being a dope fiend, to soften the blow for readers, censors, reviewers, police, critical eyes in walls & publishers' rows, god knows who. Carl wrote a worried introduction pretending to be the voice of sanity introducing the book on the part of the publisher. Perhaps he was. A certain literary description of Texas agricultural society was excised as not being germane to the funky harsh non-literary subject matter. And I repeat, crucial medico-political statements of fact or opinion by Wm. Lee were on the spot (in parentheses) disclaimed (by Ed.).

As agent I negotiated a contract approving all these obscurations, and delivering Burroughs an Advance of $800 on an edition of 100,000 copies printed back-to-back—69'd so to speak—with another book on drugs, by an ex-Narcotics Agent. Certainly a shabby package; on the other hand, given our naïveté, a kind of brave miracle that the text actually was printed and read over the next decade by a million *cognoscenti*—who did appreciate the intelligent fact, the clear perception, precise bare language, direct syntax & mind pictures—as well as the enormous sociologic grasp, culture-revolutionary attitude toward bureaucracy & Law, and the stoic cold-humor'd eye on crime.

ALLEN GINSBERG
September 19, 1976 NYC

# NOTES

## PROLOGUE

1. "Prologue": originally titled "Preface," it was retitled "Prologue" for *Junky* (1977). Note that the whereabouts of the MS. for this text are not known.

4. "put down an out-and-out con": corrected from "put me down as an 'out-and-out con'" (in *Junky* [1977], xiv); see Appendix 3.

5. "junk-dependent cells": at this point Ace inserted a note in *Junkie* (9): "Ed. note: The foregoing is not the view of recognized medical authority."

5. "phenomenal age": at this point Ace inserted a note in *Junkie* (9): "Ed. note: This is contradicted by recognized medical authority."

## JUNKY

14. "he said, pulling up his pants": restores an unused line from the "Junk" MS.

**21.** "Herman and I": from here to "gave us static" was an insert added to the 1950 "Junk" MS., sometime in either 1951 or 1952.

**23.** "Here are the facts": before this phrase Ace inserted a note in *Junkie* (33): "Ed. note: Authorities maintain that the marijuana-smoker usually forms a psychological habit pattern; under present laws, the use of marijuana is in itself a crime."

**23.** "Anyone who has used good weed": before this phrase Ace inserted a note in *Junkie* (34): "Pub. note: This opinion is contradicted by recognized medical authority."

**24.** "spatial relations": note a final phrase deleted on the "Junk" MS.; **"since space-time is an inseparable continuum."**

**31.** "my old lady": after this phrase Ace inserted a note in *Junkie* (42): "Ed. note: This is, undoubtedly, the 'common-law wife' to whom the author alludes later."

**35.** "crippled": note a following line deleted on the "Junk" MS.; **"He was stupid as a man can get without being classified as defective."**

**45.** "mediator between man and junk": note a final phrase deleted on the "Junk" MS.; **"who alone could receive the contributions of the faithful."**

**48.** "I knew Nick was": from here to "pack him in" restores an unused line from the "Junk" MS.

**55.** "take their business to Walgreen's": note a following line deleted on the "Junk" MS.; **"We'd be better off without their business anyway."**

**67.** "Benny was another oldtime Jewish shmecker": from here to "pink face and white hair" (55) was an insert made in March 1951 (see *Letters* 81).

**70.** "outside the city limits": note a following line deleted on the "Junk" MS.; **"It is unthinkable that you could find anyone in Houston who has never been outside the city."**

70. "The residents are surly": note a final phrase deleted on the "Junk" MS.; **"like most populations that subsist on tourists."**

73. "In the French Quarter": from here to "After three quick beers I felt better" (61) was an insert made in early 1951. In his letter of March 5, Burroughs refers to this as a sample of the "connections between junk and sex" that he now wanted to develop (*Letters* 81).

74. "He couldn't have been anything but Irish": restores an unused line from the "Junk" MS.

75. "as though it were actually changing color": restores a phrase unintentionally omitted from *Junky* (1977) (74).

77. "There were a few others": from here to "We ought to find another place" was omitted from *Junkie*, and restored for *Junky* (1977) (76).

78. "prosecute anything": Ace inserted a note in *Junkie* (89) at this point: "Ed. note: This statement is hearsay and the publisher accepts no responsibility for its accuracy."

92. "now. I have to go to court. If I possibly can, I'll take": these words, present in the "Junk" MS. and *Junkie* (103), were unintentionally omitted from *Junky* (1977) (92).

94. "I lay on the narrow": from here to "the neck snaps" was an insert almost certainly made in April 1952.

99. "deeper and tougher front": the "Junk" MS. continues with the struck lines, probably cut when the later chapter on Wilhelm Reich was removed in summer 1952; **"If anyone ever braces the doctor directly so he can't slide away, he will likely go into protein cleavage and end up a pile of protozoa—'a bionous heap,' as Reich puts it."**

104. "A three-lane highway": from here to "she will be ten years untangling" (90) was omitted from *Junkie*, and restored *for Junky* (1977) (105–8).

**107.** "A lot of people made quick easy money": from here to "a vast muttering of banal regret and despair" (91) was omitted from *Junkie*, and restored for *Junky* (1977) (108–9).

**108.** "I had gone into partnership": from here to "pull out of the Valley" (92) was omitted from *Junkie*, and restored for *Junky* (1977) (109–10).

**109.** "No one in the Valley had ever heard of quinine water": at this point in the original "Junk" MS. came the start of Chapter 28, the section on Wilhelm Reich; see Appendix 1.

**109.** "remain in Mexico when I got there": the "Junk" MS. continues with the deleted lines; **"Travel books never give the information I want. I am in a process of deciding whether to go to a place or not. I want to know what I can buy there with how much money, and what is the political and legal picture."**

**111.** "The Chimu Bar": from here to "we separated at a corner, shaking hands" (94) was an insert made in summer 1952. Burroughs wrote to Ginsberg on July 13: "I enclose a chapter on a Mexican queer bar which they can use or not as they see fit. It is to be inserted back in the original manuscript of JUNK at page 150 as indicated" *(Letters* 135). This material was in fact first written as part of his *Queer* MS., which Burroughs transposed from third to first person.

**112.** "I dropped my shirt and shorts on the pistol": when transposing this material from his *Queer* MS., Burroughs omitted the following lines; **"Though he was near forty Lee had the thin body of an adolescent. His shoulders and chest were wide across and very shallow. The line of his body curved in from the chest to a flat stomach. Body hair was sparse and dark in contrast to the light brown hair of his head."** Clearly indicating when this material was written, and why he would drop it, Burroughs quotes these lines in his letter of April 5, 1952, in the context of discussing the problem of deciding which person he should be writing *Queer* in, first or third (see *Letters* 111).

**112.** "The boy smiled and lay down on the bed": when transposing this material from his *Queer* MS., Burroughs omitted the following lines; **"Lee's body was moving in rhythmic contractions, every muscle caressing the smooth hard body of the other, the amoeba reflex to surround and incorporate. His body tensed convulsively rigid, sparks flashed behind his eyes and the breath whistled through his teeth. Slowly his muscles relaxed away from the other's body."**

**112.** "Some time later": from here to "queer bars brought me down" was an insert probably written and made in summer 1952. These passages did not appear in *Junkie*, and were restored for *Junky* (1977) (114).

**113.** "The meaning of "*mañana*": from here to "Do you want to score?" (96) was the last page of the original "Junk" MS. completed in December 1950. This page did not appear in *Junkie*, and Burroughs complained about the omission in his 1959 letter to A. A. Wyn (see Appendix 3).

**113.** "A user may be": from here to "indelible" (96) restore unused lines from an insert that was never made.

**114.** "There is only one pusher in Mexico City": this marks the start of the forty pages of additional material Burroughs was required to write by Ace to make the novel up to length (see *Letters* 134–35).

**115.** "An addict may be ten years off": from here to "but you are never off after the first habit" were omitted from *Junkie*, restored for *Junky* (1977) (116–17).

**116.** "One script will last a day": from here to "trying to shoot this crap" was omitted from *Junkie*, and restored for *Junky* (1977) (118).

**118.** "During this time": this section was introduced on the MS. under the subheading "Attempts at Cure: Anti-Histamines."

**119.** "Our Lady of Chalma": this paragraph was an insert, probably made in 1952.

**120.** "the arm swinging out": from here to "limp wrist of the fag" restore unused lines lightly deleted on the "Junk" MS., which clarify this ironic gesture of group identity.

**120.** "with a few exceptions": this phrase was unintentionally omitted from *Junky* (1977) (123).

**121.** "Aside from junk itself": from here to "the intervals of sickness" restore unused lines marked for omission on the "Junk" MS.

**121.** "The end of the month": from here to "shaking her head" (103) derives from a page out of MS. sequence, probably written and inserted in spring, 1952; like all the material from this point until "Junk short-circuits sex" (104), it did not appear in *Junkie* but was restored for *Junky* (1977) (123–24).

**121.** "My old lady looked at me": from here to "shaking her head" restore unused lines from the "Junk" MS.

**122.** "You can't stop shooting C—as long as it is there you shoot it"; restores an unused line from the "Junk" MS.

**122.** "You don't want another shot right away": restores an unused line from the "Junk" MS.

**123.** "I tried the Chinese cure": from here until "best go back to the needle" (105) restore unused passages marked for omission on the MS.

**124.** "control over my actions": at this point, the "Junk" MS. has a further, deleted line; **"But I knew sooner or later the time would come to quit and then I would be able to do it."**

**124.** "One morning in April": from here until "His toothless mouth was twisted with hate" (119), the material originally derives from the *Queer* MS.

**124.** "the magic of childhood": at this point, the original *Queer* MS. has a significant line, cut when Burroughs transposed this material into his "Junk" MS.; **"The glory and the freshness**

**of a dream.**" Quotation is from William Wordsworth's *Ode: Intimations of Immortality from Recollections of Early Childhood.*

126.  "A junkie does not ordinarily kick": from here to "a self cured junkie" restore unused lines marked for omission on the "Junk" MS.

126.  "than drink like this": the original *Queer* MS. version of this material continues with what became the beginning of *Queer* when reedited for publication in 1985 ("Lee turned his attention . . .").

130.  "lay on the table": the original *Queer* MS. version of this material continues, in a way that clarifies the kind of cuts Burroughs had to make when transposing to his "Junk" MS.; **"He was naked. Wonder who paid for the room? Lee sat up in bed. Sore ass. 'My God!' Lee thought, 'I been beat for my virtue!'"**

130.  "no loss either": the original *Queer* MS. version of this material continues; **"Cheap bastard. He makes me for all my valuables, avails himself of my person and doesn't even leave me 15 centavos car fare."**

130.  "What do you carry it for?": the original *Queer* MS. version of this material continues; **"'It's passive and feminine.'**

**'How do you mean?'**

**'A provocation. Look what happens last night. You end up getting pogged by a middle aged Mexican cop . . . or maybe he was just probing you for your money. *Thees gringo, he got it somewhere.*'"**

131.  "the way you've been acting lately": the original *Queer* MS. version of this material continues; **"And if you want to go to bed with a member of your own sex, of which I certainly disapprove, I should think you would want to dress well and come on a little. At least take a bath. You won't get anywhere waving a rusty pistola."**

**131.** "horror that has grown inside it": the original *Queer* MS. version of this material continues; **"Lee saw penises grow centipede legs, others moving about like jointed caterpillars. Lee watched curiously. 'Very artistic' he said in a pansy voice. He did not feel fear."**

**132.** "I sent my wife": from here to "I will try" restore lines inserted on the *Queer* MS. version of this material at the time Burroughs prepared the material for transposition to "Junk."

**133.** "with the cellular stoicism that junk bestows on the user": restores unused phrasing from the "Junk" MS. (cf "stoically" in *Junky* [1977] 134).

**136.** "play with the cat some time": the "Junk" MS. continues with lines marked for omission; **"When I am on junk, I take pleasure in tormenting and terrorizing cats. I hold a cat out the window or provoke the unfortunate animal into biting or scratching, then slap it across the face with brutal force. I give the cats a bath and hold their heads under water."**

**137.** "where everything is exactly": from here to "possible" restore lines struck through on the "Junk" MS. Note that in the same line, "inanity" is a correction of "insanity" (in *Junky* [1977] 139).

**137.** "Every time exactly that much less": restores a line struck through on the "Junk" MS.

**137.** "with the children": restores a phrase struck through on the "Junk" MS.

**140.** "twisted with hate": this marks the end of material transposed from the *Queer* MS. (which carries on as per *Queer* 18).

**142.** "free junk and immunity": at this point, Ace inserted a note in *Junkie* (143): "Ed. note: This statement is hearsay and the publisher excepts [*sic*] no responsibility for its accuracy."

**143.** "I kept a little on hand": from here to "dropped in sick" restores a line struck through on the "Junk" MS., which did appear in *Junkie* (144), but not in *Junky* (1977) (145).

147. "Lexington is full of young kids now": a retyped page of the "Junk" MS. continues; **"I fixed Bill up with Old Ike, but Bill wasn't satisfied. He couldn't limit himself to a schedule, so he was always running short. Besides he didn't really like M, and kept asking me to find him an H connection."**

147. "One day I was in the Opera Bar": from here to "it was so full of crisp money" (126) did not appear in *Junkie*. This material, introduced on the MS. as "The Bad Piece of H," was originally written as a separate piece from "Junk" during late summer 1952, and was inserted for *Junky* (1977) (149–51).

## GLOSSARY

151. Glossary: Burroughs' first draft (Ginsberg Collection, Stanford University) begins with a different opening paragraph, and a different first line to the second: **"The purpose of a glossary is to explain the meaning of words and expressions used in a book. It seems logical to put the glossary at the beginning so the reader will be able to understand what he is about to read. I don't know why glossaries are always found at the end of a book. Anyway, here is my glossary at the beginning of this book.**
**" 'Jive talk,' which seems to be largely a Negro invention, is used more in connection with marijuana than junk."**

This draft was divided into four separate sections of entries. The second was introduced as "largely 'jive talk'"; the third as "specific to 'lush workers'"; and the fourth as "miscellaneous expressions."

153. **"Heat":** this entry is restored from Burroughs' first draft glossary, and seems to have been lost in revision.

154. **"Nembies"**: after the phrase "to take the edge off," Burroughs' first draft glossary continued; **"Sometimes injected intravenously. If you miss the vein you will surely get an abscess. Barbiturates are more dangerous than junk because a user of barbiturates—eight or more capsules per day—gets the horrors when he is cut off barbiturates, and he is subject to epileptic fits with frequent head injury from flopping around on concrete floors. He is most likely to find himself cut off in a place where the floors are concrete."**

154. **"The People . . .** Narcotics agents. A New Orleans expression"; corrects a continuity error (cf "Another New Orleans expression" in *Junky* [1977]) introduced because in Burroughs' first draft glossary, not made in alphabetical order, his entry for "The People" followed the one for "Pusher."

155. **"Score:** To buy junk or marijuana"; restores a correction made in Burroughs' first draft glossary (cf "To buy weed or marijuana" in *Junky* [1977] 157).

156. **"**For example, 'Fey'"**: in *Junkie* this was followed by "also now (1953)"; deleted for *Junky* (1977).

APPENDIX 1: CHAPTER 28 OF
THE ORIGINAL "JUNK" MANUSCRIPT
(Ginsberg Collection, Stanford University)

157. "he calls 'orgones'": on the manuscript Burroughs spells it "Orgonne," an error that suggests he wrote this material without refreshing his memory by reading any of Reich's books. Note the glossary definition: "ORGONE ENERGY: Primordial Cosmic Energy; universally present and demonstrable visually, thermically, electroscopically and by means of Geiger-Mueller counters. In the living organism: Bioenergy,

Life Energy. Discovered by Wilhelm Reich between 1936 and 1940." (See Wilhelm Reich, *The Mass Psychology of Fascism* [Harmondsworth: Penguin, 1975], 34.)

## APPENDIX 3: LETTER FROM WILLIAM BURROUGHS TO A. A. WYN [1959]
### (Ginsberg Collection, Columbia University)

**169.** *"Preface. Page 8, Line 8"*: see "Prologue" xlii.

**170.** *"Page 21, Line 1"*: see *Junky* 4.

**170.** *"Page 85, Line 22"*: see *Junky* 68.

**170.** *"Page 93, Line 5"*: see *Junky* 75.

**170.** *"Page 120, last line"*: see *Junky* 110.

**170.** "Page 150 in the original M.S.": see *Junky* 107–8.

## APPENDIX 4: *"JUNKIE*: AN APPRECIATION"(1952) BY ALLEN GINSBERG

**171.** *"Junkie*—An Appreciation": excerpted from a letter to Ace Books, April 12 1952, previously published in Allen Ginsberg, *Deliberate Prose: Selected Essays*, 1952–1995 (New York: HarperCollins, 2000), edited by Bill Morgan, 380–82.

## APPENDIX 6: FOREWORD TO *JUNKIE* (1964) BY CARL SOLOMON

**177.** "Foreword": the text of this piece is reprinted from the 1973 Bruce and Watson edition of *Junkie*.